DesRon 3,

The Ocean Red

Charles Johnson

authorHOUSE

AuthorHouse™
1663 Liberty Drive
Bloomington, IN 47403
www.authorhouse.com
Phone: 1 (800) 839-8640

Published by AuthorHouse 03/11/2020

ISBN: 978-1-4969-7428-0 (sc)
ISBN: 978-1-4969-7427-3 (e)

Library of Congress Control Number: 2015903516

Print information available on the last page.

Dedicated to the heroic men and women who have served, are serving and will serve in the Armed Forces of the United States of America, and to those who have died in action defending our great country. Your sacrifice will never be forgotten.

Acknowledgments

Sharon Bauer
Noel Reynolds
Ruben & Ada Reynolds
Donnamae Reynolds
Harvey Benko
William (Bill) Leoni
David Grimm
James McGarvey

Disclaimer

Reference toward the enemy (Japanese) during the period this story encompasses reflect the attitude and feelings of the time and do not in any way reflect those of the author or publisher.

Contents

Chapter 1

The morning began like so many others before; the sun had risen to shine down on the beautiful island and the peaceful fleet at anchor. While the war continued to rage on the other side of the world, it was the furthest thing from anybody's mind here. There were rumors of war, the Japanese had invaded China and were committing atrocities on the Chinese people that were in the local papers almost daily. But American diplomats were working their magic and the fear of a war seemed almost nonexistent. Still, with the possibility there, steps were being taken to ensure the safety of the fleet and those stationed there. Aircraft were lined up along the runways in plain view where they could be watched instead of in the big new hangars. The biggest concern wasn't from an enemy air/surface attack, but from a raid of 5th columnists. There were several hundred thousand Japanese living on the islands. The navy considered them the biggest threat. They knew the difficulty of steaming a fleet from Japan to the Hawaiian Islands without being discovered. But that threat was why the fleet had been moved from San Diego to Hawaii in the first place.

What a sight it made. Four aircraft carriers (Lexington, Yorktown, Enterprise and Saratoga) along with the tender Langley. Eight battleships, (Pennsylvania, West Virginia, Arizona, Oklahoma, Tennessee, Maryland, Nevada and California were present at Pearl Harbor. Then there were the hundreds of supporting ships from the heavy and light cruisers to the destroyers and submarines and transports and tankers. However, on this day, the carriers were gone. The Saratoga and the Langley were in San Diego for some repairs and modifications, the Lexington and Yorktown were delivering some aircraft to Wake Island, and the Enterprise was on patrol. Under normal circumstances the battleships would also have gone on patrol, but the captain chose to leave them behind. They would only slow him down.

There wasn't a cloud in the sky that Sunday morning as sailors lay about deciding what to do. Some were on duty, but the majority weren't. Christmas was just around the corner, so many were readying cards and gifts to send home. Some were even planning their leaves to be home with family and friends. One such sailor, a gunner's mate on the battleship Arizona, Steve Wiler, sat on the deck against the barbette of B turret, writing a letter home to his girl. He was having difficulty with the letter. His girl wanted him to leave the navy as soon as his tour was up (in 2 months) and get married. She wanted him to work in her father's department store. She was sure that their marriage would fail if he didn't leave the navy. Steve loved her, but he also loved the navy. He was only 23 years old and felt he wasn't ready to settle down and was trying to figure out a way to tell her. Hearing a low drone in the sky, he looked up and saw a large number of planes approaching. There seemed to be something menacing about them, not just their number but the direction they were coming from. Nearby, some men were shooting dice on the deck. One of them was a friend of his and fellow gunners mate, Gary Weiss. He looked up and saw another formation of ten or twelve planes coming in low on the water. This wasn't all that strange; the navy was always doing practice runs on the ships. Still there was something different about this. At first he couldn't put his finger on it, and then it came to him. These planes looked different, and they were carrying what appeared to be ordinance. He ran to the bow to watch. Steve also ran to the port side rail to watch. There wasn't anything better to do.

Sammy Gore sat on a stump near the seaplane hangar at Ford Island, fishing. The area was off limits to civilians, especially to kids. But Sammy's grandfather was Admiral Fred Moore, the naval base commander, so the gate sentries let him in and everybody else just looked the other way. If the "old man" didn't care, why should they? Because the big planes took off regularly, fishing usually wasn't that good here. Sammy chose this spot so he could see the battleships. But today, Sammy caught his limit quickly. He considered going home for more bait, then as quickly dismissed the idea and decided to sit back and watch the big ships. It was, after all why he fished there in the first place. Leaving his catch behind, he walked past the patrol plane hangars along the beach so he could see the battleships clearly. Usually he couldn't see all of them at the same time. They had all come in the night before. The California was to his left, though he couldn't see her very well. A tanker blocked his view. The outboard battleships were the Oklahoma, West Virginia and the Nevada. The inboard battleships were the Maryland, Tennessee and Arizona. The auxilary ship Vestal lay outboard of the Arizona and the tail end battleship was the Nevada. Sammy made sure to stay out of sight of the Nevada, his father was aboard the Nevada and today he was officer of the deck. Sammy knew he'd be in trouble if his dad saw him there. Looking them over, he thought to himself, "what a sweet target they'd make for a torpedo attack." Someday he would command one of them, he knew. Then his attention was drawn to the sky as he heard the sound of aircraft. It seemed neat until the first bomb fell. Shaken by the explosion, Sammy ran to the seaplane hangars to hide. Minutes later, nine high level bombers dropped their bombs on the hangars. As the seaplane hangars were blown sky high, so disappeared Sammy's dreams of commanding a battleship.

Harry Vanka was hot. The interior of a ship at anchor was always hot. He decided to go up to the crow's nest to cool off and relax. There was a .30 caliber machine gun up there, but still enough room to kick back and maybe write a letter or two. The crow's nest was above the cage mast, at the very top of the ship. From there he could see everything. The breeze was always great up there. Harry had joined the navy four years ago to see the world. He quickly realized that he loved cruising the high seas and he rarely left the ship when it arrived in port. The Oklahoma was his new home. He loved the navy and couldn't imagine ever leaving it. Taking out his writing gear, he began to write his mother, describing what he saw going on around him. Looking towards the harbor opening, he saw a small minesweeper coming in. Glancing up from his letter, he noticed some low flying planes, then looking around; he began to see many more. It wasn't uncommon to see this sort of thing, but this was Sunday. The navy never practice on

Sundays, especially Sunday morning. He could see that the army planes were still parked along the runway, and he knew the carriers were at sea. Something didn't add up. Almost on instinct, he began loading the .30 caliber machine gun beside him. As soon as he saw the torpedos hit the water, he lined up a plane in his sights and squeezed the trigger. The first opposing gun fire the enemy felt.

Ensign Bill Hunt was a recent Annapolis graduate and had only arrived at the base a week before. He was assigned to the battleship Tennessee as a gunnery officer. The Tennessee was moored inboard of the West Virginia on battleship row. He soon learned, (as others knew) that the inboard position was the worst position, that the outboard battleship got the breeze. The big ships were old and had no air conditioning. Fans only blew the hot air around. Bill had graduated at the top of his class, and his father had been awarded a medal of honor in the last war, posthumously, so he could have got which ever post he wanted. And he did. He requested duty with the pacific fleet, based at Pearl Harbor. His big brother was stationed here. Or so he thought. Quickly he found out that his brother (Sam) had transferred to the Asiatic fleet, based at the Cavity naval base in the Philippines. Sam was the executive officer on a destroyer, the U.S.S. Jackson. Bill liked the Tennessee. As gun captain of A turret, he teased the other gunnery officers that he was closer to their targets than they were. But some officers resented Bill and Sam. Because their father had been a decorated hero in WW1, it had been easy for them to get into the academy. But then they had had the opportunity to grow up with their fathers, Sam and Bill hadn't.

The Tennessee was a very old ship, commissioned in 1919. But she was still one of the most powerful warships in the U.S. Navy, or any navy for that matter. She displaced 32,000 tons, was 908 feet long, and was armed with 12-14 inch guns, 22-5 inch guns and 4-3 inch guns, plus 3 seaplanes that could be launched and recovered when needed. She was what Bill referred to as a powerhouse. Bill was saddened that his brother was no longer here, but reasoned that it was a small navy, he'd run into him sooner or later. Today he was O.O.D., officer of the deck and senior officer aboard. He felt like he was the king of his own realm. "Too bad," Bill said to those around him, "I would have liked to take it out for a spin."

One minute it was peaceful and the next minute planes were swarming in like angry hornets. Alarms began going off all around him as all hell seemed to break loose. Bill watched two planes make a low level attack on the Oklahoma, torpedo attack. As the torpedos made their way towards the ship he heard a machine gun firing and saw one of the planes wobble a bit. Seconds after it dropped its fish, it nosed down into the water, the first enemy plane shot down in the attack.

Minutes later, Nevada's anti aircraft guns opened fire. Then, as if on que, other ships opened fire as well and all hell seemed to break loose. Up in the crow's nest of the Oklahoma, Harry Vanda began shooting at all of the planes diving around him. There were so many to shoot at. When the first torpedo had struck the ship, he had half expected the ship to blow up and sink. Instead there was just a slight shudder and an even slighter list to port. He noticed a plane flying towards him and he directed his fire at it. He saw his rounds hit the right wing at the root and was surprised to see the wing sever from the plane and fall free. Harry was surprised at how easily the aircraft was shot down. As the plane burst into flames and crashed, he quickly switched targets. Then the ship was struck by two more torpedo and the list to port increased. Harry waited for the toppling motion to stop, but it didn't seem like it was going to. Everybody knew that a battleship couldn't turn over. But the motion didn't stop. As the Oklahoma rolled over, Harry stepped out of the crow's nest and into the water, and started swimming to get away from the ship before the suction pulled him down with her. Shaking his fists at the attacking aircraft, he screamed "I'll get you, you bastards", and swam to the next battleship astern, the West Virginia.

The Wee Vee, as the West Virginia was affectionately called by her crew, had her own problems. She was also an outboard battleship like the Oklahoma, and like the Oklahoma she was struck by two torpedos early in the attack. But her captain was aboard and as the ship began to list, he ordered her counter flooded immediately. With water flooding her starboard compartments right after the port side hits, the ship settled to the bottom of the harbor on an even keel, instead of rolling over like the Oklahoma. Thus saving hundreds of her crew from the suffocating death that many Oklahoma sailors were now facing. Safe from turning turtle, she wasn't protected from the bombs, and collected five, which set her afire amidships, forcing her captain to flood her magazines to keep her from blowing up. As her crew struggled to save their shipmates, her guns continued to blaze away at the enemy planes.

At the port side rail of the Arizona, Steve Wiler watched the strange aircraft as they came in low, flying towards the Oklahoma and West Virginia. He didn't recognize the planes and he was still thinking practice. Even as he watched something fall from the planes, he was still thinking, "Dummy torpedo." But as they hit the ships and exploded, all thoughts of drill faded away. Steve, (a gunner in X turret) ran to his battle station. He never saw his best friend (Gary Weiss) again. Suddenly in a flash, the world seemed to come to an end. And for one thousand one hundred and two men it did. A bomb, modified from an 18 inch armor piercing shell struck the Arizona abreast of her B turret, penetrating several decks to her powder magazine and exploded. The forward part of the ship seemed to leap out of the water, then settled back in a black cloud of smoke and a ball of flame. More than a thousand men disappeared in the explosion as the ship as far aft as the boat deck lay in a crumpled mass. The dead lay everywhere and in this instance there were few survivors to rescue the wounded. Also in this case, there were few wounded. Men were simply vaporized. The survivors, men who were aft of the boat deck, continued to fight on as best as they could, which in this case meant saving themselves and the few others they could find. The ship was destroyed. The bow had been blown into junk by the magazine explosion and her fuel tanks were ruptured. Burning oil now flowed from the ship, further endangering the men in the water. In fact, the ship would burn for three days. The smoke from the Arizona carried by the wind obscured battleship row, but that didn't stop the bombs from continuing to rain down.

Quickly realizing that the West Virginia wasn't the best choice, Harry Vanda climbed a hawser line and boarded the Tennessee. He spent the rest of the day helping with the wounded. At A turret, Bill Hunt had little to do. Ammunition was locked away for an inspection that was scheduled for the next day. So he reported to the bridge. Being in an inboard position, Tennessee was spared from torpedo hits, but she was still a target for bombs. One of the first hits struck the ships dispensary, killing the doctors and nearly all of the pharmacist's mates. A call to the other ships for medical assistance had gone unanswered. The dead and wounded lay everywhere. On the bridge, the captain sent Hunt to the mail room where many sailors from the West Virginia were coming aboard. Hunt went down and put them to work on the anti aircraft guns, replacing the dead and wounded. The captain of the Tennessee had his own troubles. Being an inboard ship meant that the main and secondary armaments couldn't be fired without hitting the ships to the port side. The smoke from the Arizona obscured everything fore and aft, so the big guns were useless anyway. Also, the Tennessee, which had steam to leave, couldn't leave because she was wedged against the quay by the sunken West Virginia. All she could do was sit and take it.

Americans have always been at their best when the chips were down and this day was no different. Everywhere one would look, he would see heroism, above and beyond the call of duty. Smoke and fire was everywhere. The skies were dotted with anti aircraft fire as sailors tried to bring their tormentors down. Then, like a vision, a gray shape materialized from the hazy, smoke. A gray dragon spitting fire and flame moved out of the line and began making its way through the harbor to get to the channel and the open sea, the stars and stripes flying proudly from her stern. It was the Nevada. Of all the things that sailors saw that day, all of the horror and heroism, the one thing that many would remember more than anything else, was the sight of the battleship Nevada attempting to escape to the open sea. It also didn't escape the enemy's attention either. Planes that had been in their dives on other ships suddenly pulled out of their dives and turned to attack the Nevada instead with the obvious intention of sinking her in the channel and bottling in the fleet. Signals flew from the HQ towers, ordering her to stay away. Her captain, a brave man, had no choice but to obey orders and he instead beached her. What a shame that those in command had so little faith in her that they stopped her from realizing her destiny. Still, what a sight she made, geysers of water spouting up around her as bombs fell on and around her like drops of rain upon the water. There was smoke pouring out of her bow and stern as the bombs and torpedo struck her and at her stern proudly flew the stars and stripes. Then another proud moment, the cruiser Oakland, (the little acorn) slipped past the beached Nevada, and headed for the open sea. Her commander ignores the signals and cruises along at thirty knots, even as the bombs fall around her. With her guns blazing, she picks up speed, even as the enemy planes converge on her. With bombs dropped on and around her, and all torpedos missing their mark, the little acorn makes it through the channel and the open expanse of the sea. The luckiest cruiser in the U.S. Navy.

Before anybody knew it, the planes were gone. Behind them they left the U.S. Pacific fleet devastated, with fewer than 30 planes operational, 3 destroyers sunk, 2 cruisers heavily damaged, 2 battleships destroyed, 6 battleships heavily and lightly damaged and many other ships damaged as well. More than 3,700 men killed and wounded. The next day, the Japanese struck the naval base of Cavite in the Philippines. Though only one merchantman was sunk and one destroyer damaged, the supply and repair facilities were blown into scrap. Following the Cavite airstrike, units of the imperial Japanese navy began converging on Indonesia to capture its oil refineries. Troop transports came with them. All hopes of stopping them fell to the Asiatic fleet. Due to the losses of the battleship H.M.S. Prince of Wales and the battle cruiser H.M.S. Repulse the warships of the four predominate countries, (American, British, Dutch and Australian) were combined to form the ABDA Flotilla Float. Placed under the command of Dutch Admiral Helfridge, the largest vessel in the fleet, (numbering 32 warships) was the American heavy cruiser, U.S.S. Houston. The cruiser, commissioned in 1930, was also the youngest ship in the fleet. Twenty three of the ships in the fleet were destroyers, eighteen of which were commissioned between 1916-1919. All of these destroyers were obsolete, with armaments and engines that were worn out and continually breaking down. Facing the allied fleet were one hundred and seventy seven enemy warships that included twelve aircraft carriers, nine battleships, thirty four cruisers and ninety four destroyers. Most of the enemy destroyers were modern. The allies had no carriers available and their airfields had been pulverized to the point that they had minimal aircraft available that were able to take flight much less fight. The ABDA ships went out on patrols without air cover and were often found by enemy planes. Soon the bombers and torpedo planes found them. A damaged ship had no repair facilities to go to. Spares were soon gone. They either fabricated parts or jury rigged the ships to fight on without the parts, the ships were scuttled by their crews, or sunk by the enemy. Some attempted the voyage to Australia for repairs, but very few of these made it. There were just too many enemy warships and aircraft in their way. Shortages of fuel, supplies and ammunition were also common.* An oil embargo which the United States placed on Japan for attacking China was the chief reason why the Japanese attacked in the first place. When the US transferred their navy from their base in San Diego to Pearl Harbor the Japanese saw it as an immediate threat. War was inevitable. So down the Celebes Sea came a juggernaut of enemy warships hell bent on destroying everything that stood in its path. Tarakan was easily captured on January 11th. On the 21st, the enemy steamed down the Makassar Strait to capture Balikpapan, which lay to the north and east of Bali. By this time there was very little to stop it, 2 CA's, 3CL's and 10 DD's.

Admiral Hart (USN) ordered admiral Glassford to take two Cl's (light cruisers) and eight DD's (destroyers) to intercept the invasion force in the Makassar Strait. So began an unfortunate chain of events. One cruiser developed engine trouble and had to turn back with a destroyer escort. The second cruiser ran aground, got off but was damaged and also had to return to base, also with a destroyer escort. That left only five destroyers of DESRON 3, (destroyer squadron 3), Jackson, Barr, Stewart, Pope and Oliver to turn back the enemy. Despite the reports, they were facing unbelievable odds.

The destroyers of DesRon 3 were old four pipers of WW1 vintage. They were of the Wickes and Clemson classes. The common specifications of the ships were a length of 314 feet long, with a beam of 31 feet. They displaced 1,149 tons. The 4 pipers or cans, (as they were known) were powered by steam turbines generating 2,610 shaft horse power which gave them a maximum speed of 35 knots on two shafts, when they were new. Now their speed was closer to 22 knots with great difficulty. They were armed with 4-4 inch guns, stern mounted depth- charges, 6 torpedo tubes and a 3 inch AA battery. The three inch gun, when functioning, was capable of shooting at low flying aircraft, but was unable to reach high flying bombers. Some of the ships had had their 3" guns replaced with1.1 inch guns, but these were always breaking down. Additionally they also couldn't reach high altitudes and were very slow firing.(The modern 20mm Oerliken and 40mm Bofors were being put on the newer destroyers of the US Navy, but none of these ships had them.) Sadly, their inept anti aircraft battery made them easy meat for the enemy aircraft. The destroyers of DesRon 3 were scheduled to be recalled to the United States in the first half of 1942 to be scrapped. They would've been replaced with newer destroyers with the new AA batteries. Then there was the torpedo problem. A problem that wouldn't be solved for two years, the torpedo had a bad magnetic exploder and firing pin that was too light. This caused most fish (torpedos) to misfire and fail to explode. All in all, the destroyers of DesRon 3 were practically useless. Their engines were worn out, their deck guns too small, and their fish were faulty. These inefficiencies were offset by the fact that the ships were crewed by the sailors of the best trained navy in the world. As such, they went out. As luck would have it, they didn't locate the enemy and returned safely. Day after day the destroyers went on patrol. Day after day they were attacked by high and low level bombers. Unable to shoot them down, they could only maneuver to escape the deadly rain. At chasing salvos they got very good, it was their only defense.

Of the five survivors of DesRon 3, the Stewart was the oldest, vintage 1916; she was 25 years old, which is very old for a first line ship. The ship was tired. Minor things continued to break down, and when several minor troubles occurred, they became major problems. And without a repair facility, even minor problems could become hopeless causes. The engineers became masters at keeping their engines running. There were no spare parts, so the machinists became wizards at fabricating parts. With aircraft, when one was destroyed, it could be cannibalized. But when a ship was destroyed it was sunk. Parts couldn't be taken from a damaged ship because of the shortage of ships. In fact, the shortage of ships was becoming acute, with not enough destroyers available to escort the larger cruisers. Soon, due to losses of the cruisers, the shortage wouldn't be felt. It was a toss up which were more important, fuel and ammunition or engineers and machinists. In reality, there was a shortage of all four, as well as food and medical supplies. Without either one, the destroyers weren't going anywhere.

The fighting had been difficult and costly since the attack on Pearl Harbor and Cavite. Ships, reinforcements and supplies had been promised, but nobody really expected to see any. The Japanese had cut their supply lines and were sinking everything they found afloat. The few submarines that made it through brought very little, some food and medical supplies, but mostly ammunition for the ground troops. About the only thing they could talk the subs out of was torpedoes, and they couldn't get them to function properly. Some of the luckier wounded were taken out, but most would be left to die in the jungles or at the hands of the advancing enemy.

As Lt. Marcus D. Hawkins stood on the bridge of the destroyer Stewart, he thought about the chain of events that had landed him in his current command. Five years ago he had graduated from Annapolis, third in his class. Then gunnery school where he finished seventh. With a very promising career ahead of him, he requested duty with the Pacific fleet where he served as gunnery officer aboard the USS Arizona, first as gun captain of A turret then B turret. Then a transfer to the Asiatic fleet as executive officer of the USS Stewart. Like her squadron mates, she was an obsolete destroyer, scheduled to be scrapped until war caught up with her. For two years Hawk had served aboard her, with promises of a command of his own. Those dreams ended on December the 7th. A lot of dreams ended that day. Now, with most of her squadron mates rusting hulks on the bottom of the Java Sea, the Stewart seemed to be awaiting her turn. But not quietly waiting. Her 4 inch guns, upon which her crew's lives depended, were continually breaking down. Her secondary armament, the 1.1's, couldn't fire high enough to reach the high level bombers that attacked the ship. Nor could they shoot fast enough to hit the lower flying planes with anything but a lucky shot. Then there were the torpedos. They were crap faulty. How many blue jackets had lost their lives when their captains had fought their way within 5,000 yards to fire their fish, only to see them jump from the water like playful bass and fail to explode? With all of the mechanical troubles aboard the Stewart and DesRon 3, somehow the men were in good spirits and continued to perform their duties valiantly. But they were tired and would require some r&r soon. They had been under nearly steady combat conditions since Cavity had been attacked and destroyed. That was December 8th. That day the ship had been on patrol and so had escaped the blasting in Cavite. They were cruising the Java sea, when 9 high level bombers had appeared overhead. As the ship began to maneuver defensively, it became immediately apparent that the ships anti aircraft guns were useless. The 4 inch guns had contact fuses, so only exploded if they hit something. The chances of hitting an aircraft dead on was rare. So the captain did the only thing he could. He chased splashes. As Captain (James) Palmer stood on the port side bridge rail and Hawk stood on the starboard side, they yelled out orders to the helmsman as to which way to turn. "Left rudder, right rudder, hard to starboard, hard to port." For an hour they fought off attack after attack without damage. But when the 2nd and 3rd waves arrived simultaneously, they knew they were in for it. Eighteen bombers flew overhead and dropped at the same time. They maneuvered radically. The luck of the gods was with them, for they only took one hit. But it was a costly one. A 250 kg bomb struck the port side torpedo mount, destroying it. In itself, it wasn't a bad hit, the torpedo were useless anyway. But the resulting explosion also blew off the port side bridge wing. It disappeared in the blast, and with it went Captain Palmer. Ironically, he was the only casualty. Captain James Palmer was buried the next morning at 0700 hours with full military honors.

That was two months ago that command of the Stewart fell to the Hawk. In addition to other shortages, experienced captains were also in short supply. The loss of Captain Palmer moved Lt. Hawkins into the command position. Although in this case, Hawk was more than experienced. On the thirty missions and patrols since the attack that took Captain Palmer's life, Hawk had more than proved he was fit for the command, for the ship hadn't taken a single casualty. Perhaps the Stewart was a lucky ship after all. Standing on the bridge Hawk pondered the last two months and wondered what would become of his promising career. Then this morning from fleet headquarters ordering all vessel commanders to report to the flagship at 1100 hours. Knowing this probably meant action, Hawk ordered his subordinate officers to report to his wardroom. First to arrive was his gunnery officer, Lt. (jg) Kevin Cummings. "Guns, I've been ordered to report to the flagship. We may be seeing more action. Check with the gun crews as to any problems we may have with the 4 inchers and give the exec a status check on the ongoing repair of mount B. Also check the magazines and make sure we have all the 4 inch ammunition we can carry." "Aye aye sir," answered Lt. Cummings. As he left the engineering officer came in. Lt. Mark Wilkes was one of those irreplaceable engineers. How he kept those ancient power plants running, Hawk could never understand. Wilkes was also a very capable officer and only junior to Hawk by one week. Hawk and Wilkes had become very good friends in the two and a half years since he had come aboard. Wilkes was a walking encyclopedia on naval knowledge and strategies. When alone, they used their first names, but Wilkes had begun calling him Hawk, as had all of the officers. Even the enlisted men referred to their captain in this manner. Of course not to his face. Strict military decorum prevented this. Wilkes was very impressed with the Hawk, how quickly he took command when the captain was killed, and even his ability to grasp a situation and turn things around to their favor. Since taking over, Hawk had already saved the ship and crew from certain annihilation several times. Something that was also noticed by their squadron commander as well. "Mr. Wilkes, how are the engines?" "Fine captain. There's scuttlebutt that we may be seeing some action again. Any truth to that?" I have to report to HQ within the hour," said Hawk." I'm guessing that means something is about to hit the fan." "I hope it's not us", replied Wilkes, chuckling. "Mark, make sure we are topped off with all the fuel we can carry. Check with the chief on that port shaft we repaired last week and check with the machinists as to whether we're still losing fuel from the port side fuel tank. Then give your report to the exec." "Aye aye sir." said Wilkes as he turned and left. Next to report were ensigns John and Jerry Webb. The Webb's were brothers, in fact identical twins. John was in charge of damage control and Jerry was the ship's doctor. That was the only way they could be told apart. Jerry's uniform was always spotless and John's always had a trace of grease or oil on his. Both had been aboard the Stewart for seven years and knew the ship inside and out, front to back. "John," said the Hawk," we may be heading into action soon. Make sure you have plenty of oxyacetylene and foamite. Make sure everything is secured. Make a checklist of anything you need and give it to the exec." Turning to his medical officer, Hawk said," Jerry, check your supplies, and let Lt. Wilkes know if you need anything." The last officer to report was ensign Clemson, the supply officer. "Gene," said Hawk, "I need you to check that your stores are completely stocked. We'll probably be going out shortly. We may be gone for only several hours or several days. Make a list of anything you need or think we'll need and give your list to Lt. Wilkes." Minutes later Hawk went up to the bridge where his exec was standing his watch as OOD, Lt. Wayne Benson. "Wayne," said Hawk, "I've been ordered to report to fleet. I'm sure it means action. I've asked for status reports from Cummings, Wilkes, the Webb's and Clemson. As soon as they put them together, compile them and give me a report when I return." "Yes sir." replied Benson.

Aboard the flagship, the USS Houston, Admiral Doorman (Dutch) reported that a sub had located an enemy convoy comprising nine merchantmen and troopships escorted by two destroyers making for Surabaya, before he was forced under by one of the escorts. "Gentlemen," said the admiral, "we're going after that convoy. Task Force 7 will take care of the escorts. DesRon 3 will enter the harbor and destroy the troopships and supply ships with torpedo fire. Then on my order, as soon as the escorts are removed, the destroyers will pull out and we'll finish off the ships in the harbor with heavy gunfire." Next, the admiral's aide stepped up and gave the hour of departure, the course and speed they would travel, and the expected hour of attack. Then Admiral Doorman returned to the podium and finished. "Gentlemen, return to your ships and prepare them for battle. This is going to get bloody. I'll send a radio to the fleet a half hour before we sortie. Good luck to you all." As everyone stood to leave and began to filter out, Hawk saw Cmdr. Adams seated at the far side of the wardroom and went over to speak with him. Commander Stuart Adams was ComDesRon 3; (Commander of destroyer squadron 3) Cmdr. Adams liked Hawk. Some said Hawk was one of his favorite officers, and many believed he looked out for Hawk. He did. Hawk was one of his youngest and most, promising officers. His actions since taking command of the Stewart hadn't escaped his attentions. Although unknown to Hawk, Cmdr. Adams had already put the Hawk in for several decorations. Hawk was also one of his most inexperienced officers, but thus far that had been an asset.

Because of his inexperience, Hawk was able to see things in a mission that his more experienced officers overlooked or took for granted. Hawk had a keen sense of seeing things before they happened. It was a sense that all great warriors possessed. He saw greatness ahead for Hawk. "Cmdr., may I speak to you for a moment?" asked Hawk. Cmdr. Adams motioned Hawk over to an empty corner of the wardroom. "I know what you're going to say, Lt." said Cmdr. Adams. "A convoy that valuable has to have an escort of more than two destroyers. But the japs know we don't have much left to send out. The admiral thinks the enemy may be over confident." "But sir,' answered Hawk, "If the enemy does have a force larger than what the sub saw before it was forced to submerge, we could be facing a very large force. We could be wiped out. This could be a trap, get us to send out everything we have. We steam out there, see only the two destroyers and commit ourselves. Then they come in with a much heavier force and slaughter us." "Yes," said Cmdr. Adams, "I see your point. I'll speak to the admiral. But looking at it from his point of view, Lt. If the Jap admiral is over confident, we could surprise him and wipe them out and escape before they knew what hit them. One more thing. The captain of the Barr has been relieved of command due to health reasons. I want you to transfer your exec to replace him." "But sir, "protested Hawk, "he's very inexperienced. Isn't there anyone else you can send over?" Shaking his head, Cmdr Adams answered, "I'm afraid not. There's a shortage of officers too." "Then Cmdr., I request that the Barr follow the Stewart on the patrol so I can give him as much help as possible." "That's a good idea Lt., Now return to your ship and I'll let you know what the admiral says. But I wouldn't hold your breath, once the admiral makes up his mind to do something; it's pretty hard to change it." "Yes sir "said Hawk. Saluting, he turned and returned to his ship. "Good luck, Lt.", Hawk heard the Cmdr. say as he left.

Prior to Captain Palmer's death, Hawk had always envisioned he'd feel a sort of excitement before going into battle. But since taking command of the Stewart, all he felt was a sort of sick feeling in his stomach. He reasoned it was the burden of responsibility placed upon him. Two and a half hours after reporting to the flagship, Hawk wished he was an ordinary seaman. Then he would be oblivious to what he knew now. Returning to his ship, Hawk walked past the other four ships in the squadron that made up DesRon 3. They were all of the same destroyer class as the Stewart, but commissioned after her. Hence all had the same ailments, mechanical and weaponry failures that his ship had been experiencing since the war began. The Pope, Jackson, Oliver (flagship, Com DesRon 3), and Barr had all fought ferociously and heroically thus far. He wondered if any would survive this coming battle.

Aboard the Stewart, Hawk sent for his executive officer to report to the captain's cabin. Once there, Hawk began briefing his exec on the next mission. Lt. Benson also shared the same concerns about the details as Hawk had voiced with Cmdr. Adams. "Why would the enemy send out such a valuable convoy without a proper escort?" asked Benson. "Maybe it's the intention of the enemy to draw us out, sucker us into the open, and then send in his aircraft or heavy ships. Damn it sir, they could easily wipe us out on this one mission. Take out the rest of the Asiatic fleet in one battle." "That's how I see it," said Hawk. "I said as much to Cmdr. Adams. He said he would speak to Admiral Doorman. But I wouldn't expect any change in orders. Benson had long ago learned to trust Hawk's judgment on matters of combat. He too had found that Hawk had a keen sense of what was going to happen in battle before it actually happened. He seldom spoke out about planned missions but when he did, Hawk was right on the money. Benson thought it was uncanny at first, but then he realized it was to his and the crew of the Stewarts advantage. As soon as the Hawk finished briefing his exec, Benson handed him the report on the status of the Stewart. "Sir," started Benson, "we've only got five torpedoes aboard, all on the starboard side. The port mount is still inoperable. B turret is still inoperable as well, but the mechanics say they'll have it on line within the hour. Mr. Wilkes reports that his engines are up to snuff, the port screw looks like it'll work alright, fuel tanks are topped off, but he reports that the #4 fuel tank is still losing fuel, though it's a minor leak and it shouldn't reduce our speed. However it will leave a trail for an enemy sub to follow. The doc reports that all medical supplies are aboard, and John has reported damage control is ready for action, though he has requested new fire "hoses." (That was a sort of private joke aboard. Everyone knew there wasn't an extra hose available in all of the Asiatic fleet, much less a new one.) "Captain," said Benson, "The ship is squared away and ready for action. Or as ready as she will ever be." "Well Ben," said Hawk, "if everything goes according to plan, we might give the japs a little back. But if not, be prepared to get the hell out of there as quick as you can." Hawk saw that Benson was confused, so he continued, "You're being transferred to the Barr. Her captain is being relieved due to a medical condition. You're to report to him as his relief." Going to his locker, Hawk took out a bottle of medicinal brandy and poured a glass for himself and one for Benson. Then he continued, "I spoke to Cmdr. Adams and suggested that you follow the Stewart in for the attack." An expression of fear crossed Benson's face and Hawk placed his right hand on his exec's shoulder and said, " relax Ben, you'll do just fine. You won't have time before we leave to get to know your officers, but as soon as we return look over your files on your officers. Study their strengths and weaknesses. Interview them, find out which of them you can lean on and trust the most when the chips are down. And above all else, remember, just because they have the rank doesn't mean they know their jobs." Hawk let things sink in a little then continued.. "Ben, you're a damn good exec. You'll be a damn good captain. Just follow your orders and when you're not sure, follow your gut instincts. Keep your head and never let your subordinates see you panic. Tonight, just follow my lead, stick to the plan, and do what feels natural when we go into action. And remember that once the action starts, despite following the plan of attack, if you see a way to inflict maximum damage on the enemy, jump on it." Raising his glass to Bens, Hawk toasted, "To the captain of the USS Barr, may success follow your banner." With their glasses empty, they shook hands and Ben left to gather his gear, and then left the ship to report to the Barr, leaving Hawk alone on the bridge of the Stewart, feeling as though he had just sentenced his friend to death. Going to the bridge voice tube, he called down to the engine room and asked Lt. Wilkes to report to his cabin. Reporting to the captain's cabin, Lt. Wilkes saw Hawk rinsing out a glass and saw the bottle of brandy on the small table. The bottle didn't surprise him. He knew that many of the captains in the fleet kept a bottle in their cabins despite the navy regulations pertaining to alcohol aboard. They had them for stress and tense times. And these were very stressful times. "Sir," said

Chapter 2

Sitting in his quarters one hour later, Hawk was wishing he could get drunk. But years of naval discipline and the responsibility of his men wouldn't allow him to. Benson's leaving seemed to be a bad omen. Even though it was his idea, and was for the good of the mission, he told himself. Now his exec was in the engine room instead of up on the bridge. Another bad omen he thought to himself. This mission seemed like a risky proposition and the closer it got to sortie, the worse things looked. Personally he didn't think the chances of success looked very good. It just didn't make sense to him that the Jap convoy would be so lightly protected. Over confident or not, no admiral in any navy could be so fool hardy. But Admiral Doormann was willing to bet every ship they had, and the lives of thousands of Blue Jackets that the jap admiral was that foolish. Maybe, thought Hawk, Admiral Doormann was the foolish one. At 0130 the radio message flashed to the ABDA fleet to prepare to heave to all ships. And Hawk prepared himself for the worst.

At 0200 the small fleet upped their anchors and one by one the 12 ships steamed out at 20 knots, on a direct course SE, 225. Because of the distance, the hour of attack, (just before dawn, about 0600) and the shortage of fuel, the fleet took a direct course to the target. "Again another bad omen". Hawk thought. At 0548, with Surabaya 20,000 yards to starboard, Doormann turned his four cruisers and four destroyers 20 degrees to port to attack the two escorting destroyers. Des Ron 3, with Oliver in the lead, followed by Pope, Jackson, Stewart and Barr began making smoke to cover their attack on the merchantmen. At 6,000 yards, USS. Oliver ordered Des Ron 3 to fire all port side torpedoes (except for Stewart, whose port mount was inoperable) then open fire one minute later with their four inch guns. All torpedoes missed or failed to explode. Gunnery however was excellent. The four inchers were small caliber, but the targets were unarmored, and the gunner's aims were deadly. According to the mission's goals, destroyer Barr's first shots were star shell. With the left side of the bay lit up. Des Ron 3 began picking out targets. The troopships were quiet, probably already unloaded. The merchantmen were low in the water-still full, so they were targeted first. One cargo ship, obviously loaded with ammunition, exploded in a fire ball after just three hits, illuminating several other cargo ships. It also illuminated a cruiser. Why it had withheld fire was thus far was anybody's guess, but now it opened up with its eight inch guns and Des Ron 3 was suddenly surrounded by shell splashes. The destroyers swung 90 degrees to starboard then 90 degrees to port in an S maneuver, and then fired all starboard side torpedoes at the cruiser. Just 2,100 yards distant, there was no way they could miss. But they did- or they failed to explode.

At 0627 the USS Oliver took an eight inch round in her forward engine room and forward boiler. Flooding rapidly, she took on an immediate seven degree list to starboard and her speed dropped to ten knots. Turning to port to retire, Cmdr. Adams ordered Des Ron 3 to continue the attack. Limping away for home, screams suddenly were heard over the TBS (talk between ships). Two battleships and three cruisers had their escape route blocked. It was a trap! As the Oliver began taking 6,8,14 and 15 inch gun fire, the Barr rushed to her aid. Before anybody could order Benson back, the Oliver and the Barr were blasted to pieces. Dozens of enemy high caliber shells struck the two hapless American destroyers with terrifyingly destructive blows that decimated the small ships, turning them into crematoriums. In seconds the shell twisted hulks disappeared beneath the waves. There would be few, if any survivors. The Pope, Jackson and Stewart continued their gun duel with the cruiser. Hawk, taking command of Des Ron 3 ordered Pope to resume the attack on the cargo ships as Jackson and Stewart continued to shell the cruiser. Hawk then realized why the torpedoes hadn't hit the cruiser. She was high and dry aground.

Since she wasn't firing her secondary armaments Hawk figured she was partially abandoned. Just as the cruiser appeared to be getting the worst of it, a call came over the TBS from Admiral Doorman himself ordering Des Ron 3 to retire.

Admiral Doorman's cruisers had had a surprise of their own. As they opened fire on the convoys two lone escorts, three enemy battleships, seven heavy and light cruisers, and twenty four destroyers appeared off both bows (port and starboard) and began to pummel the admirals ships. With nowhere to run, all they could do was fight and be annihilated. It was at this point that Admiral Doormann ordered Des Ron 3 to retire. Three minutes later the USS Houston received several 15 inch hits to her bridge structure, killing nearly everyone there, including Admiral Doormann. Within the next six hours, the ABDA fleet would cease to exist.

Knowing that his avenue of escape was blocked, evidenced by the destruction of destroyers Oliver and Barr, Hawk decided to retire in the direction least expected. He had no idea the firepower he'd soon be facing. Calling down to the engine room, Mark answered, "Lt. Wilkes". "Mark", Hawk asked, "we've done all we can here, we've been ordered to withdraw. Apparently the Admiral has run into trouble. Our escape route is blocked by two battleships and three cruisers. They've just sunk the Oliver and Barr. We have no clear path of escape. I plan to withdraw to the south, maybe assist the Admiral. There may be a straggler or two we can pick up. We'll circle Celebes Island and swing North back to base. You're the exec; you have to know my intentions. We'll be facing unimaginable odds, but I think it's our only chance. What I need to know from you, is can the engines take flank speed for the next three to four hours?" "Well sir," said Lt. Wilkes, "They can do it, but I'll have to stay down here to head off any problems." "I don't like it, but OK", said Hawk. "Stand by to shoot the works". Ordering the Pope and Jackson to close up, Hawk called down to the engine room, "Give me everything she's got". Turning to the helmsman, he ordered, "left full rudder, course 180, speed full ahead. Pulling the speed enunciator to flank, the Stewart heeled sharply to port, and then came back to an even keel, her speed picked up and she flew faster than she had for many years. In the engine room, Lt. Wilkes winced at the high speed and higher rate of fuel consumption. Then he shrugged to himself. "What the hell, we'll probably all be dead in the next couple of hours anyway."

Ten minutes later Hawk found his worst fears realized. Steaming into the battle area he came upon what he was certain was the entire Japanese navy. Flotsam, wreckage and burning oil was everywhere, marking the final resting place of each of Doormann's ships. There were a few survivors in the water, but at the high rate of speed the destroyers were traveling, there was no way they could stop to pick them up. However as they passed, they through some life preservers overboard to help them stay afloat. For now it was as much as they could do. With enemy heavy units as far as the eye could see in every direction, Hawk knew his plan couldn't work. Turning to his helmsman, he ordered "Reverse course," and calling down the voice tube to the engine room he ordered "Lt. Wilkes, "I need flank plus. We have the whole jap navy bearing down on us." The Stewart was now racing north, back through the oil slicks that marked the final resting places of the Oliver and Barr. On his own initiative the helmsman weaved through the patches of survivors in the water. Heavy shells began falling around the ship, killing and maiming the men in the water. With the survival of his ship at risk, Hawk couldn't worry about them now. "Sir, masts ahead to port and starboard." screamed the spotters, as a wall of splashes appeared all around the three destroyers. "Port ten degrees," screamed Hawk, then as soon as the destroyer began to swing into the turn, "starboard ten degrees. As the ship steadied on course, shells began falling where the ship would've been had Hawk not ordered the course change. Chasing splashes was an old defensive maneuver to avoid being struck. But Hawk knew he couldn't do it for long. Because of the sheer volume of the number of shells falling around the three American destroyers, eventually one of the big shells would find its target. And one of those 15" shells could sink any one of the destroyers. With enemy ships coming from ahead and both quarters, Hawk knew they'd soon have him boxed in and once that happened, they were dead. Going to the TBS, Hawk ordered the Pope and Jackson to scatter. Then told his helmsman, "Left rudder 20 degrees." As the ship heeled violently into the turn, Hawk had no time to check if the rest of DesRon 3 was following him. He had to concentrate on saving his own ship. Then the first hit arrived, there was a flash, a horrendous explosion and B turret disappeared in an angry cloud of smoke and flame. Another flash and a hole appeared in the fore deck, twenty feet ahead of A turret. When the smoke cleared, A turret was still there, but silent. Then another hit, aft of the bridge, destroying the radio room and sending the mast flying overboard. Too busy maneuvering the Stewart, Hawk can only hope that the other two destroyers of DesRon 3 are faring better. Through the smoke and flame of battle and the splashes caused by the near misses, Hawk spots a rain squall to starboard and orders the helmsman, "Starboard twenty five degrees." As the ship turns, Hawk looks behind him to see if the other two cans are following him. Jackson is right behind him. Then he sees the Pope coming out of a smoke screen provided by the Jackson. Pope is following, but is losing speed due to battle damage. In a few brief seconds he sees that her bridge has been demolished by several direct hits, both of her masts are gone as are her last three funnels. Being "tail end charlie," the Pope has received most of the shells coming from the enemy warships behind. Her X and Y turrets (her rear guns) are wrecked lumps of unrecognizable machinery. In fact, nothing on her stern is discernible. It's a miracle she's still afloat. Suddenly they are in the squall and safe for the moment. A few shells continue to drop around them as the enemy lobbed a few shots blindly, hoping for a lucky hit. (Distrusting the early radar apparatus, Admiral Yammamoto had few sets placed aboard his warships, relying on Japanese eyes instead.) Hawk knows that at this moment the enemy is surrounding the squall to catch them when they come out. Des Ron 3 stayed in the squall as long as they could. Thankful for the respite, they're able to repair some of the battle damage, bring up ammunition from the magazines, tend to the wounded, catch their breath, and maybe say a prayer or two before the rain dissipated and they have to face the enemy one last time. They knew death is near. The rain would only last for so long. Then they would be in a shell storm. A hell storm. Still, there's no panic. Every man knows his duty. Discipline reigns.

Wounded are treated, damage is shored up, weapons that can be repaired are repaired and those able to rest, rest. The gunners slump in exhaustion at their mounts. Sandwiches are brought out to the crew to eat at their posts, from a galley that somehow escaped the blasting.

Then as the rain begins to slacken, Hawk and his men prepare for their final battle. A battle they have no hope of winning or even surviving. With all operational guns manned and the crew standing by, the ships slip out of the squall into a bright blue sky ready for a deluge of gunfire. Except, all is silent. The enemy is nowhere to be seen. The lookouts report the horizons clear. The ships steam ahead slow, the only speed they can manage, while the lookouts continue to scan the horizons, wary of yet another trap. Baffled by the absence of the enemy, Hawk takes advantage of another apparent respite. More repairs are made. Hawk places the Stewart and Jackson on each side of the Pope. Lines are passed over and they begin pumping out her flooded compartments. When her engines seize up, Hawk sends the engineer from the Jackson to the Pope to assist with repairs. All the while Hawk is confused. He's not alone. Where is the enemy? They were just 10,000 yards outside of the squall. Why would they leave? DesRon 3 was finished, meat for the dogs. And how could their entire fleet get away so quickly? Why wasn't there any trace of battle? Where was the flotsam, the oil slicks? The smoke? Doormann's four cruisers and two destroyers as well as the Oliver and Barr were sunk in close proximity. There were some survivors in the water. They had thrown out life preservers to them. Now the preservers and the survivors were gone. Everyone was confused. Were they dead? Had they passed to some sort of Valhalla? Were they now ghosts? Being reasonable men, they knew that was absurd. There had to be another reason. But what could it be? Things just didn't add up! The Pope's stern compartments, now free of water, rises out of the water. Holes are plugged making the ship more water tight. The engineers get one of her engines back on line, her engineer advises Hawk that the Pope can move under her own power at 10 knots. The ships move out, heading back towards base, a base that Hawk desperately hopes is still there. He orders the Jackson to stand off to starboard of the Pope in case her engines fail again and the Pope needs another tow. Stewart takes the lead. Miraculously the Jackson's and Stewart's engines were not damaged in the battle they were now leaving behind. A battle that took the lives of many of their friends. Hawk sends a signal to the Jackson ordering the ship to follow the Pope at 500 yards, but if the enemy is sighted the Jackson is to abandon the Stewart and

Pope and steam at best speed back to base and report the loss of DesRon 3. Jackson had also taken damage amidships; her radio room was also damaged. She could receive, but not send. As the battered remnants of Des Ron 3 continued towards their base (Cavite), Hawk kept his crews at action stations, his lookouts still searching the seas for enemy ships and the skies for enemy aircraft. Repair parties continued to repair what they could. Dr. Webb was kept busy with the wounded and Ensign Webb with damage control and search parties looking for sailors trapped in any compartments. The dead were gathered and counted against the ships roster. And still the enemy did not come. The men, carrying out their duties were becoming uneasy and nervous. Nobody could figure out where the enemy had gone. By the following morning, the dead were accounted for and placed in the wardroom. The search of all compartments for the missing began. Pope, the most heavily damaged suffered 123 dead, Jackson-78 and Stewart-91. A complete search of the ships took several hours. Once finished, Hawk has a good idea of DesRon 3's casualties; Pope - 123, Jackson - 78, and Stewart - 91. Haw then called an officers conference aboard the Jackson - the least damaged of the 3 destroyers.

In the officers wardroom on the Jackson, the Popes captain, Lt. Rivers reported, "Sir, we've plugged all of the leaks below the waterline and halted all of the flooding. The welders will have the hull watertight within the hour. Engines 1 and 3 are back on line, but are operating at 43% efficiency. I'm afraid engines 2 and 4 are unrepairable without a shipyard repair facility. Turrets X and Y have been destroyed as well. The after magazine was partially flooded but is now dry. Both the masts are gone, and the radio room took a direct hit and is out of commission as well. Maximum speed is 10 knots but in a pinch we can make 12 knots for a very short time. Turrets A and B are operable, but only in manual control." "Thank you Lt. Rivers. Give yourself and your crew a well done." Then turning to the captain of the Jackson, Hawk continued, "Lt. Hunt?" 'Sir," Hunt began, "We were hit by what appeared to be 4-8" hits amidships. The first took out the ships dispensary. Our doctor, Lt. Meadows was killed as well as seven men. The second hit took out our forward mast, however it has been jury rigged. The radio room was slightly damaged, the radio receives, but we can't send. I have technicians working on it, but they don't seem very hopeful. The third hit was aft and starboard of C mount. It must have been armor piercing because it went through the deck and came out the side of the ship without exploding. Damage was minimal, except for the holes. The last hit was on the starboard torpedo director and torpedo mount. Since we have no torpedoes, it won't affect the fighting capabilities of the ship." As Lt. Hunt gave his report, Hawk was thinking about another report, Hunt's service record that he had read shortly after the battle had ended the day before.

Lt. Samuel Hunt had begun his naval career on a bad note. He had barely graduated the academy. His grades were outstanding, but he had had an incredible chip on his shoulders, perhaps because his father had been a hero in the last war. The elder Hunt had received the Congressional Medal of Honor, posthumously. Maybe his ego would have been smaller had his father been around to guide him in his youth. While at Annapolis, Cadet Hunt had had a problem carrying out orders that he didn't agree with, like policing cigarette butts. Hunt didn't smoke. All others he carried out with enthusiasm. Anybody else would have been tossed out, but his father's medal carried a lot of weight. Nine years in the navy had seen him rise and fall in the ranks due to minor infractions. His career began in naval aviation, flying a scout plane off of the cruiser Helena. Then a transfer to the battleship Arizona as captain of X, then Y turrets. From there, due to a disciplinary action he was transferred to the Asiatic fleet as executive officer of the Jackson. Sam Hunt was due to be discharged in late December, but the war had marooned him. Because of the war, all discharges were put off. Experienced officers were needed. Even the bad ones. But then Lt. Hunt changed. Perhaps it was the damage sustained to his old ships. Maybe it was the deaths of his shipmates and friends aboard his old ships. He knew he had a brother serving on the battleship Tennessee, whom as yet he hadn't heard if he had survived or not. Whatever the reason, Hunt had been transformed by the war. When the captain of the Jackson had moved up to exec of the cruiser Ajax, Hunt became the Jackson's new captain. And since taking command, Hunt had proven himself to be a very capable and resourceful officer.

Lt. Maxwell Rivers was another good officer, Captain of the Pope. He was two years junior to Hawk. When the war started, he was third officer aboard the Pope. Like Lt. Cummings, he was a master gunner. He found himself her captain due to attrition, the deaths of his commanding officer and executive officer very early in the war. Like Lt. Hunt, he had done an excellent job since taking over. From the time he had reported for duty three years ago, he had shown that he had a propensity as a scrounger. It wasn't long before Cmdr. Adams had made him the squadron supply officer. However when war came, he requested a return to the Pope. When the captain and exec were killed in the air raid on Cavite, Lt. Rivers became the Pope's new Captain. Like Lt. Hunt, Lt. Rivers had done a splendid job thus far. They were both men he knew he could count on.

Hawk stood and looked at everyone in the room. The men were uncertain and puzzled, but not scared. He was very proud of them. What bothered him was he knew they were looking to him for leadership. The problem was that he was as confused about the absence of the enemy as they were. "Men" Hawk began, "The disappearance of the enemy has got me stumped. I don't know why they left or where they went. But their absence has given us the time we needed to repair our ships. That was their mistake. We're going to steam north back to base. Our speed will be ten knots to allow the Pope to keep up. If heavy enemy units are sighted Sam (U.S.S. Jackson) and I (U.S.S Stewart) will make smoke to cover Jim's (U.S.S Pope) escape. When the Pope is clear we will attack. If things appear to be going badly for us, Jim, you'll have to abandon, don't open the sea cocks. Set your scuttling charges for twenty minutes. The enemy will board your ship and maybe we'll take a lot of them out. Just get your men as far from the Pope as you can. Sam, if we sight the enemy, you take the lead and go straight for him. My forward turrets are inoperable. I'll steer forty degrees to port or starboard to bring my after turrets to bear. If things go badly, you circle back for Popes crew. I'll attack to create a diversion." As Hawk finished, Lt. Hunt started to protest. But Hawk held up his hand and said, "That is all gentlemen. Let's return to our ships and prepare to get underway." As soon as Lt. Rivers had left, Lt. Hunt confronted Hawk. "Sir", he said "You're the squadron commander. My ship should create the diversion." "No" said Hawk. "Your ship is the least damaged and has the best chance of picking up the Pope's crew, and getting back to base. But Sam, if picking up the Popes crew means getting yourself sunk-leave them and proceed back to base at top speed. One of us has to get back to base. If we still have a base, and remember, that damned jap fleet is still out there somewhere."

Two hours later found the three ships still steaming towards their base, with still no trace of the enemy. The Pope was having difficulty keeping up, (obviously her ten knots was slower than that of the Stewart and Jackson) so Hawk had ordered a speed of eight knots. Hawk also ordered twice as many lookouts on duty. He didn't want to be caught by surprise. The only thing he could figure was that the enemy had hauled off and steamed to Cavite to destroy the naval base. That meant they would be at the base waiting for them or close by the base. As they had approached Surabaya Hawk had noticed that there weren't any troopships or merchantmen in the harbor. Even the grounded cruiser was gone. If the troops had moved inland and the cargo ships had unloaded, they may have moved out. And if they had pulled the cruiser off of the reef, they may have towed her to safety. But Hawk still couldn't figure out why there wasn't any debris. Since he didn't think the japs could have pulled the cruiser free, he reasoned they must have blown her up. Then again, why no debris? Equally perplexing was the lack of debris as they passed through the area where the Oliver and Barr went down. Hawk had hoped there might be blue jackets in the water. But the surface was void. No survivors, no debris, no slicks, and surprisingly, no sharks which were always present following a naval battle. At 1400 lookouts spotted smoke on the horizon, but the distance was too far to make any positive identification as to whether the ship was friendly or enemy. At 1800, as the three destroyers neared Cavite a ship was seen coming out of the harbor. As it closed on DesRon 3, it was seen to be a tanker. As it drew closer, it was seen to be flying a Japanese flag from her stern post. Calling the squadron to action stations, Jackson and Stewart veered off and steered for the enemy, increasing speed to twenty eight knots. The enemy ship must have mistaken them for two of their own, because she didn't attempt to escape. At 8,000 yards Lt. Hunt ordered his gunners to open fire. 'A' turret was right on the money, the first three salvos landed amidships, starting a large fire. As the tanker turned away to try to escape, 'B' turret hit its bridge with their second salvo. Then 'A' turret hit them again, then before another shell could hit the tanker, it exploded in a flash that left no doubt that there wouldn't be any survivors. As the three destroyers continued to steam toward Cavite, another ship was seen to be departing the harbor. As the Jackson's turrets began to train on this new target, the lookout announced that the stars and stripes were flying from the new target ship. As Lt. Hunt watched this new ship, (a cutter) wary of a trap, he was mildly surprised to see that it was only armed with a light machine gun on its bow. But what really caught his attention was that the three sailors manning it were training it on the Jackson. Believing the ship was sailing under false colors, Hunt ordered his gun crews to open fire. This didn't escape Hawk's attention either. He was about to order the Jackson to commence fire, it had after all just come out of a harbor following an enemy ship. With the Jackson only 5000 yards from the cutter, her A turret resumed fire. At that distance they could hardly miss. They didn't, the first shot struck the bow, and when the smoke cleared, the machine gun and its crew had vanished from this world. As the second round went out, a radioman came running to the bridge. "Sir, we've just received a radio, she's one of ours." Running to the TBS, Hawk screamed, "Cease fire, cease fire." Following the destruction of his deck gun, the cutter commander had radically changed course. This alone had saved his ship from the next two salvos, and they landed 100 feet away from his ship. With the cutter disabled and disarmed, Hawk ordered DesRon 3 to surround the cutter. This done, he ordered Lt. Hunt to send a boat to the cutter and bring its commander to the Stewart. As he watched the Jackson lower its boat, he muttered, "What the hell is going on?" It didn't make sense why an American ship would be coming out of Cavite behind an enemy vessel. Nothing had made any sense since they had emerged from the squall.

Hawk was sitting in the wardroom when the cutters captain came in, escorted by Lt. Hunt and two armed seamen. The seamen quickly left, posted outside the door. A steward came in with some coffee, set it on the table, then left, leaving the officers alone. The cutters captain, wearing the insignia of a Lt.Cmdr. was a portly man of African American descent. He introduced himself as Cmdr. Thomas

Williams. Hawk had never seen a black officer before, much less a high ranking one. "Officer shortages", he guessed. Seething, Cmdr. Williams screamed at Hawk," What the hell gives you the right to fire on an American vessel?" "Sir," answered Hawk, "we are at war". We sank the enemy tanker as it came out of the harbor. When you came out of the same harbor, with your gun crews ready to open up on us, it was natural to assume that you were enemy as well." "What enemy? And by what authority do you attack any vessel in these waters?" Standing and pointing to the commission plaque mounted on the wall, Hawk answered, "My authority comes from the President of the United States and the War Department." The Cmdr. glared at Hawk a moment, and then asked, "Are you nuts? We haven't been at war with Japan for more than a hundred years. Where did these old ships come from, Lt., If you are a Lt. You have committed an act of aggression against a peaceful nation. A nation allied with the United States. As area commander, I order you to surrender your vessels to me. You and your officers and men are under arrest for the murder of twenty nine Japanese nationals, as well as the deaths of four of my men aboard the cutter USS Palanka." "That's absurd," said Hawk. "Japan attacked Pearl Harbor just three months ago. Three days ago they sank four cruisers and two destroyers under the direct command of Admiral Karl Doormann, and two destroyers under the command of Cmdr. Stuart Adams, ComDesRon 3 of the Asiatic fleet. I will not surrender any of my ships or men without a direct order from Franklin D. Roosevelt, the war department or Admiral Glassford, Commander of the Asiatic Fleet." Somewhat subdued by Hawks outburst, the cutter captain stared at Hawk and asked, "Who the devil is Roosevelt?" Sitting at the wardroom table, he looks around him, then slowly rises and walks over to the bulkhead and looks out the porthole at the Pope. Hastily repaired from her last battle, the previous damage is unmistakable. The fire blackened metal, the patches welded over the holes made from shell penetrations, the twisted remains of X and Y turrets, the absence of three of her four funnels and their bases are all evident, all obviously recent battle damage. Turning and glaring at Hawk a moment, he walked over to the starboard side and gazed out at the Jackson. Though not as heavily damaged as the Pope, her damage is equally evident. He rubbed his eyes as though looking at a mirage, as surely this must be. He looked at Hawk and asked, "How is this possible?" Then thinking a second, it hit him. "Did you say the ABDA fleet under Admiral Karl Doormann?" "Yes sir," answered Hawk. "We were placed under his command one week after the Japanese sank the HMS Prince of Wales and the HMS Repulse. Three days ago we attempted to disrupt an enemy landing in Surabaya Bay. We sank a tanker and two cargo ships and heavily damaged a Mogami class cruiser that had run aground. When we were ordered to withdraw, we found our escape route blocked. Trapped, we lost two destroyers, The Oliver and the Barr. Our squadron commander was aboard the Oliver. As senior surviving officer I took over command of what was left of DesRon 3." The cutter commander shook his head and repeated over and over to himself, "No, this can't be. This is impossible." Hawk got up and walked over to the cutter captain and asked, "What are you talking about sir?" Looking up at Hawk and Wilkes he asked them," Lt's., Do you know what year it is?" Lt.Wilkes answered, "Of course, it's 1942." "No," replied the cutter captain. "It's 2042"!

Hawk and Wilkes turned white. Now things began to make sense. Why the enemy warships had disappeared, the absence of wreckage and survivors. But how could such a thing have happened? Even though the results made sense, how was it possible? Leaking as his ships were, the disposition of DesRon 3 was up in the air. According to history, the destroyers no longer existed. Until Washington could verify their claim they decided the ships couldn't be allowed entry into the military base. So the mangled destroyers of DesRon 3 lay anchored outside the harbor of Cavite. From a distance they appeared to be blockading it. But a closer examination would show that the ships were actually wrecks, and if they were aboard they would see that only a steady pumping was keeping them afloat. Within the harbor there were repair facilities that could fix all of their troubles, but until Washington decided what to do with them, the base was off limits to DesRon 3. As soon as word of the arrival of DesRon 3 had been made public, the press descended on the backwater base. Scientists swarmed to the base attempting to solve the riddle as to how the naval squadron had jumped across a period of a hundred years to arrive at the present date. The Japanese didn't care how they had done it, they wanted Hawk tried for the murder of the crew of the Kobe Maru and its sinking. Sensing a ticklish situation, the president ordered four frigates from Pearl Harbor and three more from Wake Island to steam to Cavite and form a protection detail for the ancient destroyer squadron until a decision could be made on their disposition. Within a week everyone was talking about their heroic return from the dead and the sinking of the tanker was quickly forgotten by everyone. Everyone but the Japanese, that is. They still wanted Hawk tried and beheaded. There had even been threats that ranged from leaving the United Nations (if Hawk wasn't handed over to the Japanese) to purchasing warships and engaging DesRon3 in battle. Weeks later the periodicals were still filled with stories of DesRon 3. Included were stories about their heroic battles during the war, and historic accounts of how the Japanese had caught the destroyers as they came out of the squall and rapidly sank all three destroyers. Their crews were slaughtered on the ships and in the water. No sailors were picked up. Those that had survived the shelling and the machine gunning were left to the sharks. It was the way of the enemy. One Nagato class battleship had been lost in the battle. Reports were sketchy. All that was known was that the battleship had followed them into the squall and had never come out. It was assumed that DesRon 3 had sunk it. Now, 100 years later, that's what they wanted to do to the Pope, Jackson and Stewart. About that time the Erickson battle group showed up. The battle group was built around the nuclear powered aircraft carrier John Erickson, CVN 144. Their duty and responsibility was to protect the men and destroyers of DesRon 3. A decision had been made as to their disposition. Ghosts from the past or not, they were still warships of the US Navy. Even if nobody could figure out how, A) they had survived the blasting as they came out of the squall, and B) How they had managed to teleport themselves 100 years into the future. The only thing that was certain was that it took a special act and vote in congress to list the ships on the active duty rolls of the United States Navy again.. That was the only way that DesRon 3 could utilize the naval repair facilities. And none too soon, the destroyers had begun to spring leaks. When the destroyers finally were able to enter the harbor, all were in a sinking condition. All headed directly into dry docks.

Chapter 3

Chartered yachts and aircraft began to arrive filled with newspaper reporters and satellite/cable crews in the hopes of interviewing Hawk and his crews. But it was to no avail. No interviews were given and navy fighter jets kept all non military ships and planes away. A small naval fleet even surrounded the final resting place of the Kobe Maru long enough to blow the wreck to smithereens. It was reported that the wreck posed a threat to navigation, but many believed it was with the idea that if the wreck was out of sight, it would be out of mind as well. That probably wasn't a good idea though. Immediately conspiracy theories began to surface. The captain and crew of the cutter were sworn to secrecy about details of DesRon 3 and the sinking of the tanker, and then transferred to a place where they could be watched. This contributed to more conspiracy theories. When the press was unable to get their stories, they fabricated them. Soon the papers were theorizing that UFO's had abducted DesRon 3 and destroyed the Japanese battleship Nagato. It was as believable as the truth, that DesRon 3 had teleported themselves 100 years into the future. Then a naval research ship came in and interviewed the destroyer men. They couldn't discern anything, so they left, tracing the exact path of DesRon 3 including entering a squall that happened to be at the same coordinates. They were never seen again. There was even a story that a group of researchers were going to charter a ship from the Woods Hole Oceanic Institute to dive down and see if the ships that the japs claimed to have sunk were really there. WHOI denied the report. As the squadron received more publicity, more people showed up to see the now famous ships. So a second battle group was sent to Cavite. This was the aircraft carrier John F. Kennedy, CVN 169. For some reason the protection of DesRon 3 was now given the highest priority. Of special interest to the current President of the United States was that his grandfather was a chief petty officer aboard the USS Stewart. The President, Anthony Williams, soon arrived on the presidential yacht. Accompanying him was the new base commander, Cmdr. John Thomas. His great grandfather was a famous submarine skipper of WWII, Cmdr. Dudley (Mush) Morton.

Not everyone was kept away. American scientists and naval engineers we allowed aboard inspecting the ships and interviewing Des Ron 3's officers with questions as to how they were able to transcend the ages, to escape the enemy warships and arrive here in another century. Hawk and his officers had no idea. They informed the officers that in the last fifty years the United States had stepped up their explorations of space. But they were faced with the age old problem of how to get astronauts across the galaxy alive. The spaceships would have to be enormous to carry enough food and fuel. If they were somehow able to bend time or find a space portal to cross time, their problem would be solved. Hawk and his officers listened attentively. They couldn't believe that the world had evolved so much in the last hundred years. But neither did they have any useful information for them.

The men of DesRon 3 were held almost like prisoners at Cavite. As the ships were in a dry dock, they were required to leave their ships and were housed in a barracks near the dock. A beach was sectioned off for them and nobody was allowed to speak with them. They were told it was a matter of national security as well as their own safety. Food and refreshments were trucked in for them. They were closely guarded. The navy also brought in jamming equipment which was installed on several frigates to ensure that no information got out. This seemed odd to Hawk and his officers, as none of the radios on his ships could transmit. And only Jackson's could receive. Small naval craft continually patrolled the entrance to the harbor. And a combat air patrol was kept over Cavite. They were told it was for their own safety, but they seemed as intent on keeping them in the dark as much as the rest of the world. There were reports that the Japanese had threatened them again, this time with a kamikaze attack, the likes of which hadn't been seen for a hundred years. When it was explained to Hawk what a kamikaze attack was, he had a hard time believing that anybody would do that intentionally.

Early one morning as the sun was coming up; Lt. Hunt was walking the decks of his destroyer. It was his favorite time of the day. Nearly all of his crew were asleep and there wasn't anything for him to do so he could take his time and relax. Rounding the stern as the sun came up off of the horizon, he was suddenly faced with a ghostly apparition. At first he was startled, then calmed, as though by an old friend. He knew he was hallucinating. He had to be. There was no way she could be there. She had to be a mirage, brought on by a mind hungry for something familiar. She was dressed in gray, looking as formidable as the day he had first met her, and trailing the colors of the great nation she represented. He closed his eyes, expecting her to have disappeared when he reopened them. But she was still there. Still believing her a mirage, and not wanting to lose sight of her, Hunt leaned over the railing and watched her approach, afraid that if he blinked, she would be gone. The sun rose behind her, slowly revealing her silhouette. Only when she had dropped her anchor did Hunt truly believe she was there. But there she was. The battleship Texas had come to call.

Lt. Cmdr. Samuel Hunt Sr. was the third officer of the USS Texas in 1916. During the naval battle of Jutland the Texas was heavily damaged while in combat with a German battleship and a couple of cruisers. Taking several heavy shells to her bridge, the captain was seriously wounded and the exec was killed. Lt. Cmdr. Hunt assumed command and steamed the heavily damaged battleship out of the battle area. Bringing the ship safely out of harm's way, he learned that the flagship was being taken under fire by several enemy battleships. Reversing course, he advanced through an enemy destroyer's smoke screen and crept undetected towards the enemy battle wagons. Coming out of the smoke screen a mere 5,000 yards from the enemy ships (point blank range) he opened fire with all starboard guns and began blasting the enemy battleships to pieces, buying time for the flagship to escape. In the short melee, one enemy battleship was seen to explode and sink, while another turned away heavily damaged. The Texas then turned away and left the battle area. She didn't escape unscathed though. She received one torpedo hit near the bow and three large caliber hits to her bridge. Lt. Cmdr. Hunt was severely injured and died from his wounds later that day. For his commitment and courage above and beyond the call of duty, he was awarded the Congressional Medal of Honor, posthumously.

The U.S.S. Texas was a New York class battleship armed with 10-14 inch guns. She was conceived on the drawing tables in 1914 and took three years to build and was commissioned in 1916. By 1941 she was already obsolete. She was based at the Mare Island navy yard when Pearl Harbor was attacked and so escaped destruction. Obsolete as she was, she was still a powerful ship. Transferred to the Atlantic fleet following re modernization, she served with distinction as a bombardment platform preceding nine invasions and fought the Italian battleship Jean Bart in a short sea action that all but destroyed the Italian battle wagon. In 1945, (following the surrender of Germany) she was transferred to the Pacific fleet, again distinguishing herself as a floating gun platform for pre invasion bombardment at Iwo Jima and Okinawa. At the end of the war, she was decommissioned, having been awarded thirteen battle stars and four meritorious unit citations. Sold as a memorial, she spent the next ninety five years moored near Houston, Texas. Lt. Sam Hunt (Jr.) had served on his daddy's ship then transferred to the U.S.S. Nevada for further training. The Nevada was of a class preceding the New York class. For Hunt, seeing the Texas was like seeing an old friend. Very old indeed.

As the days passed, more ships appeared. Many of them as old as the Texas. Some of them more modern. The modern ships were understandable, if one believed that the warships were there for DesRon 3's protection. But the arrival of the old ships was perplexing. None of Hawk's officers could understand it. Nor could Hawk. They obviously weren't there to make DesRon 3 comfortable. Then one day the Secretary of the Navy came aboard, to speak with Lt. Hawkins and his officers. The SecNav was accompanied by several senators and congressmen and two naval historians. Hawk and his officers stood at attention until the SecNav (Vice Admiral Frank Scott, the great grandson of an admiral killed during the Guadalcanal campaign) motioned the men to be seated. "Lt. Hawkins," said the SecNav, "I find it my responsibility and obligation to see that you men know what happened in the war that you served in, fought in and died in." With a wave of his hand, the historians began passing out books and a sheaf of papers. Now Hawk was really getting confused. He had expected some indoctrination training, but he rather thought it would be of events following the war. He was still trying to figure out why the Texas and the other old ships were there. "If you have any questions," said the SecNav, "you can direct them at these two officers here." Hawk had a lot of questions, but decided to wait and see what the admiral was up to. As the officers read, a myriad of expressions appeared on their faces. They had many questions and the historians did their best to answer them. But at the end, the one they all had, the historians couldn't answer. "What now." "What are you going to do with us?" asked Hawk? There was a moment of silence as the historians left the room, followed by the politicians. "Uh oh." thought Hawk. "Here it comes."

An officer, whom Hawk hadn't noticed before strode over to Hawk and sat down across from him,. "Yes gentlemen, we won the war, but it was expensive. There's a saying, to lose a war is cheap, but to win a war takes everything you've got. What we lost in men, we can't ever regain. And financially, we still haven't recovered completely, "said Admiral Tucker. "We have an idea that we want to run by you," said the SecNav. "The first year of the war went very badly for us. We just weren't prepared for a two ocean war. We started a rapid rebuilding of our naval and ground forces. But even as the tide changed in our favor, the losses grew to horrifying proportions. We were fighting an enemy the likes that we had never fought before." Hawk saw tears in the admiral's eyes. He now knew from the history books how costly the battles had been for the navy and ground forces. The word "Astronomical" came to mind. The admiral continued," Our losses in men and material were incomprehensible. The war very nearly bankrupted the nation. And as admiral Tucker said, we never really recovered. But your timely arrival has given us the opportunity to change that." "I don't understand," said Lt. Wilkes. But Hawk knew. Turning to his executive officer, he said, "They want us to go back!" The expression of shock on Hunt's face was immediate. "Not just go back, gentlemen," continued the SecNav, "go back and win." "Sir" said Lt. Hunt, "with all due respect, are you out of your fucking mind?" "That'll be enough, Lt.," said Hawk. "You're speaking to a superior officer." "No," said the admiral, "for what we're asking, he has a right to speak." "Sir, our ships are old, and even though they have been repaired, they're still obsolete. Even your history books say we were killed. Not just killed, wiped out. No survivors. Why should we go back to face certain annihilation." "Lt.," said Admiral Tucker, "you're still in the United States Navy and you'll follow the orders given you by all officers senior to you, do you understand?" "Yes sir," said a subdued Hunt. "But that's another thing. I haven't been on duty for a hundred years. And I haven't been paid for more than a hundred years. I was removed from the active duty lists when our ship was confirmed lost, so technically," Hawk cut him off. "That will be enough." Turning to the SecNav, Hawk asked him, "Sir, I assume you have a plan. Since your history books say we were all killed as we came out of the squall, it wouldn't make sense for us to return for that, unless there was a way to change that outcome. Otherwise, what would we accomplish by fulfilling the destiny of DesRon 3?" Giving Hunt a scowl, the SecNav turned his attention to Hawk. "Yes Lt.,"he said. "we have a plan." We intend to, not just repair your ships, but rebuild them, cover them with coats of armor and place heavy guns on the decks. We'll turn your ships into something between a battle cruiser and a battleship. Then we're going to send you in with additional ships, also heavier armed and armored. So when you emerge from that squall, you'll be able to escape from the trap that the enemy has for you. And maybe you can sink some of them as you make good your escape." The SecNav had Hawk's attention. Even Hunt was curious. Knowing that Hunt was navy through and through, Hawk knew he was only blowing off steam. Besides, he was only saying what was on every one's mind. He knew, given the opportunity, Hunt would charge the Jackson out of that squall and into the guns of that jap force with or without any repairs or modifications. That's the kind of officer he was. The SecNav continued "The enemy had two battleships that carried 18 inch guns. We've modified the Texas with 28 inch guns and we've tripled the armor she carried in the war. As she sits now, the enemy doesn't have anything that can penetrate her armor, or anything she can't penetrate with her guns. Since 28" guns didn't exist then, we'll have to send some supply ships with you. In addition to the Texas, we'll be sending the battleships Colorado and Mississippi with you. Of course rearmed and re-armored like the Texas. We'll also be sending at least 10 heavy and light cruisers and 12 destroyers with you, all with heavier armor and armaments. And you, commander, (emphasizing commander, the SecNav had just made it clear to Hawk that he had just been promoted.) will take command of this new fleet." "Sir," said Hawk, "if you hang armor and place guns that heavy on my old destroyers, they'll come apart at the seams and sink like rocks." "Cmdr.," said the SecNav, "by the time your ships come out of dry dock, the only thing old about them will be their officers." Turning to Lt. Wilkes, who had thus far remained silent, the SecNav said, "Lt. Cmdr, you'll take command of DesRon 3. That will include the 12 destroyers. You can choose your own flagship." "Sir", blurted Wilkes, "the Stewart will continue to be the flagship for DesRon3." Hawk smiled his approval at Wilkes, and wondered which would be his flagship. The SecNav continued, "The additional ships will be crewed by volunteers, but the captains will come from your original crews. I'll bring in some candidates tomorrow that you, Cmdr. Hawkins and Lt. Cmdr's. Wilkes and Hunt will interview. With these more powerful ships, I'm confident you can win the battles we lost, re win those we won more decisively. Keep in mind though, that as you change history, everything changes with it. By changing the outcome of the battles, by sinking more of the enemy ships in each battle, you'll be ending the war faster. Do you have any questions?" Hawk conferred with his officers a moment, and then came up with a few.

* What about tankers? His ships would need fuel.
* What was to stop the enemy from blowing them out of the water as they came out of the squall?
* What would they do if / when they ran into the navy of 1942?
* What would they do when / if they lost supply ships? There would be no place they could replenish 28 inch ammunition in 1942.

Listening to the questions brought up by Hawk, the SecNav took notes and said he'd see what he could come up with. Standing, he handed Hawk and his officers little boxes, which held their new rank insignias. After a brief ceremony, the SecNav and Admiral Tucker turned to leave. Lt. Cmdr. Hunt asked, "Sir, why not send us in with a few new battleships?" "There are none," answered the SecNav. "By the end of the war they were found to be obsolete for anything but shore bombardments preceding invasions. Since it took planes to protect them, we built more aircraft carriers. Soon after the war it was found that the aircraft carrier had replaced the battleship as queen of the seas. Most of the battleships we had were scrapped. The only few we have left are memorial ships. We'll send what we can find with you. But it looks like the only battleships you'll get is the Texas, Colorado and Mississippi. Now then gentlemen, we'll talk again tomorrow at 0900.

The next morning at 0900, Hawk was in the wardroom when the SecNav arrived with three other officers who turned out to be naval architects. Following the usual pleasantries, the senior architect, a rear admiral named Fred Fletchman, began, "Gentlemen, as you know, your vessels were extensively damaged. Even with a full and complete overhaul they wouldn't stand much of a chance against what the enemy has amassed against you. All of the ships we'll be sending with you have been beefed up. That is to say that they are more heavily armored, heavier gunned, and carry a more powerful propulsion system. We plan to do the same to your destroyers. I'm not going to bore you with details of how we're going to do it, since you're not up on modern ship building techniques, you probably wouldn't understand anyway. Basically, we're going to strip everything from the decks, raise the main deck five decks, slice off the bow and stern, and add 312', lengthening your ships to 626'. Your 4.5" guns are being scrapped. They'll be replaced with 12-16", 20-10", and 10-8" guns. Then we'll add about 200-20 and 40mm anti aircraft guns. Your ships width will be widened to 78' to accommodate the additional guns. The draft will be increased 72' to allow for the additional weight. Your torpedoes are also being upgraded from 21" to 32 inch, with homing capabilities and 8 quadruple mounts per side. I know that your torpedoes in 1942 weren't very good. The problem was the firing pin and the magnetic exploder. That problem was fixed by 1943. The fish we're giving you are much faster and deadlier. Your fish had a maximum range of 8,000 to 10,000 yards depending on the speed set, and a warhead of 320 kg. And a speed of 32 knots. These new fish have a maximum range of 40,000 yards, a warhead of 1,000 kg., and a speed of 75 knots. The Japanese had a torpedo that they used against us called a long lance. When it hit one of our cruisers, it would usually blow off the bow. In some cases, one hit would sink it. These are 4 times as powerful. One hit should sink one of their battleships. All of this extra firepower will increase the tonnage of your destroyers to 102,000 tons, making them the heaviest destroyers in creation or equal in tonnage to a modern battle cruiser. Your vessels will be faster and more heavily armored than any vessel has ever been, and more powerful than any battle cruiser ever built. Your battleships will have no equals. Are there any questions?" Looking up for the first time since he had started talking, he could see the amazed expressions on each face. "I assure you gentlemen," he continued, "this is what we will be doing to your destroyers." "And in how many years will our ships be ready," asked Hunt. "Well normally", said Admiral Fletchman, "we could build a ship such as this in three months, but since we have to take yours apart first and modernize it, it'll take about four and a half months, maybe sooner if we don't have to deal with too much rust. And I did forget to mention, your engines will be scrapped as well. Your new engines will give you a maximum speed of 70 knots." "Seventy knots?" asked Wilkes. "Well yes, I'm sorry," said the architect. "We would have hoped for a higher speed, but with all of this weight, it's the best we can get."

Matsamudo Inishi was a wealthy man. No, wealthy was an understatement. For the last 70 years his family had prospered. His grandfather had become rich in electronics. His three uncles had branched out, one in aeronautics research, one in deep sea mining, and the third in banking. They increased the family's wealth. To say they were filthy rich was also an understatement. The family was literally worth hundreds of billions of dollars. Financially, they could purchase just about any country they wanted for a tiny fraction of the money they possessed. Intelligence agencies of the major powers (USA, France, Germany and Great Britain) kept a close eye on the Inishi family. For the most part, they were clean and honest. Their business practices were all above board. But they had enemies. Many Americans felt they did in peace (and finance) what their country had failed to do in war. As well as his uncles had done, Matsamudo had managed to even further increase the family holdings. Purchasing several satellite relays and keeping a close eye on the stock market, he had bought several automotive companies. He used the technology from the aeronautical companies to design fuel efficient engines merged with aircraft and automotive designs. He became the first to mass produce hybrid cars that flew instead of drove. Countries found that they no longer had to build and maintain roads, since his cars no longer rode on the surface, but 4 feet above it. The Inishi family became the wealthiest family, a million times over.

In the years since the war, the island nation of Japan had attained a financial freedom from the United States that few countries dared dream of. Her leaders, seeing the folly of their ways after the war, signed a treaty of non aggression, vowing they would never again wage war. Being the only country (at that time) that had ever been atomic bombed and not wanting to re live it, they signed an accord with the United States. So while every country began a technology race, Japan placed her safety in the hands of the United States and concentrated on the peaceful technology of electronics. Within 30 years, Japan was a technological super power. By 2042 every country on the planet was in her debt financially. When Lt. Hawkins and DesRon 3 came onto the scene an idea and plot was born. The history they wanted changed wasn't military history, but the history following the war. The war was just the starting point. The dark secret of their motive was kept in the white house basement among a very select few that included the heads of the four most powerful nations.

Of course Hawk didn't know this. Nor did Matsumudo. What Matsumudo did know was that the United States was harboring a murderer.

In 1940, the Japanese had a vision for their nation; the term was "Hakko Ichiu", which meant bringing the eight corners of the world under one roof. Theirs! The Japanese military expansion during the war was to make it a reality. The loss of the war ended that dream, for a time. By 2042, that dream had been realized, by the Inishi family. It was this history the four super powers meant to change.

Over the next few months Hawk, Hunt and Wilkes were kept busy, all three were very interested as to how their destroyers were being modified, but they weren't allowed to see. They were told that they couldn't pass on the technology. All they were told was that the technology was now available to compress the molecular structure of steel down to one fourth of an inch. That meant that the equivalent of eight inches of steel was only two inches thick. Hawk and his officers were kept busy learning the electronics of the computer systems, ironically designed and manufactured by Japan. The destroyers were placed in a covered dry dock, so nobody could see what was being done to them and how. When entry was attempted, they were met by armed guards. Unable to view the reconstruction of his ships, Hawk instead delved into the designs and illustrations intended for his ships. He kept the Webb's involved to work into the designs the damage control and first aid stations that they would be using aboard the ships. With Lt. Cmdr.'s Wilkes and Hunt, Hawk studied the propulsion and armaments systems. Neither the engines nor the guns were at all like they were a hundred years earlier. For one thing, both would be computer controlled. Both the engines and the guns could be controlled from the bridge or any number of other places. In fact, every function aboard the ship could be controlled from the bridge. There were also 3 bridges, all heavily armored in case one was was destroyed, however unlikely.. To Wilkes, who was now stuck on the bridge as captain, it meant that he could still control the engines. To Hawk, it meant that if casualties or damage got high enough, he could fight with or without men to fire the guns. Since the battles could be controlled by a computer, it also meant that all he had to do was feed his orders into the computer and if he was injured or killed, the computer would continue to control the ship and the fighting would continue until the battle was won or the ship was sunk. Yes, the computers could even do his job. The computers, tied together and voice activated, placed the Stewart as DesRon 3, Command 1, and the Pope as Command 2. Task Force 1 as yet hadn't been programmed into the computer, since Hawk hadn't chosen his flagship yet.

Then one day on an overcast afternoon an alarm sounded, a tri jet came winging towards the anchorage. Ships alarms went off throughout the fleet, warnings were sent in several different languages to turn about; they were entering a restricted zone. The plane turned away. An hour later it returned from another direction, lower on the water, as though trying to come in under the radar. Again warnings were broadcast and again the plane turned away. It seemed to be testing the harbor defenses. And it seemed to Hawk that it wasn't piloted by a human, but by remote control. Something about the way it maneuvered. Eight days later, it was back. It came in from one direction, left, then came in from another direction and left again. It definitely seemed to be testing something. One week later DesRon 3 emerged from their respective dry docks. Or rather cocoons, as Hunt had begun calling them. As Hawk, Hunt and Wilkes looked on; they could scarcely believe their eyes. The flush deck had remained the same, and except for the huge size of the additional and heavier guns and a variety of other equipment, they looked somewhat the same except for the obvious massive increase of their size. A tour of the interior of the ship disclosed enlarged areas such as magazine and engineering spaces due to the increase in weaponry and larger and more powerful engines. However the ships retained their four funnels. Hawk was confused; the designs had only called for two funnels. As he would learn later that day, only two of them were functional. The other two were added to retain their original design. There was one added benefit, if one funnel was shot away; the exhaust could be re routed to an unused funnel. Another benefit was that it would give the enemy the false impression they were fighting a 1919 class destroyer instead of something they had never seen the likes of. "Yeah," thought Hawk, "When they get a load of all of this fire power, they'll shit their pants." Going aboard to the bridge, Hawk found the original commissioning plaque attached to the bulkhead (wall). Looking at Wilkes and Hunt, and with a tear in his eye, Hawk remarked, "a nice touch." The crew came aboard a couple of hours later and began reacquainting themselves with the ship. Despite being enlarged, the ships complement was reduced by the electronics that controlled the many duties aboard the ship. This allowed many of the crew to transfer to one of the other twelve destroyers that would be going with them. Most sailors weren't accustomed to this type of ship, since frigates had replaced destroyers some fifty years before. The following day the Pope, Jackson and Stewart began their sea trials. Gunnery practice was also held. Sleeves, towed by tugs and aircraft were the targets. Hunt was especially pleased. The radar controlled guns performed better than he had dreamed possible. Radar controlled weaponry was just being developed in 1941 and was in its infancy, which is to say it wasn't very accurate. But one hundred years later, with computers far more advanced, the shells hit the targets with pin point accuracy. The computers and radar controlled weapons systems were surrounded by 20" of armor, making it highly unlikely they would ever get damaged in battle. Even then, there were backup systems in case they did get damaged. Even in local control, his gunners were very good. Hawk had insisted that they practice in local control in case the impossible happened and the computers went off line. Any concerns Hawk had about his ships disappeared that morning.

That afternoon the tri jet reappeared. As it neared DesRon 3, the escorting frigate sent out a broadcast warning the plane to change direction. Not only did it ignore the warning, but a second tri jet appeared behind the first. The frigate, the USS John Paul Jones sent another warning, which was also ignored. As Hawk watched from the bridge of the Stewart, he was aghast to see the first tri jet suddenly dive into the side of the USS Pope. On the bridge of the Pope, Lt. Cmdr. Hunt had been watching the tri jet. As he was moving towards the computer to put it in attack mode, the jet dove at his ship. It occurred to him to evade, but he knew it was too late. The jet screamed down in a power dive and seconds later it struck the 40mm gun tub at the base of the mast, behind the bridge. There was a thud and a dull roar. Then the alarm bells went off, followed by a swish as the damage control system came on and the retardant began putting out the fire. The last time Hunt looked, the armor was hardly scratched. This time Hunt got to the computer and the ship began changing course to evade the second tri jet, which was already starting its attack. This one seemed to be targeting the bridge area. Hunt went inside of the armored bridge structure and activated the attack computer. In a split second, the guns were firing. The jet didn't stand a chance, but in dying, it still struck the ship, close to where the first had hit. The jet crumpled on impact and sprayed hi test fuel all over the deck. As before, the damage control computer took control and the fire was soon out.

By the time DesRon 3 had returned to Cavite and pulled into their moorings, word of the attack had already spread through the base via scuttlebutt. As soon as the Pope docked, Admirals Fletchman and Scott boarded to inspect the damage. The naval architect was pleased to see that the armor plate had withstood the impact and the resulting explosion and fire. The SecNav, however, ordered the Pope back into the dry dock where the armor plate could be inspected more thoroughly. The fire had burned off the new paint and that would be touched up as well. An hour later a conference was held in the wardroom of the Stewart. "Admiral," asked Hawk, "do we know who is responsible for the attack on the Pope?" "Yes and no," answered the SecNav, "Pearl Harbor received a cryptic message forty five minutes ago stating that the attack was a belated response for the sinking of the Kobe Maru." "But the Pope didn't sink the Kobe Maru. The Stewart and the Jackson did." replied Hawk. "Yes," said the SecNav, "but the Pope received more media attention than the Stewart or Jackson, probably due to her being so much more heavily damaged." "Sir, who claimed responsibility for the attack." asked Hawk. "All we know is that the message originated in Japan," answered the SecNav. Hawk nodded. He knew there was information about the mission that he wasn't privy to. He still didn't believe the motives they gave him. But he had learned a long time ago that in the navy it was always "need to know." They obviously didn't believe he needed to know. Turning to Hunt, Hawk asked," Cmdr., do you have a damage report for me?" "Yes sir, eight 40mm's destroyed, two 20mm's damaged, and sixteen men dead. One man is missing. Seaman second class George Raby was in the main mast birds nest when the plane hit at the base of the mast. A search by the captain's gig failed to find any trace of him. He's MIA and presumed dead. Sir, a search of the two wrecked planes found no pilots aboard. But their bodies may have been blown overboard by the explosions" Thinking about his earlier suspicions, Hawk replied, "I doubt it." "Cmdr.", said the SecNav, "we were planning to send DesRon 3 to Pearl Harbor for a shakedown cruise, but now I don't think that would be wise. Not after this morning's attack. What do you think?" "Well sir," answered Hawk, "I've never been one to run away from a fight, but if I'm going to fight japs, I'd rather it be in 1942 where I won't be vilified for it. I'm sure my officers will agree with me." Hawk didn't have to look at Hunt or Wilkes to know that they were nodding in agreement. The next morning the Pope emerged from her cocoon. Her guns had all been replaced and the paint touched up. She looked as good as new, for a ship that was a hundred and twenty three years old, that is. Prior to sortie, all crews were given two days off for R&R; however the rest was spent on base since the risk couldn't be taken that anyone would talk to the wrong person about the upcoming mission. Those who stayed aboard had the thrill of seeing the rest of the ships arrive that would follow DesRon 3 to hell and back. In a perfect line ahead formation, they anchored outside Cavite on the morning of the mission's sortie, the battleships, Texas, Mississippi and Colorado, followed by five heavy and light cruisers, and twelve destroyers. When they left, the cruisers and destroyers would form a circle around the battleships and DesRon 3. Several hours before they were to leave, the SecNav came aboard to give Hawk his final orders and some information. "Sir," asked Hawk, "what about my supply ships?" The SecNav smiled and led Hawk to the flying bridge of the Stewart. "They're already here, Cmdr." Hawk looked and at first he didn't see anything. But as he looked hard, he saw them. Ten periscopes were off his port bow. Turning to the admiral, the SecNav explained. "As you said, cmdr., any supply ships we sent in with you would be subjected to enemy fire. And obviously they would be targeted by the enemy as soon as they were spotted. So we decided we should send the supplies in submarines, but the subs of the Second World War were much too small, we'd have to send in twenty or thirty subs. There aren't that many in existence. And building that many would risk a security problem. So we did the only thing we could. We gave you ten nuclear subs. We gutted out the rockets from their insides so they could carry the twenty eight inch ammunition. They do, however carry their torpedoes, which are the same as your ships carry. But here's the thing, the nukes can't be seen once you're on the other side, by anyone outside of your command. That is imperative. You may use the ammunition they carry quickly, but before you send them back through the squall, remember, you may need their torpedoes. And keep in mind that these new torpedoes are much too large and heavy to re load. But when you do send them through the squall to re supply your fleet, we'll load them up and return them as soon as we can. For us, from the time they arrive to the time they leave, a year will pass. For you it'll be a return on the same day." The SecNav sat down a second and his mood seemed to change. From a speaker phone in the wardroom, he gave a sort of pep talk to all of the ships in the force, telling the men of the importance of the mission. He gave high praise to the men of Des Ron 3 and the rest of the men who had volunteered for this assignment and he promised they would be remembered despite its success or failure. When he was finished and the men were making preparations to sortie, the SecNav had one last conference with Hawk and his officers. "Gentlemen," said the admiral, "There's one more thing, this is ultra top secret. There have been a lot of sinking's in the south pacific and the south china seas over the last few months. We think the Japanese are behind it, but we're not sure. All we do know is that the small number of survivors claims that a very old ship blew them out of the water." "We haven't heard anything about that." said Hawk. "Yes," continued the SecNav, "we kept you and your officers and men in the dark. The whole base has been in a media blackout. You see, you have the only old ships in this part of the world. Your ships haven't left port, so we're convinced that the Japanese are behind it, and plan to blame you and the United States for the cover up." "Would they go to such extremes?" asked Hunt. The admiral nodded and said, "Well, since our security has been so tight, maybe this is the only way they can get at you. All we know for sure is that survivor reports claim that a nineteenth century warship sank them. You, gentlemen, have the only nineteenth century warships. So if you didn't do it, then somebody else is out there sinking ships with another nineteenth century warship. After you leave, if you see anyone out there that shouldn't be out there, sink them. But don't radio an action report. And above all, don't pick up survivors. Not only on this side of the squall, but especially on the other side. Remember, as soon as they know about you, they'll send everything they have against you. One more thing, the battleships you have with you are memorial ships. Try not to lose them. We have to return them." The SecNav stood up and shook hands with Hawk, Hunt and Wilkes and wished them luck. At the door he stopped and turned and said, "May the Gods of war watch over you, and may the rest of the Gods forgive us." Then he was out of the door and gone, leaving the three officers as confused as they were as they came out of the squall.

Chapter 4

The time of sortie came, destroyers Franklin, House and Shaver leading. They were followed by Cru Div 1 and 2, (comprising of the heavy and light cruisers) ringing DesRon 3, and the battleships. They were followed by destroyers Monroe, Lake, Jolie, Ladd, Smith, Hanson, Peterson, Waverly and Grant encircling the fleet. Somewhere ahead, to port and starboard and behind was the nuclear attack subs/supply ships. The navy's secret service. Hawk remembered reading in the historic archives that the submarine service had brought the empire of Japan to her knees during the Second World War by sinking most of her merchant marine and many of her warships. He fervently hoped these attack boats would do the same. Once at sea, the fleet made several course corrections to discourage any sight seers from following them. But the radars showed the seas clear. As they neared the location of the squall, a battle formation was formed. The battle plan, which had been rehearsed and gone over repeatedly over the last two weeks called for the Stewart, Pope and Jackson to enter first. They'd be followed by six destroyers, then the battleships. Then the cruisers and then the last six destroyers to mop up. The subs would enter when they wanted, since they would be deep in the water and unseen. (Nobody was certain if the squall would allow the other ships besides DesRon 3 to come out of the squall in 1942.) Coming out of the squall, DesRon 3 would turn ninety degrees to port, make smoke and haul ass as they opened fire. (The enemy, expecting 3 dilapidated destroyers to come out of the squall would be surprised when 3 much larger ships came out, traveling at a higher rate of speed.)

As the other ships came out they would do the same. When broadside of the enemy, all ships would fire torpedoes. The subs, if they made it out would take up stations ahead, beside and behind. They would not take part in the battle at this time. It was hoped that the enemy would concentrate their fire on DesRon 3 as they emerged from the squall, then as the battleships came out they would target the enemy with their twenty eight inch guns and destroy them. As the cruisers came into the fray, they and the battleships would then encircle the enemy and along with DesRon 3, would wipe out any enemy warships afloat. If for whatever reason that only DesRon 3 came out, DesRon 3 would follow plan B, which meant that they would come out and turn ninety degrees to port, make all possible smoke, fire all starboard torpedoes and open up with gunfire. They would take as many of the bastards with them as they could. Every contingency had been thought of and covered, including Murphy's law. In the squall, destroyers Franklin and House could be clearly seen about 200 yards astern. But when DesRon 3 came out, they came out alone. All of the other warships disappeared. (In the squall, all radars and sonar's were inoperative. This was believed to be because the squall was a time portal of sorts.) Steaming through the squall at 60 knots, DesRon 3 passed through it rapidly. When they came out, the Japanese were taken completely by surprise. Expecting three severely damaged (and slow) destroyers, they suddenly found themselves facing three very large and fast ships. Three heavy gunned undamaged ships. They had been so confident that they weren't even prepared to fire their torpedo batteries. When they opened fire, their shells landed astern in the water. Meanwhile, Stewart, Pope and Jackson made their turns to port and unleashed half of their torpedo batteries. Then, making smoke they opened up with their 16, 12 and 8 inch guns. The enemy, taken by surprise in more ways than one, sat for several seconds before they opened up at the destroyers. Several seconds was more than enough time for Hawks ships to gain speed and proceed to circle the enemy fleet. As the enemy guns began to bark in defense, they found themselves firing into a very solid seeming smoke screen. Hawks destroyers, however, were firing on full computer control. And the firing was deadly accurate. As Hawk began to swing to starboard to circle the Japanese ships, another enemy formation was seen to port, converging to assist the japs they were already fighting. Hawk ordered another turn to port and headed his ships towards those ships. As the speed enunciator hit 77 knots, Hawk felt the old Stewart leap out of the water. And just as suddenly the ship shuddered as all of his guns opened up together. Standing in the armored bridge, Hawk was surprised at all of the hits and no misses. He tried to imagine the thoughts of the enemy aboard the ships. Smiling to himself, he thought, "They must be punch drunk by now." Turning his binoculars to the rear of the Stewart, he saw the Pope and Jackson, also firing rapidly. He saw the flash as the guns go off, but no smoke. The shells are smokeless. The enemy can't range in on their smoke. If the Japanese had fired fish, they missed. Now, as the destroyer's raced towards these new targets, their torpedoes began to hit. As DesRon 3 raced SE, the ships were suddenly rocked by a violent explosion. The Stewart shook as though a doll in a child's hand. Hawk sprinted aft; sure that one of his destroyers had blown up. But the Pope and Jackson are still there. A Japanese battleship in the center of the enemy formation had gone to meet their ancestors; a series of salvos had struck vital areas of the enemy warship, causing its destruction. The rest of the Japanese ships didn't fare much better. In addition to being powerful, the torpedoes are wakeless. They never saw them coming. Turning his attention to the fast approaching ships ahead of him, Hawk is vastly amazed at the accuracy of computer controlled fire. The results are beautiful and devastating The ships are struck by repeated hits. There are no misses or near misses. Already their casualties have to be high. An enemy destroyer steered into the path of a torpedo approaching an enemy battleship in an attempt to save the capital ship, but the radar controlled fish dove under the destroyer and struck the battle wagon anyway. The explosion was massive and when the smoke cleared, the ship had lost her bow clear up to the bridge. It rapidly lost speed and veered out of formation. As Hawk watched their shells falling on the enemy ships, he realized that he could sympathize with the enemy commander. "Now you know what it feels like," he said (to no one in particular) remembering a year ago when his ships were under fire and trying to escape into the squall. Twenty thousand yards from the enemy Hawk returned to the armored bridge and ordered, "DesRon 3 seven degree turn to starboard on my mark, stand by torpedo battery C, port side." Forty five seconds later Hawk ordered, "Stand by." Then as the ships steadied on course, "DesRon 3 fire torpedoes." With the turn, the turrets and the guns, controlled by the computer continued to strike the jap ships. Now the fish flew out of their tubes at the enemy warships. The Japanese, unaccustomed to having American torpedoes actually explode when they struck a target never saw them coming, nor expected the terrible result of the warheads actually going off. They didn't even bother turning away to avoid them. Then again, these were wakeless and they couldn't see them anyhow. Twenty seconds before they would've hit, the air was pierced by what Hawk reasoned sounded like a drum beat magnified a thousand times over. Startled for a second, he assumed one of his torpedoes had circled back and struck one of his ships. The explosions came from astern. Running to the starboard bridge wing and looking aft he saw that the first enemy formation was under attack again. Instinctively he looked towards the squall, the only place the gun fire could be coming from. When he saw the Grey shapes emerging from the squall, he knew. Running back into the bridge, he reached for the TBS and nearly screamed, "Tallyho boys, the rest of the guys are here." Task Force 1 had finally emerged and according to plan had fired torpedoes then opened gunfire. The japs, distracted by their attempts to save their ships, hadn't seen these new ships come out. Nor had they expected another formation to come out. After all, only three ships had entered the squall. A split second after the fish hit, the guns opened up and the shells began blowing more big holes in their ships. The explosions caused by the twenty eight inch guns seemed unrealistic. Huge pieces of the jap ships were blown off, sent flying into the air and eventually falling into the water. They certainly wouldn't have to worry about survivors. There wouldn't be any. Now death, that seemed so imminent just minutes ago, was the furthest thing from Hawks mind. Watching the desolation befalling the japs. Hawk saw a big battle wagon turn and try to escape some of the shells from falling on it. In doing so, it literally ran down one of its escorting destroyers, cutting it in half. The "tin can" instantly exploded, which in turn blew a large hole into the side of the battleship (or maybe it was a torpedo). Time almost seemed to stop as all attention turned to the stricken battleship. With an enormous burst of flame, it rolled over and disappeared beneath the waves. It amazed Hawk how such a large ship could be gone so quickly. Within the steady din of heavy caliber hits the enemy tried to fight on as best they could. But they stood little chance. Their guns were blown off their turrets before they could range in on the American ships. The few that did manage to fire back, saw their shells bounce off the armor. A quick glance at the radar showed one blip after another disappearing from the scope. Returning his attention to the ships in front of him, Hawk saw that they had changed course and were trying to escape. A bell rang on the bridge, "Sir," said the radioman, "they're trying to call for help." "Jam their transmissions.", ordered Hawk. A moment later the radioman responded, "Jamming their signals, sir." Hawk asked, "RadCom, have you translated their last transmission?" "Yes sir, but it was fragmented. Transmission reads, "Have engaged.........sunk..... sinking. That's all they got out sir." Looking behind him, Hawk saw that all five enemy battleships have sunk. Two of the three cruisers have also gone to Nippon. The destroyers have attempted to scatter, but they can't escape the radar controlled weapons of TF 1. One cruiser is still afloat, listing heavily to port. Two destroyers are standing by to pick up survivors. Hawk sees a command pennant flying from the cruiser. Reaching for the TBS, Hawk orders, "ComTF 1 to Texas, bury those last three ships." Minutes later the seas are clear of any enemy ships afloat. "RadCom, sir the cruiser Los Angeles is requesting permission to pick up survivors." Turning quickly to the talker, Hawk orders, "Permission denied." Then, "send to all ships, No, repeat no survivors will be picked up. Let the sharks have them." Turning away from the voice recorder, he quietly remarked, "At least we don't machine gun them in the water." With the rearward enemy ships disposed of, Hawk ordered the task force to switch targets and take the forward targets under fire. There wasn't much left to shoot at. The fish had done their duty. What ships hadn't been sunk initially from the torpedoes; the guns of DesRon 3 had hurried under. What ships were left, were in a sinking condition. As the Texas, Mississippi and Colorado came into range of these last floating japs, they were quickly dispatched. With the seas clear as far as seventy miles and no enemy aircraft close, Hawk ordered the task force to regroup, formation C. That called for all ships to form a diamond shape with the heavier ships in the center. When the ships were in position, Hawk asked for a damage report from all warships and while they were coming in, he turned to the computer and said, "Computer, send to all ships captains. Mark it sensitive. Prior to sortie a discussion took place between the SecNav and my immediate officers of DesRon 3. The orders were simple. No enemy survivors will be picked up. No humanitarian aid will be given to the enemy. No rafts or supplies will be thrown to the enemy. This may sound cruel to you, but remember that any survivors will report our position and strength. And also remember that we have no air cover, while the enemy has many aircraft to search for us and attack us. Remind your subordinates that the only supplies the enemy has given Americans in the water is lead."

No sooner had Hawk finished that an alarm bell went off at the radar console. Flipping a switch, the computer answered, "Three enemy cruisers and seven destroyers coming in fast, fifty one miles, twenty degrees on a parallel course. They'll be in range of the battleships in six minutes." The enemy ships were not trying to open the distance between them. Either they didn't know the exact position of the American fleet, or the ships they could see (from that distance they should have been able to see the masts of the American fleet) they believed to be friendly. It was a natural assumption. The allies weren't supposed to have anywhere near that number of ships, and since the sinking's of the HMS Prince of Wales and the Repulse, there wasn't anything sizable this side of Pearl Harbor. Hawk was sure they thought they were coming to the assistance of the ships that had sent the earlier radio message. But if that was the case, very soon they would realize that the masts they could see were not of their ships. Going to the computer, Hawk dialed in his command code, then entered attack plan 4-G. Instantly the computer sent the command to all of the other bridge computers, whose captains then logged in their codes. The navigational computers then sent the required course and speeds to the engine rooms. All hull frequencies were then automatically entered into the main battle computer so there wouldn't be the danger of the ships targeting a friendly ship. (Torpedo or gun fire) With the computers controlling the engines & rudders (course and speed), torpedo batteries, gun batteries, and damage control, all was in readiness. Hawk and his officers and men basically became passengers and spectators. Ten minutes later, the battle unfolded. The enemy, not expecting American units in this area, much less units of this size, were taken completely off guard. By the time they realized they were under fire, it was too late. The torpedoes were among them. The battle was a carbon copy of the last one. And as completely one sided. The warships of 1942 were no match for the computer controlled warships of 2042. The enemy commander, thinking the ships approaching him were friendly, hadn't even called his crews to battle stations. As the shells and fish began to hit home, he realized his mistake. Before he could do anything, his ships were doing a banzai charge for the bottom of the sea. The sharks would eat well this day.

(Plan 4-G called for DesRons 3, 4, 5 and 6 to cruise down the enemies starboard side, releasing torpedoes, then two minutes later,(when the torpedoes began to nip in) open gun fire. CruDiv (Battleship Division) 1 and 2 would cruise down his port side and open gun fire. BatDiv (Battle Division) would also cruise down their port side and unleash gun fire. Destroyers range to the enemy would be six thousand yards. Cruisers range would be ten thousand yards, battleships range would be twenty thousand yards. All ranges for each ship was controlled by their computers and those were controlled by the command computer aboard the Stewart.) Each ship had several backup systems in case the bridge took damage.

Nothing was left to chance. Every contingency had been considered and countered. It was zero hour minus two minutes. Hawk almost felt sorry for them. A light flashed from the leading enemy destroyer. A recognition signal. ("Maybe the enemy commander wasn't so incompetent after all.) "Computer," said Hawk, "send the correct answer." A few seconds later, the computer responded, "Pass code sent and accepted." "RadCom, check for enemy aircraft.", ordered Hawk. "Skies clear for a hundred miles, sir." Zero hour, minus one minute. "All ships standby, 4-G active minus 30 seconds. "All destroyers, open torpedo fire." Then two minutes later, "All ships, open gun fire." The fish left their tubes so smoothly that it was easy not to notice. The main armament was another story. Each time they went off, Hawk still felt compelled to see if his bow was still there. "Computer," said Hawk, "check for enemy torpedoes in the water" "Scanning," said the computer. Within twenty seconds the computer answered that the skies were clear and no torpedos detected. Suddenly all hell broke loose as night turned into day. The destruction must have been massive as the shells fell like rain, deluging the hapless enemy warships. It seemed as though there wasn't an inch of deck plating untouched by shell fire. The effect on enemy personnel must have been catastrophic. Hawk imagined that the decks must be running with blood. Remembering the casualties they had inflicted on his ships, and those on the Oliver and Barr, he realized they had this coming. He no longer felt bad for them. Going to the TBS, he spoke to DesRon 3, "Come on guys, I can't see enough hits." In amazement, the hits seemed to increase. Before the enemy could respond in defense of their ships, Hawks torpedoes had blown out their bottoms and the gunfire had blown out their guts. The enemy had no time to do anything but burn and die. And die they did. They were blown into pieces too small to attract the sharks. But there was lots of blood. Seventeen minutes later, Hawk was forced to give the cease fire order. Any other shooting would be a waste of ammunition. There was nothing left afloat to fire at. The fleet didn't even slow down. Hawk ordered, "Flank speed ahead, computer, compute course to Cavite, best time." Minutes later, the computer answered. "Course 110 degrees speed 25 knots suggested." "Make it so." ordered Hawk. Six minutes later the computer chimed, "Five warships emerging from the rain squall 30 miles astern. IFF recognized." Ordering the rest of the fleet ahead at thirty five knots, Hawk turned to the computer and ordered a reversal of the Stewart's course back to the squall, curious as to what could possibly be coming out. At 10,000 yard, Hawk saw a very large shadow emerging from the squall. He judged that it must be enormous, since he could already make out the shape at this distance. At 2,000 yards he could make her out, despite the overcast conditions. "It's the Big Stick, the USS Theodore Roosevelt. Damn, she's huge," Hawk says, under his breath. The four escorting frigates blew their horns for "Good Luck," then returned into the squall, their duty finished. The Teddy R. quickly pulled up to the Stewart, then putting on speed, pulled away, heading towards the fleet. The Stewart again reversed course and had to put on full steam to catch her. Then both raced back to the fleet that was quickly disappearing on the horizon. When they reached the task force, Hawk ordered the carrier into the center of the formation, but before he can order the destroyers to open the way to let the carrier in, the captain of the large ship deftly maneuvers the ship in to the center position. Hawk can only stare in shock and dismay, then astonishment as the carrier slips in, as though he were parking a car. Only when the ship is safely in formation and steaming along in column, does Hawk realize he had been holding his breath. "Sir," says a signalman on the port side bridge wing, "the carrier is signaling that they are sending a helicopter to our stern to pick up the fleet commander." Still in a slight state of shock, and anxious to meet the captain who was able to perform such a delicate maneuver, Hawk ordered the signalman, "Send, on my way.", then proceeded to the stern, to the only area large enough to allow a chopper to land. Coming off of the bridge and walking alongside his 12 inch turrets, he sees the chopper has already lifted off from the carrier and is heading towards his ship. The copter grows larger in size as it approaches, and when it lands on the fantail, he is surprised at its size. "Sir" said the pilot, as Hawk approaches the helicopters side door, "I have orders to retrieve the task force commander." "That's me," Hawk tells him. The pilot didn't move for a second, then stepped aside. "I'm sorry sir," he says to Hawk, "I didn't recognize you." By now, Hawk understands. He has seen that look before. He knows it is strange for an officer his age to command a task force. "But then," he tells himself, "these are strange times." Climbing aboard, the helicopter lifts off of the destroyer's deck and flies back towards the carrier. As it approaches, Hawk sees what he estimates to be 200 aircraft on its flight deck. He remembers seeing the Teddy R. as a memorial ship on his visit to Pearl Harbor, only then she was carrying jet aircraft. The planes on her deck now are WWII vintage aircraft of a type he's never seen.

Once aboard the carrier, Hawk is escorted by a marine through a maze of halls and doors, up and down stairwells until they finally reach the captain's quarters. The marine knocks at the door and a voice tells them to enter. "Cmdr., I'm captain Amos Sherman, your executive officer of Task Force 1. Please sit down and make yourself comfortable. Can I get you something to drink? Admiral Scott said you are partial to bourbon. I had the ship's doc bring up a couple of bottles. Water and ice ok?" Hawk nodded and captain poured a small amount into a glass and handed it to Hawk. Drinking slowly, Hawk was confused and getting more so as time went on. "Sir, I have sealed orders for you from the SecNav and the President of the United States. You can read them here in my cabin or next door in your cabin, if you wish.", said the captain. "My cabin?" asked Hawk. Captain Sherman smiled and handed Hawk a large envelope, then started to leave. "I'll read them here, and please stay, captain. I'm sure I'll have some questions for you." "Aye aye, sir." answered Captain Sherman. Opening the envelope, Hawk took out the first letter and read its contents.

To: Commander / Task Force 1
From: SecNav
Effective: 1 March, 1942 /2042

Cmdr. Marcus D. Hawkins is this day promoted to the temporary rank of Admiral, commanding Task Force 1.

Task Force 1 comprises of CVN 121 Theodore Roosevelt, (Flagship), Battleships Texas, Colorado and Mississippi. Heavy cruisers Houston, Nome, Los Angeles, Adak and Aguadilla. Light cruisers Cloquet, Esko, Proctor, Carlton and Duluth. Battle cruisers Stewart, Pope and Jackson. Destroyers Franklin, House, Shaver, Lake, Monroe, Jolie, Ladd, Smith, Hanson, Peterson, Waverly and Grant. SSBN's Seawolf, Scorpian, Harder, Hake, Trout, Bluefin, Archerfish, Tang, Seahorse and Wahoo.

Primary Orders

* Destroy all enemy shipping, military and merchant. DO NOT RETRIEVE SURVIVORS.
* Report to COM PAC, Pearl Harbor at earliest convenience. (Hand deliver document to Chester W. Nimitz, Admiral, USN) to gain assistance for fuel and supplies.
* Do not allow SSBN's to be seen or boarded by personnel outside of this immediate command.
* Use SSBN's to re supply as needed. Send back to 2042 for re supply.

* Use CVN to refuel and re supply as needed. Do not send back to 2042 until mission completed.
* Rules of engagement DO NOT APPLY.
* Names of mission crewmen within this command must NOT be made available to personnel outside of this command. All information is confidential.
* No records or names of vessels lost to this command will be retained.
* No equipment, computerized or not of the current date, (1942) will be turned over to anybody outside of this immediate command.
* DO NOT TAKE PRISONERS OR SURVIVORS. REPEAT, NO PRISONERS WILL BE TAKEN. NO SURVIVORS WILL BE ASSISTED.

The next two letters were the same, one addressed to Chester W. Nimitz and the second addressed to Franklin D. Roosevelt.

Date: 1 March, 2042
To: Chester W. Nimitz, Admiral USN / Franklin D. Roosevelt, Pres. USA
From: SecNav, William A. Halsey III, Admiral and Chester W. Nimitz III, Admiral and Chief of Staff to President Anthony W. Williams, President of the United States.

Sir's, these ships have come from the future to assist you and our countrymen with the winning of this war. We understand how farfetched this sounds. However these ships should be testament that our claim is true. A tour of the CVN should convince you. The only assistance we require is food, fuel and ammunition for our smaller caliber guns. Your enemy is still our enemy. Any and all assistance will be appreciated. A refusal will result in a recall of our fleet. Any attempt to detain our ships will result in an unfortunate military action.

At this stage in the war, we know that your intelligence department is having difficulty breaking the enemy codes. As a token of proof, one admiral to another, of the same nation and navy, but of a different time and era, and from a great grandson to his great grandfather, Admiral Hawkins will pass on to you all of the codes that the Japanese, Germans and Italians will use in this war, as well as the dates they will be used. This alone will greatly assist you in decisively winning the war.

The admiral commanding this Task Force is listed on your officers roles as Lt. (jg) Marcus D. Hawkins. To allow him to carry out his mission, it was necessary for him to carry the rank of Admiral. He is fully qualified to command, a testament to the illustrious training given forth at Annapolis in 1937. This promotion was authorized by Anthony H. Williams, President of the United States, 2042. We ask that you accept him as such, that you list him on your officer roles as such, and that you give him all of the assistance that is possible for him to fulfill his mission.

Respectfully,
F.A.Scott, III, Vice Admiral, Secretary of the Navy
C.W.Nimitz III, Admiral
A.H.Williams, Pres. USA

Also in the envelope were a small box and another sealed envelope. The envelope was marked "Ultra Secret, Eyes only." Opening it, Hawk found a letter from the SecNav.

To: Marcus D. Hawkins, Admiral, ComTaskForce One.

* Be advised that shortly after your departure from Cavite, it was learned that Japan is knowledgeable of your task force and your mission, possibly due to a 19th century Japanese warship in Japanese waters. Satellite footage caught what appears to be a Yamato class battleship of seventy eight thousand tons reported sunk in 1944, probably responsible for the merchantman losses reported to you before you departed Cavite.
* While your presence there is changing history, their presence due to knowledge of your presence will also change history. Keep a watchful eye on the historical documents in your

ships safe and in the computer banks of the carrier. As history changes, so will they. No documents must fall into the hands of personnel outside of your immediate command. Nor must they be seen by personnel outside of your command.

* Aboard the carrier there are 200 F6F Hellcats. (fighter planes) In the hangar there are 350 more. This aircraft does not exist in your time yet. It is the next generation of the F4F Wildcat. Also in a crate on the hangar deck, marked winter gear, is a stealth jet plane. It is a F-173. It can be remotely operated, computer operated or pilot operated. It is nuclear powered and flies at the speed of light. It can be flown in and out of the squall, however there is no guarantee that it will return to 2042. Keep in mind that it can also be programmed to explode over Japan if it becomes necessary. The Theodore Roosevelt is nuclear powered as well.

* Under NO circumstances can your historical data, the F-173, or the carrier be taken intact by the enemy of 1942. To avoid capture, any or all must be destroyed and sunk.

* Also made available before the carrier sailed are five thousand stars. Captain Sherman, your exec, is knowledgeable of these and will pass on this information.

* In the event that the USS Theodore Roosevelt is destroyed in combat, all historic documentation must be deleted from the computers before the carrier can be allowed to sink, the carrier must not be allowed to sink intact, and the F-173 must be destroyed and not allowed to sink with the carrier. These steps must be followed to ensure that no technology from the future can be salvaged.

Chapter 5

In the small box Hawk found the one star insignia of an admiral. Looking at Captain Sherman, Hawk asked, "How much do you know about the contents of this envelope?" "I know everything, admiral," said Captain Sherman. "I wish I could say good luck, but this mission seems so staggering. Since the japs in 2042 know about your mission, it's just a matter of time before they know in 1942. If they change their missions and dates of their missions and change their codes, then the only advantage we have is our extra armor and fire power." Hawk thought a moment and answered, "No. If they change their codes or battle plans regarding locations of the battles, that will be recorded in the historic archives. We'll know about it as they change. It's the things that aren't recorded in the documents that they can change that we wouldn't know about until the last moment. Things like troop and ship strengths and movements. The F-173 may be our only hope to end the war earlier. But I don't know how we'll use it yet. I guess I'll find out when I need to. But now, tell me about the stars." "Yes sir," said Captain Sherman. " The stars are surface to air rockets, similar to a bazooka. Except that these are laser guided to the target. As soon as the laser locks onto the target, a plane, a green light comes on the screen showing that the target has been acquired. If the target changes course and attempts to evade, the rocket is still locked on. It's only chance to evade destruction is to out run the war head. Jets can't even out run or out maneuver a star. In fact, there's only one plane ever built that can out run a star. And that's an F-173 stealth plane, and we have the only one. The stars range is 122 miles, and can lock onto a target from a maximum distance of 15 miles. These rockets were designed to hit jets before they could run away, no propeller driven aircraft is ever going to out run a star." "I see," said Hawk. "And we have five thousand aboard?" Captain Sherman nodded. "Sir, with the limited number we have, I suggest we use them only as a last resort." "I agree," said Hawk. "And I think we'll distribute some of them to the destroyers as they'll be the next likely target after the carrier. As I understand it, the battleships and cruisers are equipped with surface to air racket mounts, correct?" When Sherman expressed a look of surprise, Hawk asked him, "What?" "Sir, I wasn't aware you knew the technical data on the assorted armaments of the ships beyond DesRon 3." As commander of Task Force 1 it's my responsibility to know everything I can about all of the ships in my command. Don't you agree?" "Yes sir, I'm sorry sir. I didn't mean to suggest that it wasn't.", said Sherm, realizing that there was a lot about Admiral Hawkins that wasn't in the briefing. He was beginning to think that the SecNav's choice of command may have been the right one after all. Hawk continued, "Because of the nature of this mission, it is imperative that we don't give aid or assist the enemy in the water. It is important that every man in this command understand this. Any man who disagrees with this directive can turn in his resignation and we will do our best to transport him back to the year of 2042 on the next available ride, probably on an SSBN when we send one back to re supply. Captain, send that message to every ship in the command." "Sir," said Sherm,"that order is contrary to the rules of the Geneva Convention. I had a discussion with Admiral Scott on this same subject." "And what did the admiral say," asked Hawk. "He said it would be up to the discretion of the commander. You sir." said Sherm. "Well captain," continued Hawk, "any survivors assisted in the water will most likely survive to be picked up. They will undoubtedly reveal our strength, capabilities and position. Even given the unusual capabilities of the ships in the fleet, the enemy could still amass a fleet to oppose us that would be far stronger than us in numbers alone. We won't machine gun them in the water, like they do to our men; we're not the butchers they are. We're civilized, but we won't help them to survive either. If they live to be rescued, it'll be by luck alone. Is that clear, captain?" "Yes sir," answered Sherm. He still didn't agree with Hawk, but he could see his point. And on one point he did agree. "The enemy could surely amass a fleet of ships large enough to give TF 1 a good fight. "However," said Hawk, "should the opportunity arise to spring a trap on the enemy, we may allow them to see a part of our force to draw the enemy to a position where we could fight him on our own terms."

Changing the subject, Hawk said, "I didn't recognize the aircraft on the flight deck as I came aboard. My instructions say they're the next generation after the wildcats. Does that mean we can use the wildcats for parts?" "Yes sir," said Sherm. "All of the shell can be taken from the wildcats. The F4F's carried six machine guns, three per wing. The F6F's carry four machine guns per wing for a total of eight. The self sealing tanks have been improved and the plane has a much tighter turning radius, enabling it to out maneuver the Japanese zero. The F6F can also carry bombs, which is why Admiral Scott chose to give us all fighters instead of some bombers as well. Our planes were also modified to carry two additional machine guns, for a total of five per wing. The wildcat was powered with a twelve hundred (1200) horse power Pratt and Whitney engine. The Hellcat was powered with a fifteen hundred (1500) horse power P&W. Our Hellcats are powered with an eighteen hundred (1800) horse power engine. According to the historic records, this plane was the best fighter plane developed during the war. Also according to the historic records, the Japanese zero is the fastest, most maneuverable plane in the air at the start of the war. It is powered by a thirteen hundred and fifty (1350) horse power Sakae engine. It has no armor protection for its pilot, and no self sealing fuel tanks." "What can you tell me about the carrier?" asked Hawk. "The Teddy R. was commissioned in 2003 and spent the next twenty five years primarily stationed in the Mediterranean Sea in actions against the Iraqi and Iranian forces. She was built to accommodate one hundred jets on her main flight deck and another hundred on her hanger deck below. Since jets are much larger than the planes we carry, were able to carry three hundred above on the flight deck and four hundred on the hanger deck below. A study of the historic records showed that the WWII carrier was most vulnerable when taking aircraft aboard. So after choosing the Teddy R. for this mission, Admiral Scott had the carrier modified so she could take aircraft aboard over the bow on the flight deck and simultaneously launch from the hangar deck, aft. This will speed up carrier operations and create less possibilities of hazard. The Teddy R. is nuclear powered and can cruise for a period of six years before needing to recharge her reactors. When we steam her into port, it'll be to pick up supplies and ammunition. Any re fueling will be to top off tanks of aviation fuel for our escort. She's two thousand six hundred and fifty feet long (2650), three hundred and fifty feet wide (350), and has a draft of sixty five feet (65). The navy had to dredge Pearl Harbor an additional thirty feet to allow the carrier to enter the channel and the harbor. The ship is equipped with six, ninety thousand (SHP) ship horse power engines, using seven screws, giving it a cruising speed of sixty (60) knots and a maximum speed of seventy two (72) knots. She has tanks in her hull that carry a million gallons of aviation fuel, protected from the keel to the fourth deck by an anti torpedo blister. Remember that the steel is compressed four to one? Four inches of steel n 1942 is compressed down to only one inch. We found that a ship build of compressed steel produces an ultrasonic sound that produces and impenetrable under water barrier projecting our from the hull for a distance of 100 yards. This barrier or force field protect the ship from torpedos and any other under water weapons. The Teddy R has a triple bottom to protect her keel from mines. Her hull is protected by eighteen feet of armor and another ten feet of armor along the blister. Her flight deck has thirteen feet of armor plate and her hangar deck has an additional fifteen feet. Admiral, there isn't a bomb, mine or torpedo that can penetrate the armor on this ship to damage anything vital. Our only concern is that an atomic or nuclear bomb could theoretically overturn her. As for the ships armament, we have twenty two hundred Phalanx guns, Ten twenty eight inch guns, thirty two twelve inch guns, and two ten inch guns. The phalanx is a sort of a Gatling gun. It's radar and computer controlled, firing three thousand rounds a minute, using armor piercing, white phosphorous and tracer rounds. The maximum range is thirty two hundred yards, but they're deadly at twenty five hundred. We have a thousand per side and a hundred fore and aft. The phalanx and stars should make us untouchable to attacking aircraft. The Teddy R. carries five hundred and fifty aircraft. She is the heaviest carrier ever built, weighing in now, after all of her most recent modifications, at three hundred and sixty nine thousand tons. (369,000) In addition to the aviation fuel tanks along her hull, she also has tanks in her keel that can hold as much as a half a million more gallons of fuel." Giving Hawk a moment to digest all of the information, Sherm continued. "The carrier has the most sophisticated radio, radar and sonar equipment in the world by 2042 standards. In addition to being able to pick up every type of frequency, we're capable of jamming every frequency from a distance of four hundred miles, which is the maximum range of our radar. The ship is crewed by six thousand nine hundred and ten men, including the pilots. The ships stores are ample enough to supply her crew at sea for extended periods of time up to six months. In the event that we somehow take heavy losses, all of the ships armaments can be operated by computer control. A little about the F-173, the fighter flies at the speed of light, is nuclear powered and has stealth capabilities. Nothing can track it. Not in 1942 or 2042. Not even a radar controlled phalanx gun. It's the only plane in existence that can out run a star. It can be radar and radio controlled from here or another F-173, but we only have the one. And it can be programmed to fly to a location and return and land on the carrier, or any other location. Since they're brand new in 2042, the Admiral could only get us one, and he practically had to steal it. If I understood the SecNav, the use of the F-173 was limited to reporting the loss of the fleet." Hawk wondered if Sherm was aware of the other use that the admiral had authorized in his letter to Hawk.

Captain Sherman took Hawk to the next cabin (the Admirals cabin) showing him around. The cabin was much bigger than any Hawk had had before. It was palatial compared to the captain's cabin on the Stewart. Hell, the head (bathroom) was larger than his cabin on the Stewart The admiral's cabin even had a bar. Next to the cabin was his ward room and it had a bar also. Hawk thought, "They must think I'm a drunk." Unlike the British Navy, the United States Navy doesn't allow alcohol aboard its vessels, except for medicinal purposes. All of the bottles were brandy and marked medicinal. Brandy (bourbon) was Hawk's drink of choice. But he was certain if beer was his choice, the admiral would have had it aboard labeled medicinal also. In wartime, nearly all captains kept a small bar in their quarters for periods of stress. These were very stressful times. Because of this, Hawk was certain the brass looked the other way. Filling two glasses from the bar in the ward room, Sherm gave one to Hawk and held the other one for himself. Raising his glass to Hawk's, he said, "To the United States, the United States Navy and all the best things they stand for. May success follow your flag." Hawk then returned the toast, "To the success of our mission."

An hour later, having returned to the Stewart to gather his belongings, Hawk called Lt. Cmdr. Wilkes to his quarters. Upon arriving and seeing the star on Hawk's collar, Wilkes saluted and congratulated his commander and friend. Stepping up to Wilkes, Hawk removed his collar insignia and replaced it with his old insignia, telling him, "I'd consider it an honor if you wore mine," thus promoting his friend to captain. "In addition to being the new captain of the Stewart, you're also the new commander of the DesRons." When Wilkes started to protest, Hawk held up his hand to stop him. "Look Mark, I know that except for me, nobody loves this ship more. I won't take no for an answer. And next to me, nobody except Captain Sherman is as knowledgeable about our mission. My second has to be from our time and era. Somebody our crews know and trust and will follow into the gates of hell if need be. You follow that bill, Captain Sherman doesn't. As 3rd officer in command of the fleet, I should be placing you aboard one of the battleships and if you choose to relinquish your command of the Stewart, I'll understand. But as you know, the Stewart was built as a flag destroyer and rebuilt as heavy and heavily gunned as a battle cruiser, so I'll leave it up to you where you place your flag." "Sir, unless I'm moved up to command another ship, I'd rather fly my flag from the Stewart." Hawk nodded, shook hands with Wilkes, then left the ship and returned to the carrier. Years later Wilkes would swear that Hawk had tears in his eyes when he left his beloved Stewart.

With the Teddy R.'s radar and sonar showing the water and air clear for a distance of four hundred miles all around the carrier, Hawk ordered the fleet on a direct course for Cavite, speed thirty six knots to accommodate the use of the sonar. Also, Hawk was unsure of what he would find when he got there and took a slow approach to the naval base. An hour later, Hawk was called to the bride. Radar showed there were large ships in the harbor and the entrance was blockaded by thirteen other ships. Five hours later, as TF 1 approached their base, flashes could be seen on the horizon. As they got closer, gun fire could be distinctly heard. Except for Hawks battleships and heavy cruisers there were no other allied heavy vessels in this part of the world. So Hawk knew the base was under enemy attack. Ordering the fleet to battle stations, Hawk continued his approach, assuming that the enemy would believe that the approaching ships were Japanese. Using the radar, then eye sight, Hawk drew up his battle plan, based on the disposition of the enemy fleet. The enemy formation was made up of two Kongo class battleships and three Mogami class heavy cruisers inside of the harbor bombarding the base from within. Outside of the harbor and along the shoreline were thirteen destroyers. Apparently their attention was on the harbor and shore, because they either didn't notice TF 1 coming, or they had seen them coming and disregarded the approaching ships. That was their mistake. Programming the computer for plan "Charlie one," (the command computer sent the details to the other computers within the fleet.) By using the computers, Hawk didn't have to use the TBS, which reduced the possibility that the enemy would be alerted that the approaching ships were American. Plan Charlie one called for four destroyers to steam across the entrance and open torpedo fire on the destroyers at the mouth of the harbor, twelve thousand yards away. The other eight destroyers followed grouped in fours, one thousand yards behind the group ahead. Each DesRon would open fire with torpedoes at the same time. As soon as the fish struck their targets, they would open up with gun fire. Simultaneously the battleships, Mississippi and Colorado would be ten thousand yards beyond, and they would open fire with their twenty eight inch guns, firing over the destroyers heads, at the Kongo and Mogami class warships. This plan held the Texas, the cruisers and DesRon 3 in reserve in case they were needed. The enemy was wholly unprepared to defend themselves from the sea. As the torpedoes struck the hulls of the enemy destroyers, japs, who were happily killing Americans on the shore suddenly found themselves in the waters swimming for their lives. It didn't take long for the sharks to arrive. The waters, already beginning to turn black from oil escaping from the breaches in their hulls, would soon be stained with the color of blood as well. And the sharks would feast today. A sea battle is an awesome sight to see. No other man made creation is as devastating. No form of nature can be compared to the destructive power of mans most powerful ships in combat with each other. For every explosion you see, there are fifty more that you don't see. As the fish hit and the warheads went off, they blew huge sections of the sides of the ships into the air. Pieces of steel and iron went flying into the sky, men and pieces of men also flew into the air, to land back in the water with big splashes. Then the guns went off and the explosions grew in number and magnitude. As they hit, the destroyers disappeared in flashes of flame and clouds of smoke. More guns, turrets, men and armor plate flew towards the heavens. Then thunder, louder than any ever heard began to go off. The twenty eight inch guns began sending their shells towards the enemy ships in the harbor. The enemy battleships and cruisers, firing their port side guns on the harbor had stupidly neglected to man their starboard side guns, and had ammunition stacked behind their turrets, on the starboard side. The colossal shells of the battleships Mississippi and Colorado created a chaos unimaginable to those who have never experienced their destructive nature. In the time it took for their crews to man those guns, their ships were afire and starting to sink. Escape was impossible, except for the escape to die, for death was close. Very close. These japs died the most horrible deaths imaginable. They were either blown apart or were devoured by the sharks if they were unlucky enough to survive the blasting and ended up in the water. Task Force 1 ceased firing as the last enemy warship slipped beneath the water. As much as Hawk wanted to enter the Cavite Naval Base, he decided that he couldn't risk the fleet being spotted by any enemy who may have gotten ashore. Instead, pulling his ships into formation, he ordered a course for Pearl Harbor. He had a rendezvous to keep with Admiral Nimitz.

Over the next week, as Task Force 1 made its way to Pearl, Hawk spent his every spare moment studying the designs and capabilities of the carrier. If he thought he had had a lot to memorize from the capabilities of the rest of the ships, it was nothing compared to just the carrier. He walked every inch of her decks and got lost more times than he would ever admit. He read every document he could find in the ships library and the computers on the capabilities of the electronics and her armaments. He spoke to his engineers to learn about the propulsion system. Having nearly no understanding of nuclear physics, he had to start at square one so he could understand what they were talking about. He studied the schematics and blueprints of the ship and familiarized himself with the weapons systems, radar systems, and sonar systems. He visited the wardrooms and pilot squad rooms, spoke with his pilots and asked them questions about the jets they flew and how they compared to the F6F fighter planes they were now flying. And he got to know his pilots so well that he could name everyone on sight. (The pilots were so impressed with Hawk, that he took the time to get to know them.) By the time the week was up, Hawk was confident that when a crewman reported a compartment damaged or a system off line, he would know what they were talking about. He also knew he could depend on his crews. And more importantly, they knew they could depend on him. During that week, he wasn't the only man working. He kept a constant combat air patrol (CAP) over the fleet and had all of the squadrons practicing gunnery, bombing techniques, formation flying and (most importantly) carrier deck landings and take off's. The rest of the crews practiced their duties. There was drill after drill, the loud speaker going off, blaring the alarm gong of battle stations, (surface action) and (anti aircraft action), damage control stations, alerts to the medical teams directing them to certain areas and compartments. It didn't take long before the crew was doing their duties in their sleep. There was no complaining though. The men knew that all of this training would save their lives. And they knew their officers, including the task force commander was drilling as hard as they were. In addition to the CAP, Hawk put up scout planes, sending them just beyond the range of the radar. It was good practice for them and Hawk didn't want any surprises. He thought five hundred miles was a good range, far out enough to do some good, yet close enough to get them back quickly if he needed them. One day out of Cavite the radar detected planes a hundred and twenty miles away. The F6F's took off and nineteen minutes later the radio rang out the tallyho of a sighting of the enemy planes. Within a minute, Lt. Radcliffe sent out the all clear, two zeros splashed. The scouts quickly dispatched them with a combination of jet and propeller techniques, speed and multiple gun attacks. The jap pilots never stood a chance against the jet aces of the future or the F6F. The gun cameras recorded the attacks for study later, showed the zeros flaming after only a few hits. It was impressive. Thinking an enemy carrier might be close by, Hawk sent his SSBN's to search for it, but they must have been shore based, because no sighting of an enemy fleet was found. Four hundred miles from Pearl Harbor the radar detected another plane, the computer showed that it was sending IFF signals. Hawk sent the scouts out to check it out. Lt. Radcliffe had it in his sights in ten minutes, and confirmed that it was an American patrol plane, probably from Pearl. Being the highest ranking pilot present, he sent the other two planes on their patrol, while he shadowed the Catalina. After a few minutes, he flew off to rejoin his patrol. Not more than three minutes later, a submarine surfaced and a plane was launched. This was detected on the radar as soon as the sub surfaced and launched. Since American subs didn't have that capability, the computer read the plane as enemy and immediately dispatched an order to Lt. Radcliffe to the scene, which was within twenty miles of the Catalina. Upon his arrival, he found the patrol plane already under attack. One engine was already afire and the patrol pilot was trying to get the fire out and feather the prop. On his own initiative, he pulled up behind the enemy float plane and with a short burst of his weapons, scattered the Jap all over the Pacific Ocean. And in plain sight of the crew of the patrol plane! He then flew off in search of the enemy submarine. Not finding any sign of it, he joined up with his patrol group and flew back to the carrier. Meanwhile, the Catalina reversed its coarse and returned to Pearl to report the attack of the zero and their subsequent rescue from the American fighter plane.

Upon landing on the Teddy R., Lt. Radcliffe was ordered to report to the squadron commander. Arriving, he found himself facing the boss and the big boss, Admiral Hawkins. "Lt.," asked Hawk, "Who gave you the authority to shoot down that enemy plane?" "Sir?" asked the Lt. "You flamed that Jap in plain view of the crew in the patrol plane. Now they're going to fly back and report that they were under attack by an enemy plane, but an American plane came to their defense and shot it down. Then they're going to wonder whose plane shot down the enemy plane. We know the Lexington and Yorktown are near Wake Island and the Enterprise is at Mare Island Naval Yard for repairs and re supply. So whose plane shot down the enemy float plane?" "Sir," returned Lt.

Radcliffe, in an attempt to defend his actions, "I was dispatched to the scene by the attack computer of the carrier. When I arrived, the patrol plane was already under fire with an engine disabled. Had I allowed the enemy plane to attack again, the Catalina would have been shot down. I didn't radio for permission to fire because I didn't want to risk the enemy picking up my transmission and losing the element of surprise. I don't believe I reacted irresponsibly. When the crew of the patrol plane reports that they were saved by an American fighter, won't that tell Pearl that friendly forces are near? Wouldn't it be worse if Pearl picked up a transmission that they are under attack that they are going down, that an American fighter is nearby, but it isn't responding to their defense?" Considering this, Hawk answered, "Next time, Lt. You will radio the carrier and request permission to fire." Hawk waited a moment, then continued, "How many kills does that make now Lt?" "Three sir."answered Lt. Radcliffe. Hawk thought a second or two then turned to the squadron commander and said, "Mr. Radcliffe is our highest scoring fighter pilot Jim, I believe that has earned him a captaincy. What do you think?" "He's a good pilot sir, one of my best pilots. He's worked hard, like all of my pilots. I think he rates it." "Very well," said Hawk. Then turning to the Lt., he said, "You're excused Captain."As soon as the pilot had left, Hawk turned to the squadron commander and said, "Jim, I want a secured radio channel installed in the cockpit of every fighter before it flies off of this deck. We don't want any more unauthorized actions. Captain Radcliffe was correct in his actions to shoot down the Jap. But we don't know how that attack will affect our arrival. We're bound to see more reconnaissance planes before we get to Pearl. Make certain that all of our pilots understand that when they come across any more patrol planes, keep an eye on them, but stay out of sight." The following day, as luck would have it, Captain Radcliffe was again on patrol when the computer detected a patrol plane at four hundred miles and flying on a course that, unless they changed course, would intersect with the Task Force 1's position. The attack computer vectored the scouts to the position of the recon plane. In minutes Captain Radcliffe was above and behind the patrol plane, out of sight in the sun. "Rover to Master, Rover to Master. Watching the sheep. No wolves present. Shadowing to Spike. Out." (Translation: Radcliffe had arrived at the location of the

Catalina and was shadowing, keeping in the sun. No enemy in sight, he will continue watching until relieved by the next level of protection, which is the CAP patrolling 200 miles out from the carrier.) The attack computer then sent the appropriate answer, a single ding. (Two dings would mean repeat, and three would mean discontinue shadowing and resume your patrol.) Hawk, on the bridge with Captain Sherman and Cmdr. James Sterling, (the squadron commander of the fighting 48th) turned and smiled at his officers. "That's better. Even with the secured frequencies, it doesn't hurt to be safe."When Captain Radcliffe returned from his patrol, he stood before the squadron commander and gave his report. "Sir, upon arriving at the position of the patrol craft, we flew into the sun where we were in his blinds. We shadowed him until we were relieved by the combat air patrol. I'm positive we weren't seen. Other than his hourly status checks he didn't send out any sighting reports. Once I was relieved, I flew back to the carrier to end my patrol mission." "Good job, captain. You're excused." Task Force 1 continued on its course, with the patrol plane from Pearl Harbor still approaching. Two hours later the reconnaissance planes was within the range of the naked eye, and obviously close enough for the crew to see the task force. "Sir," said RadCom, "picking up a radio transmission from the patrol plane. They're reporting our disposition and position." "Thank you, RadCom." said Hawk, "Please keep me advised." Seconds later, "Sir, Pearl is asking for conformation as to the identity of our ships." Sensing trouble, Hawk ran to the TBS and in plain language sent to the fleet, "Attention all ships, we will be overflown shortly by a patrol plane. Do not fire, the plane is friendly. Repeat, the aircraft is friendly." It wasn't long before the plane flew over, and as it did, Hawk held his breath, certain that someone may not have gotten the word and would open fire. But the ships guns remained silent. Then to RadCom Hawk ordered, "Send the correct recognition signal." Surely a sign to the pilots and Pearl Harbor that the task force approaching them was friendly as well.

The following day, with Pearl Harbor within two hundred miles, Hawk was on the bridge as the sun came up, watching the radar scope and monitored all radio frequencies. A radar blip was watched to rise from the sea plane base and fly a direct course towards the task force. Fifty miles away, "Blue one to big stick, blue one to big stick, friendly recon approaching fifty miles. Requesting instructions." It was Captain Radcliffe, careful not to piss off the boss. "Blue one, this is big stick. Blue one and blue two will fly wing tip escort so they see your insignia and can report that we're on the same team. But maintain radio silence. Repeat, maintain radio silence. Fly escort until 100 miles from Pearl Harbor, then fly return course Zulu. Repeat, return course Zulu. Acknowledge." "Blue one, Blue two acknowledges. Out." (Course Zulu required the pilot to fly a box pattern on the return to the carrier so that the planes, if followed, wouldn't lead an enemy to the carrier. When their course is parallel to the carrier, the enemy planes could then be intercepted by friendly fighters and shot down before coming into contact with the carrier.) Also being watched for the morning was the enemy submarine that had launched the float plane the previous day. Captain Radcliffe had requested permission to search for it, but had been denied. Now, as it lay on the surface charging its batteries, Hawk sent orders to the SSBN Seawolf to "take care of it." Forty five minutes after it had surfaced, as Hawk watched the scope, he saw the blip (representing the sub) disappear from the scope and he knew it had been reduced to a twisted hulk on the ocean bottom. USS Seawolf could paint a rising sun on her sail tower. The wolf was a killer.

Transmissions, intercepted and deciphered (encoded) from the patrol plane reported the presence of the two planes that were escorting them, describing the fighters as a type similar to the wildcat and wearing an American insignia. Pearl Harbor had radioed back the information that no friendly carriers were in the vicinity, and so the planes couldn't be friendly. The PBY then radioed that one of the planes was the one that had shot down the enemy air craft that had tried to shoot them down the day before. Pearl repeated that no friendly carriers were in the vicinity, so any carrier aircraft must be enemy. They were told to use extreme caution. Two hours later, as the carrier came into their sight, they transmitted a sighting report. Part of their report described a very large American flag painted on the flight deck next to the island superstructure. As the PBY approached closer, they came into contact with seventeen additional F6F's, the combat air patrol. The planes flew as though the patrol plane wasn't there, as though ignorant of their presence. Hawk's orders were carried out to perfection, and once again the guns of the fleet remained silent. "Sir," RadCom called, "The PBY is sending a report of the fleets disposition, do you want to jam it?" "Negative," said Hawk. "Decode it for me." "Aye aye sir, decoding. Sighted 1 fleet size carrier, 6 battleships, 10 cruisers and10 destroyers, course 225, range 169 miles from base." The PBY flew over the fleet a couple of times then turned and flew a return course back towards Pearl. Fifteen hundred feet below on the bridge of the Teddy R., Hawk breathed a sigh of relief. Pearl now knew that an exceptionally large fleet was approaching them. Even though the patrol plane had reported that the fleet was friendly, Pearl had to wonder, "How could any fleet coming from that direction be friendly? The British didn't have anything so large in this part of the world. It must surely be an enemy ruse." The PBY pilots had mistaken the three destroyers of DesRon 3 for battleships. But except for that, their report was accurate. The misidentification of Hawk's destroyers was an honest mistake. After all, they had been modified and were now nearly as long as the current battleships of the time. They certainly weren't armed like the destroyers of 1942. Admiral Scott (of 2042) had referred to them as battle cruisers. Hawk guessed they were probably closer to a battle cruiser than a destroyer. At this distance, Pearl had been on the radar since dawn. Hawk could see there was a lot of activity, and the closer they got, the more active the base became. Shortly after the PBY left the area, several large blips were seen leaving the harbor and a few miles from the naval base the radar showed them separating until they were about 70 miles apart, then they began steaming towards TF 1, as though they were planning a pincer attack. Of course they had no way of knowing that TF1 was watching their every move and if Hawk had wanted to, he could have given them a surprise by dividing his forces and meeting each section with a more powerful force than they had. But he also realized that that kind of surprise could lead to their gunners opening fire when surprised. Besides, they already knew the disposition of Task Force 1. So they already knew they were vastly outnumbered. Hawk's biggest worry was that they would send out an air armada to attack the unknown fleet approaching their naval base. Hawk knew that the U.S. Carriers weren't at Pearl Harbor. Enterprise, Lexington and Yorktown were somewhere around Wake Island. Saratoga, Hornet and Wasp were at the Mare Island Navy Yard in California. Most of the fighter planes and bombers had been destroyed in the attack, but these must surely have been replaced by now. The more he thought about it, the more nervous he got. "Hell, he could be facing several hundred land based bombers at any time." Then, as if in answer to his thoughts, the bridge alarm went off. "Radar to the bridge," said RadCom. "This is the bridge." said Hawk. "Sir, Pearl is launching a large number of aircraft and they seem to making a bee line to us. Either they're sending us a welcoming party, or we should be expecting a very large air attack in the next hour or so. It looks as though they're sending everything they have against us." Hawks worst fears had come true. How could he convince the naval base that they were friendly, when they were sending their forces to attack him? Scrambling to the bridge phone, he called, "RadCom, break radio silence. Send in the currently used code, Task Force 1 to Pearl Harbor. Do not attack us. We are friendly forces coming to assist you. Recall your aircraft and warships. If we are attacked, we will defend ourselves. Recall your forces. Sign it Marcus D. Hawkins, Admiral, Commanding Task Force One. USN. Send it immediately and continue sending it until they recall their forces." Then to radar, "Radar, keep me informed as to any changes in course of the sea and air attack formations." "Aye aye sir." said the seaman in the radar room. "Aye aye sir," said the seaman hunched over the radio set. "Sending message to Pearl Harbor now." For the next ten minutes Hawk became increasingly worried, wondering whether the forces advancing on his ships would turn back or disregard his message and attack. Would he have the opportunity to offer his ships assistance or would he soon be committed in battle against his own countrymen. He considered turning about, but felt that that's what an enemy commander would do. Continuing onward, though seeming foolish, is what a friend would do. At least that's what Hawk hoped the base commander would think. Still, Hawk couldn't just sit there. Nor could he take a chance with the safety of his crews. Going to the console, Hawk ordered, "AttCom, (attack computer) send to all ships in the task force. All ships to battle stations. Stand by to repulse air and sea attack. Do not, repeat, do not open fire until given permission. Send it with my command code." Seconds later Hawk heard the buzz sound of the computer sending his command to the ships of the fleet. From the bridge, one hundred and thirty feet above the water,

Hawk could see the stir of activity aboard the carrier and the nearest ships to the carrier. He was proud of his men. There wasn't a sign of panic. Every man calmly reported to his battle station. A buzzer went off, breaking his concentration. Picking up the phone he heard, "Sir, this is the radio room. I have a coded message. Message reads, Pearl Harbor to ComTF1, do not approach within fifty miles of naval base. Anchor SW of base. Await further instructions. It's signed S.P. Johnson, Vice Admiral, Base Commander, Pearl Harbor." "Thank you radio room, send an acknowledgment, Message received and understood. Will proceed to position 50 miles, SW of base. Awaiting further instructions. Sign it M.D. Hawkins, Admiral, ComTF 1."

Chapter 6

Watching the radar, Hawk saw the three largest blips (believed to be battleships) reverse course, one began heading towards TF1, the other two returned to port. The four smaller blips stayed with the one larger, as all five then steamed towards TF1. Hawk called the radar room, "Radar, this is Admiral Hawkins. Keep an eye on those blips coming out to meet us. I'm going to my cabin. Let me know when they get within seventy miles. Also, keep an eye out for aircraft. They may change their minds and send some out to check us out." Then speaking to the TBS, "Attention all ships this is Admiral Hawkins. Stand down from general quarters. Set condition 2 watches." (Condition #2 watches called for watches four hours on and eight hours off.) Hawk then went down one deck to the captains bridge, where Captain Sherman was standing his bridge. "Sherm, can you radio the Stewart and ask Captain Wilkes and Cmdr. Hunt to join us in my wardroom in thirty minutes. Send a chopper for them." "Aye aye sir." said Captain Sherman.

With the radar watch monitoring Pearl for any ship and aircraft movements, Hawk held an officers conference in his wardroom with Captain's Sherman and Wilkes and Cmdr. Hunt. Hawk was confused as to how they should react should TF 1 come into direct contact with forces sent out from Pearl. "Surrender the fleet and let them escort you in," said Captain Wilkes. "I disagree," said Sherman. "Any surrender would call for allowing them aboard. That contradicts our orders." "I'd have to agree with Captain Sherman on that," said Hunt. "At some point we'll probably have to let them aboard to prove that we are indeed from the future, but I'm thinking that would be later, after we know they accept us as who we say we are. I think we should meet force with force. We allow them to escort us, but keep them off our ships until we actually meet with them. We'll then play it by ear." "Sir," said Sherman, "I think that will put us at a disadvantage. I believe we should go in at full speed, with our flags flying. If they put a shot across our bow and order us to heave to, we put two across their bows and order them to escort us. We have more ships, with more firepower, and many more aircraft than they have. They can't take the risk of firing on a fleet that claims that it's friendly, even if they don't know its origin. They'll figure that somebody fouled up and they just haven't gotten the word. But just to be safe, they'll send over a few ships until they're sure." "Mark," said Hawk, "What do you think about that?" "Well sir," said Wilkes, "The heaviest ships they have at hand is the Tennessee and Maryland. Their biggest guns are 14 inch, so anything they send out will be out gunned by all of our battleships. Captain Sherman is right of course, we can't let them get aboard until we know they're with us. But I just don't think that shooting at them is the right answer either. If there was some way that we could demonstrate our superior fire power without actually firing on them, I think that would be the way to go. That way we don't have to surrender and they don't have to disobey their orders to ascertain our identities before they lead us to Pearl. You can be sure of one thing though, even as we speak, at least one of their carrier groups is steaming hell bent for Pearl in an attempt to get behind us to crawl up our asses for our identity. So I think they'll send out a few ships to follow us and possibly slow us down until that carrier task force can catch up. And if I were to hazard a guess, it would be the Lexington, Yorktown or Enterprise. Maybe all three." "Sherm," said Hawk, "What do you think about that?" "Well sir," said Sherm, "that would make sense. Admiral Halsey commands that carrier group. I studied the admiral while at the academy. One of his favorite tactics was to attack from behind with far superior aircraft and bomb the hell out of the enemy, then send in his surface ships to mop up. In two years he'll do it to Admiral Ozawa's carrier force at Leyte Gulf. Only this time, he doesn't out number us in air power or fire power. Nor do his aircraft stand a chance against our planes or pilots. It would be a turkey shoot." Shaking his head, Hawk answered, "Then we have to be at Pearl Harbor before they catch up to us. Alright gentlemen, thank you for your ideas and opinions. You may return to your ships. Be ready to get under way within the next hour or so."

From the bridge of the Teddy R, Ten blips on the radar scope materialized into 3 cruisers and 7 destroyers 170 miles from Pearl, and began shadowing, then escorting TF1. Intercepted signals from the Pearl showed confusion. They recognized the Colorado, Mississippi, and Texas, but couldn't figure out how they were here when they should have been stateside at the Mare Island Naval Yard for refitting. They recognized the cruisers by American design, but not the destroyers. (Pope Stewart and Jackson were enlarged and modified and the other destroyers were of a design not yet on the drawing boards.) As for the carrier, she was 5 times longer than the largest enemy carrier in existence (the Japanese Shinano) and 8 times larger than any American carrier. Capable of carrying 553 aircraft, the largest American carrier (Lexington) could only carry 83. An accurate comparison of Teddy R. /Lexington would be battleship Tennessee/destroyer Ward. The firepower of the Teddy R, with her aircraft nearly tripled the Enterprise/ Yorktown/Lexington with all of their aircraft. * If Japan's super carrier IJN Shinano had survived long enough to be fitted out and supplied with her aircraft, she would still have carried 5 times less aircraft. Shinano, sister to super battleships Yamato and Musashi would be torpedo sunk by the submarine U.S.S. Archerfish in 1945, if history didn't change.* The thing they found the most curious was that the Teddy R. emitted no funnel smoke. At 30 knots, it seemed as though his new escorts were huffing and puffing to keep up. Hawk ordered the fleet to 40 knots and laughed as they dropped behind. It was his intention to show them what his ships were capable of. They simply ran away from their escorts and had to slow down to let them catch up. Hawk thought it was humorous. But aboard the escorts it was anything but. They had been sent to check them out, escort them in, and slow them down so Halsey could catch up from the rear, and Spruance could get into position from the west (Saratoga, Hornet, and Wasp.) What they saw was an unknown fleet, with unknown vessels steaming at very high speed, on a course to Pearl Harbor. They saw a threat! And they responded as they had been trained. The lead cruiser (Helena) fired 3-8 inch rounds across the bow of the Teddy R. What happened next was a reflexive action on Hawks part. Later he would admit it wasn't the best order he could have given. The Teddy R. and Des Ron 4 and ½ of 5 continued on at 40 knots, while Bat Div 1, Cru Div 1 & 2, ½ of Des Ron 5, all of Des Ron 6, and Des Ron 3 circled 180 degrees and encircled their Pearl Harbor escorts, all guns turned at them. The escort commander (Cmdr. Phillip Ellis,) ordered a dead stop to his cruisers and destroyers to avoid a collision with Hawks ships, and found himself looking into the biggest gun barrels he had ever seen. Aboard the carrier, Hawk boarded a helicopter and had it land on the lead cruisers (Hawk had decided it was the command ship since all of the radio transmissions to Pearl came from this ship) stern. He then emerged with 60 marines as escorts, fully armed with the weaponry of 2042.

Commander Ellis stood on the bridge of his cruiser, the U.S.S. Helena. Steady dispatches were sent to his ship, (describing the ships he was escorting) and he sent them to Pearl. He couldn't believe the size of these ships. He felt as though he was on pins and needles, waiting for Admiral Halsey to come to his aid from Midway and Admiral Spruance to come from California. Actually he didn't expect either to catch up to him in time. They were just too far away. His best hope was that the battleships Maryland and Tennessee, could be pulled away from the sunken ships that had them trapped at their moorings since the attack on December seventh. * Oklahoma had rolled over and West Virginia had sunk on an even keel, wedging the Tennessee against her mooring post.* They were only a few hours away. All of his crews were at battle stations. Even though this fleet flew the stars and stripes, they were still an unknown fleet. He couldn't stop looking at the carrier. She was as big as an island, the biggest bitch he had ever seen. The battleships he recognized, sort of anyway. They seemed bulkier, beefed up with additional armor. Even the cruisers appeared to be more heavily armored. As he studied them, they appeared to pick up speed. Then suddenly they began to pull away rapidly. He ordered full speed, but still they pulled away from him. Then, without thinking about the consequences, he ordered, "A-turret, put a salvo across the bow of the flat top.")*Navies have been doing it since the beginning of time, the understood meaning was, "Heave to and prepare to be boarded."* Cmdr. Ellis expected the ships to slow down. Instead the result gave him the need to change his shorts. The battleships, cruisers and more then half of the destroyers suddenly reversed course 180 degrees and surrounded him forcing him to order his ships to reverse speed, then stop. As the carrier and 6 destroyers continued on, he found himself looking down the longest and blackest gun barrels he could ever remember. He fervently hoped none of his gunners would be foolish enough to open fire. But just to be sure, he went to the TBS and in plain English, ordered all ships to "Hold fire" on the ships (intercom) loud speaker, then prayed nobody would disobey. Because if they did, at this point blank range, he knew his ships wouldn't survive 5 minutes, friendly fleet be damned. "Send a message" he ordered his radioman. "Am surrounded by vastly superior unknown American forces. Annihilation is probable." Within 2 minutes an answer came from Pearl. "Heavy re-enforcements en-route. Do not engage. Expect rendezvous in 12-13 hours. Acknowledge." Cmdr. Ellis acknowledged, and then sent the message to the other 9 ships under his command. "Sir unknown type aircraft approaching from the carrier", shouted the port side lookout. Running out to the port side bridge wing, Cmdr. Ellis watched an aircraft with a very large propeller above it, fly towards the stern of his ship, then watched in awe as it landed on the Helena's stern. As he wondered how an air craft could take off and land vertically, he was surprised, then scared shit-less as 50 to 60 men in unusual camouflage utilities emerged carrying the wickedest looking firearms he could ever have imagined. Running back to the bridge loud speaker, he ordered, "Do not engage boarders. Repeat, Do not engage boarders." Walking back to the bridge wing, he saw an officer now stood behind the armed boarders, and it appeared the boarders were wearing the insignia of U.S. Marines. And the officer wore the naval insignia of an Admiral. "Radioman" ordered Cmdr. Ellis "send to Pearl. We have been boarded by strange aircraft with American Naval Markings, U.S.S. Theodore Roosevelt. Fifty to sixty marines and one Admiral. Requesting instructions." "Aye aye sir," answered the radioman, then "Helena to Pearl, we..." Unknown to Cmdr. Ellis, nothing else was sent. Teddy R. jammed everything else. Ellis sent for the marine security squad and upon their arrival they went off to the stern of the Helena.

Rounding X-turret and walking past Y, they stopped 50 feet short of the armed marines and the unknown Admiral. Before he could speak, the Admiral did. "Cmdr," said Hawk, "do you make it a habit of keeping visiting Admirals waiting?" "Sir", answered Cmdr. Ellis, "by what right do you board an American warship in force?" Cmdr., I am an Admiral in the United States Navy in command of a United States Naval Task Force, a Task Force far superior in fire power to yours. Your 10 ships joined my task force. I am the senior officer present. That gives me the authority to board your ship. I can only assume you joined my task force for protection. (lied Hawk) Now by what authority do you fire upon my command? "Sir," answered Cmdr. Ellis, "we don't know who you are. I was sent to find out. Those ships, or most of them are not of our navy." Hawk interrupted Cmdr. Ellis, "Cmdr. I'm an officer in the United States Navy, in command of a fleet with sufficient fire power to send everyone of your ships to the bottom of the Pacific with the ease of one command. My mission is to kill the japs. My carrier and I, with my destroyers are going to continue on to Pearl. I'd like to bring my battleships and cruisers with me. However if I have to, I'll leave them here with you, and you can spend the next week staring down their guns, or you can hold your fire and escort us into Pearl. What's it going to be?" " Sir, I should tell you," said Cmdr. Ellis, "I have a carrier strike force and heavy unit's en-route." "No Cmdr.," said Hawk, "You don't have a carrier within a thousand miles and your heavy units, the U.S.S. Tennessee and U.S.S. Maryland are 12 hours away. We have them on radar. Pearl doesn't have sufficient long range aircraft to reach us, and I'd guess they'll keep their short range aircraft to protect the islands and the base. You're on your own Cmdr." With his ace trumped (re-enforcements) Cmdr. Ellis could only agree to continue the escort. Hawk and his marines re-boarded the helicopter and returned to the carrier. In minutes Hawks battleships, cruisers and destroyers were heading back towards the carrier followed by Cmdr. Ellis's cruisers and destroyers and every man aboard breathing a sigh of relief. Thirteen hours later the battleships Maryland and Tennessee and six destroyers came up on the horizon. Task Force 1 went to battle stations, unsure whether these ships with Cmdr. Ellis's ships would fire on them, or if the 2 battleships and 6 destroyers would fall into the escorting positions. Hawk breathed another sigh of relief when it was the latter. One hundred miles from Pearl, a large warship was seen to leave the harbor (seen on the radar scope on the Teddy R.) and stop 50 miles from the harbor entrance. As the fleet closed to 50 miles from Pearl, the large warship was identified as the U.S.S. Pennsylvania, still wearing her deck damage from the Japanese attack. At a range of 8,000 yards she signaled the fleet to drop anchor. The other 2 battleships, the 3 cruisers and 13 destroyers then pulled up port, starboard and astern of TF1, their guns trained on Hawks ships. As a show of friendship and trust, Hawk had ordered his ships to keep their turrets trained fore and aft.

Hawk first signaled, then sent his chopper to the Pennsylvania, inviting the captain and base commander to tour the Teddy R. Hawk was mildly surprised to find Admiral Nimitz in command. The Admiral declined, but sent his chief of staff, Captain F.C. Sherman, The great grandfather of the Teddy R.'s captain, Amos Sherman. Following the tour, of which Captain Sherman was very impressed, the great grandfather was introduced to his great grandson. The the two Sherman's got acquainted during lunch. Following lunch the elder Captain Sherman was given the letters from the CNO to Admiral Nimitz and the sealed letter from President Anthony Williams (2042) to President Franklin D. Roosevelt. (1942) Before he left, he was given a demonstration of the Phalanx gun in action, firing on a sleeve towed by an F6F Hell cat. (Hawk hadn't seen it in action yet either). As the elder Sherman left the ship (to report to Admiral Nimitz) Hawk could see the amazement and disbelief in his eyes.

As captain Sherman returned to the Pennsylvania he wondered how he would word his report on the strange ship he had just toured. How could he report he had met his great grandson? How could he describe the Phalanx guns capabilities, the aircraft, or the radars and sonar's, or any of the electronics? How could he make a report that didn't sound as though he'd flipped his lid? He decided he'd wait, report to Admiral Nimitz, and ask him how to word it.

For 2 days TF1 lay at anchor outside of the naval base. During that time Hawk spent time getting acquainted with his captains (and their exec's) of Bat Div 1, Cru Div 1 & 2, and Des Ron 4, 5, & 6. He had a conference with Sherm and Wilkes, placing Wilkes (as 2nd in command) on the battleship Texas, then brought him up to speed on the mission as well as the capabilities of the Teddy R., and the F-173. Lt. Cmdr. Hunt was made asst. Com Des flot. 3, 4, 5, 6, and placed aboard the U.S.S. Stewart- the command ship & flagship of Com Des Flot. 1.

On the 3rd day, Hawk received a radio message requesting his presence at the Admiralty (Naval) Headquarters. Not wanting to run the risk of the Teddy R. running aground (and allowing naval personnel to get a close look at her) Hawk sailed into Pearl aboard the Texas, commanded by Captain Richard Carlsbad. Rear Admiral Wilkes and Captain Sherman (of the Teddy R.) accompanied Hawk. At 0740, the Texas raised her anchors and was underway, heading for the harbor entrance. Captain Carlsbad was a 30 year naval officer, having begun his naval career in the Annapolis Class of 2012. In 2015, during the war with Chile, he was awarded the Navy Cross for gallantry. As an ensign and gunnery officer of mount Y he had saved his frigate when the ship had been blown in half. He managed to get the watertight doors closed amidships, thus preserving the water tight integrity. In 2030, as a lt. Cmdr. he was awarded a second Navy Cross in the war against Great Britain. Commanding the light cruiser Houston, he took his ship into the British harbor of Scapa Flow (as a diversion) sank 3 British frigates, and heavily damaged an aircraft carrier forcing a British battle squadron to break contact with a an inferior American destroyer squadron. Lt. Cmdr. Carlsbad then managed to escape the enemy naval base before the British fleet arrived. In 2042, having reached the age of mandatory retirement, he was offered command of the Texas if he volunteered for this mission.

Timing his entry just right, Hawk passed battleship row at precisely 0800. The Texas slowed to 7 knots, lowered her battle flag to half mast and fired a 5 gun salute to the wrecks of the U.S.S. Oklahoma and U.S.S. Arizona. In addition, the crew stood the rails in their whites. As taps played on the ships loud speaker, the crew rendered a hand salute. The Texas steamed around Ford island, crossed past the main channel entrance and dropped her bow anchors. The current caught her stern and swung her around so her bow faced the harbor entrance, and her stern lay 100 feet from the wreck of the floating dry dock holding what remained of the destroyer U.S.S. Shaw. Only then did Captain

Carlsbad order the stern anchors dropped. It was a maneuver perfected by the Captain over 30 years ago. The identical maneuver that allowed his cruiser to escape Scapa Flow ahead of the British fleet. As the Texas had passed the Arizona, Hawks mind had wandered back (or forward) to his visit to Pearl Harbor where he had toured the Arizona Memorial. A huge white concrete and steel structure that traversed over her hull, never actually touching it. The ship had exploded when a 14 inch shell (a bomb modified from a 14 inch shell) had pierced the main deck, Starboard of mount B, penetrating 4 decks to the powder magazine below. One thousand, one hundred and two men perished in the massive explosion. He had been told that the wreck had seeped oil from her fuel tanks for 76 years before the wreck collapsed, releasing the remaining oil in one last great spill, that had covered much of the harbor. Seeing the sunken remains of the Arizona and the Oklahoma gave Hawk a renewed hatred for the japs and an intense urge to inflict as much pain on as many of them as he could. For an instant he imagined sending the F-173 over Japan and exploding it, frying millions in one mighty flash.

From the port side aft, at 1010 dock, Hawk see's the cruiser, U.S.S. Helena, and he wonders if Cmdr. Ellis is aboard. He's also curious as to what his report said.

Hawk, Sherman, Rivers, Hunt and Wilkes, dressed in Whites, left the Texas on a launch that took them to the shore behind the base hospital. There a gray staff car picked them up, and drove them to the Naval Headquarters building. Another staff car led them, while a third followed. Both escort cars were filled with armed marine guards, making Hawk wish he had brought some of his own. Instead Hawk had posted the Texas's 40 marines at the ship's gangplanks with orders that nobody was to leave or get on the ship. Their orders were to shoot first, and check ids later. The Texas also had super sensitive radios, radars, sonars and other electronics like the Teddy R. did. Hawk fervently hoped nobody would try to board, as a battle could seriously hamper his ability to leave. Hawk asked the marine staff sergeant if all of the security was normal or if it was for him, but the driver didn't say a word. Looking around as the car sped on, Hawk saw many machine gun emplacements and anti aircraft batteries set up along the road, next to the buildings and on top the buildings, all fully manned with alert crews. Arriving at the headquarters building, Hawk saw at least one company of marines posted around the building armed with rifles and Thompson sub machine guns, everyone of them alert as well. Turning to Sherm and Wilkes, he could see they were surprised by all of the military precautions as well. "Maybe they're planning a parade for us or something," said Hawk. "Or maybe a firing squad," said Wilkes. "Or something," said Sherman. The driver stayed behind the wheel, but another marine, a corporal came to the car and opened the door so the officers could leave. "Welcome to Hawaii sirs," said the corporal, as he gave them a salute. As he closed the door, Captain F.C. Sherman came out of the headquarters building. He saluted and said, "Good to see you again Admiral, Captain." He looked at Wilkes, whom he hadn't yet met, then looked at Sherm and smiled. Finished with the salutes and pleasantries, he led them inside. He led them to a door, asked them to wait outside a moment, and then went in. Two armed marine guards closed the door. "Well Sherm," said Hawk, "does the Naval Base look the same to you?" "Apart from all the anti aircraft guns, machine gun pits, bombed out buildings, and wrecked ships and planes, yes sir, sort of", said Sherm. "Sir," said Admiral Wilkes, "I think this may have been a mistake." "What do mean?" said Hawk. "Well sir, all these armed marines. What if they don't let us leave? There's no way we can get back to the ship through all these marines. And what if they try to take the Texas by force?" "They won't get past our marines. And at the first sound of gun fire the Phalanx guns will open up in support of our marines. They couldn't get a man aboard if they stormed the ship with 10,000 men. Then of course the computers would order the 28 inch main armaments to open up with the radar control targeting every warship in the harbor. It would be foolhardy to try anything," said Hawk. "Yes sir," continued Wilkes, "but do they know it?" Hawk winced at the thought. If it looked to him that they were going to hold them, he would warn them. But what if they tried to storm the Texas before he could warn them? It would be a blood bath. And since his ship was mostly automated by computer control, the blood would be theirs, not his. Suddenly Hawk felt sick to his stomach.

A few minutes later, Captain Sherman opened the door and asked them to come in. The room was very dark. On one side there was a projection screen. When Hawk, Sherm and Wilkes had entered and the door was closed behind them, they were asked to sit down. As they did, the projector came on and they found themselves looking at the ships of TF1. "Gentlemen," said a voice in the dark, "do you expect us to believe that you have come here, from the future to fight for us?" Hawk stood and turned to speak, but before he could utter a word, another voice said, "Please sit down Lt." "Admiral," said Hawk as he turned and sat down again. "You have come to us in ships that belong to us, tell us you are from another time and expect us to welcome you. Our records show you are a Lt. Lately of the U.S.S. Stewart; the officer next to you is an ensign, also according to our records. And if we are to believe the enemy, your destroyer was sunk a century ago. Now you appear before us as self proclaimed Admirals. The officer beside you wears the insignia of a Captain, yet we can find no record of his existence. Tell me Lt., is there any reason why we shouldn't just put you in irons, and charge you for impersonating a flag officer?" "I told you so," Hawk heard Wilkes whisper next to him.

"Sir," responded Hawk, "the reason you have no record of Captain Sherman is that he won't be born yet for another 59 years. You say we showed up in ships that already belong to you? That's past tense. These ships, the Texas, Mississippi and Colorado were memorial ships in the year of 2042. Now in 1942 they are also on your commissioning list. I'm sure you've already checked and found these ships in this time are still at the Mare Island Navy Yard in California. In essence gentlemen, there are now 2 of each. As for the U.S.S. Stewart being sunk by the enemy, a look at your projection screen will show you that the Stewart is very much alive and afloat, albiet modified to fit our use. Look gentlemen. I have no idea how we moved through time 100 years. I'll leave that to men much smarter than I am to figure out. What I do know is that the destroyers Stewart, Jackson, and Pope went into a rain squall, and came out in 2042, one hundred years later. After a small altercation involving a Japanese merchant ship and a U.S. Naval cutter, we arrived back at our base, the Cavite Naval Base, in the year 2042. We reported to the Chief of Naval Operations, Admiral Chester W. Nimitz III and the Secretary of the Navy Admiral William A. Halsey III and Anthony Williams, President of the United States. We were given a mission that would begin 1 year later. During this period damage to Des Ron 3, or what remained of it, destroyer Stewart, Jackson and Pope, was repaired, then rebuilt and modified. Exact modifications are top secret and cannot be divulged. But suffice it to say the destroyers were lengthened, rearmed and re armored. The battleships have been modified along the same lines. The destroyers of Des Ron 4, 5, & 6 don't even exist and won't for 3 more years. The cruisers are beefed up as well, and also won't exist for 3-5 years. The carrier, the U.S.S. Theodore Roosevelt won't exist for 61 years. If this isn't enough proof for you, then check the codes we gave you. A simple check with your intelligence staff will show that if you combine the codes we gave you with the partial code they know about, they'll be able to read 100% of the enemy codes instead of the 10% they're now able to read. We've also included the German and Italian codes as well as the dates they will change and the new codes. If my officers and I are lying, then how would we have this information?" Hawk gave them a few minutes to think, and then continued, "Now then gentlemen, I think this meeting is over. We're going to return to our ship, and rejoin our task force. You could try to stop us, but I wouldn't suggest it unless you want a battle on your hands. Our next meeting will be on the carrier where I can promise you the hospitality will be better." Hawk, Sherm and Wilkes stood and without a salute, left the room and the Naval Headquarters building. Outside nobody stopped them. They got into the waiting car and were driven away. Surprisingly, they weren't escorted. They were driven to the Texas, which they boarded. Only then did they speak. "Holy Shit," said Sherm. "Holy Fucking Shit," said Wilkes. "And then some," replied Hawk. Hawk went straight to the bridge where he found Capt. Carlsbad. "How did it go," he asked Hawk. "I'll tell you later, Capt. Take us out of here. We're returning to the rest of the fleet." "Aye aye sir," said the captain as Hawk turned and went to the ward room to find out what was for dinner.

At the Naval Headquarters building, the lights came on as soon as Hawk and his officers had left. Seated at a table were Captain F.C. Sherman, Admiral C.W. Nimitz and President FD Roosevelt. "He's got a lot of nerve walking out on you, Mr. President," said Admiral Nimitz. "We didn't exactly tell him I was here, Chet." "What do you think Capt. Sherman," said FDR. "Well sir, one of them claims to be my great grandson. I don't know Mr. President, but he certainly knows a lot about me and my family history." "Yes," said FDR, "Chet, did you check with intelligence as to the validity of the codes"? "Yes sir", answered Adm. Nimitz. "They tell me they're now able to read 100% of all enemy codes". "Well then Chet", said FDR. "Isn't that proof that what they say is true and they are who they said they are?" "Yes sir", said Adm. Nimitz, but I still don't trust them. Why don't we arrest them, take the ships and use them ourselves? "Sir", said Capt. Sherman, "If they're from the future as they say they are, then the ships are bound to be much more sophisticated and advanced than we are accustomed to. On the tour they gave me, I didn't recognize half of what I saw. Their guns are radar controlled, operated by a computer. There are no men at the guns. Mr. President, I've been around warships for most of my life. If I didn't recognize most of what I saw, if we did steal the ships, how could we possibly operate them ourselves?" The look Adm. Nimitz gave him made Capt. Sherman say no more. "He's right Chet", said FDR, "They're obviously who they say they are. I think it would be to our advantage to let them help us. God knows we're short of men and warships now". "Is this your decision then, Mr. President?" asked Adm. Nimitz. "Yes Chet", said FDR. "Now this other matter. Since they've received their commissions from one of my predecessors, I see no reason why we shouldn't recognize them as well. I'll draw up the order for their promotions. Capt. Sherman, send a message to Adm. Hawkins requesting a list of the officers and men under his command and their present ranks. And also inform him that we'll be coming for dinner tomorrow evening to sample his hospitality". "Yes sir", said Capt. Sherman. After he had left, FDR. turned to Adm. Nimitz and said, "One more thing Chet, you're not going to like this, but I'm going to request that Admiral Hawkins assign you as my representative aboard the carrier."

"Sir, radio message from N.H.Q.", reported the radioman to Hawk. "Thank you, seaman", said Hawk as he took the message and read it, then, "Call Captain Sherman and Admiral Wilkes, and ask them to meet me in my wardroom immediately". "Yes sir", said the radioman as Hawk turned and left the bridge. "You're kidding, he's coming here?" Is all Wilkes could say as he read the radio message Hawk had handed him. Then Capt. Sherman said "Sir, the way the message reads, it's as though he was at the briefing too, this bit about sampling your hospitality". "Oh lord" said Wilkes, "Not only did you tell off the Commander of Naval Forces- Pacific (Com Nav For- Pac) but also the Commander in Chief". "Captain", Hawk said, "Talk to the chef and see if he can't whip up something extra special for dinner tomorrow night. Beans and hotdogs aren't going to cut it." "Yes Sir," said Sherm. When he left, Hawk turned to Wilkes and handed him the 2nd message. "They want a roster of all the officers and men in the fleet and their ranks." "Sir," said Wilkes, our sealed orders prohibit that." "Yes," said Hawk. "But I can give them the names of the officers and men from the original crews of the Jackson, Pope and Stewart, as well as those already lost in combat. Mark, have Captain Hunt dig up the ships rosters for Des Ron 3, list all officers and men with their current ranks. Have them delivered to me by 1300 hours tomorrow. As far as the names of the officers and men that came aboard in 2042, that's classified". "Sir, are you going to tell the commander in Chief that?", said Wilkes. "Yes Mark, I am."

Chapter 7

Alone in his cabin that night, Sherm found himself thinking about their briefing at the base naval headquarters. Though a bit rash, he knew Hawk had handled the situation well. Had he not come off as he did, they may have been arrested and imprisoned. He knew Adm. Nimitz was there, he recognized his voice. Sherm didn't like Nimitz. And he didn't trust him. If the President was there as well, that would explain all of the armed marines. He thought of Hawk again. How he didn't seem fazed at all about the armed escort. "It just goes to show" he thought to himself, "the kind of men our country breeds and the kind of officers Annapolis makes". Sherm liked Hawk, and he respected him immensely. Right from the beginning he saw how well Hawk had treated his crew. He took the time to get to know as many of them as he could. He cared for his crew and looked after them. Almost fatherly. And they respected him for it. He knew they would do anything for him. They'd follow him through the gates of hell if that's where he wanted to go. Sherm also respected him. The way he dove into the designs of the Teddy R., asked the right people questions about things he didn't understand. How he studied everything about the carrier, from her nuclear power plant and propulsion system, her damage control system, refueling methods, carrier tactics, take off and landing procedures, he studied her weapons, her aircraft, the pilots and mechanics he talked with. The man was everywhere, studying and learning everything. Then when Sherm was sure he couldn't be any more impressed, Hawk began studying naval tactics over the next hundred years to 2042. Sherm knew that if Hawk fought his way to hell, the crew would follow. And so would he.

The following morning at 0900, a radio message came in from the SSBN Scorpion. Her Captain had come across two enemy submarines on the surface, 250 miles east of Pearl Harbor, charging their batteries. The message was delivered to Sherm, and asked for permission to sink them. Sherm took the message to Hawk, on the hanger deck where he knew Hawk was every morning from 0800 to 1000. The flight simulator. The Teddy R. carried only single seat fighters, so the only way Hawk could learn to fly was in a flight simulator. Hawk had been flying since he came aboard and according to the simulator operator, the Admiral was a natural. Entering the Air Com Sim Control room, Sherm donned a headset and informed Hawk that he had a high priority message for him. "Very well," said Hawk as he hit the kill switch, ending whatever simulation he was working on. Walking across the hanger deck where they could be alone, he read the message. "The Scorpion. That's Cmdr. Grimley. A good man. If he's certain they're enemy subs, tell him to kill them. Kill them all." Placing the message in his pocket, Hawk returned to the simulator and Sherm proceeded to the radio room, impressed even more that the Hawk could remember the name of a submarine skipper under his command that he had only met once. At the radio room he found the operator intensely monitoring all sea and air frequencies. Tapping him on the shoulder, he said, "Send to submarine Scorpion, ascertain whether friend or foe. Stop. If enemy, kill them all. Stop. Sign it Com Task Force One, The Hawk." As the operator began sending, Sherman returned to the bridge. At 1100 hours, Hawk went up to the bridge where he found Sherm deep in thought. "Is something wrong," asked Hawk. "No sir," said Sherm. Then a moment later he said, "I look around us Sir, I see all of this fire power. I look on deck and see all these planes. I can't help but wonder what would've happened if we had come out of that squall and the japs hadn't attacked yet. If our surface force could've come across the enemy carrier force before they launched their attack. Or if we had been early enough to launch our planes to intercept the enemy attack force before they reached Pearl Harbor. We could've ended the war before it began. Maybe we could've warned Pearl of what was coming. "Yes," said Hawk, "I've thought about it too.

But then if we had attacked the japs before they hit Pearl, we would've been the aggressors, not Japan. Besides, if I remember history, Pearl was forewarned, twice. Once by the radar operators at Opana Point and again when the destroyer Ward reported sinking a submarine in the channel. Both warnings were ignored." Then changing the subject, Hawk asked, "Do you have that roster of the officers and men for Adm. Nimitz?" "Yes Sir," said Sherm, handing it over to Hawk. Taking out a pencil, Hawk made a small change, actually an addition. " I received a medical report from Doc Webb. He has diagnosed a Lt. Cmdr as unfit for duty, due to a heart condition. So I am releasing him from duty with this command. Also, with one exception, all of these men are from this time and era. Our sealed orders prohibit me from divulging the names of officers and men, volunteers, of 2042. However, I have included one officer of 2042. An officer already known by command here. I want him registered on the official Officers Naval Roster as a Rear Admiral. Hawk handed the Roster back to Sherm and said, "Besides, having two Captain Sherman's aboard my ship is too confusing." Holding out his hand, Hawk said, "Congratulations, Admiral."

At precisely 1600 hours, 3 motor launches approached the Teddy R. Two were escorting the third. The third launch carried Captain F.C. Sherman, Admirals C.W. Nimitz and W.A. Halsey, and 2 Cmdr.'s who carried President F.D. Roosevelt aboard, placing him in his wheel chair on the hangar deck. A boatswain mate piped them aboard and all hands stood at attention as they were escorted to an elevator that took them to the Admirals wardroom. All naval ships have water tight doors with bulkheads that are not condusive to wheelchairs. The Teddy R. included. However, the island structure is not watertight. Obviously if the rest of the ship is flooded, bulkheads and watertight integrity would be senseless. In this case, and on this day it made wheelchair access easy for the President. Given a tour, he was shown the guts of the Big Stick, her electronics, her radio and radar guidance systems. Sonar guidance was sealed off so they wouldn't see the blips representing the 10 nuclear subs that ringed the islands and covered the approaches up to 300 miles out. Then, on the bridge wings they were given a demonstration of the Phalanx guns. Having seen it before, Captain Sherman was still impressed by the destructive power of the carrier. F.D.R. was openly amazed. He could only look at Adm. Nimitz and smile. After the Phalanx demonstration, the Texas came alongside. As the guests looked on (Halsey and Nimitz were raised on battleships) the U.S.S. Jackson cruised by towing a sled. On an order from Hawk, Texas's radar controlled 21 inchers opened up. The first salvo, a broadside went off and raised an enormous splash as all 12-21" guns hit the sled dead balls on, blowing the sled into particles. Next, at the President's request, Lt. Cmdr. Radcliff was brought before FDR. Where the president personally decorated him with the distinguished Flying Cross for shooting down the zero float plane that attempted to shoot down the PBY patrol plane, thus saving it's crew. Next, also at the president's request, Admiral Hawkins was called in front of FDR where he (Hawk) was awarded the Navy Cross for the destruction of the enemy fleet outside of the rain squall. (A quick glance at Admiral Nimitz showed an expression on his face that made it perfectly obvious that he wasn't in favor of Hawk being decorated. In fact, he looked as though he wanted to shoot the Hawk.) Then Captain Amos Sherman (Commanding the Teddy R.) was promoted to Rear Admiral and awarded his pennant, with Captain F.C. Sherman looking like a proud father, or in this case a proud great grandfather. Following the awards and decoration ceremony, all went down to the Admirals wardroom for dinner, where the Admirals Chef served T-bone steaks, shrimp clusters, baked potatoes, honey yams and chocolate mousse for dessert. (Hawk was never able to learn where the steaks, fresh potatoes and the dessert came from) After wards Hawk decided they had to have guests more often. The meal was followed by coffee and then drinks from the Admirals bar. Admiral Halsey, having remained quiet throughout the visit now remarked that alcohol on a naval vessel seemed a good way to end an exceptional day. Admiral Nimitz declined the offer of an alcoholic beverage and had a glass of water instead. The President ordered a strange concoction made up of milk and gin. It was then that FDR said, "Admiral, would you mind if I asked you to allow one of my officers aboard as a liaison officer?" "I was thinking the same thing, Mr. President," said Hawk. "Who did you have in mind sir." "Well son," said FDR, "I was thinking of Admiral Nimitz." Hawk replied, "Admiral Nimitz wouldn't last 24 hours aboard the first time my crew saw that icy stare of his." Looking at Admiral

Nimitz, "Yeah that one, they'd toss him to the sharks. My crew are very protective of me. No I was thinking of Captain Sherman. The crew already knows him. They like him and respect him. I don't know about a liaison officer. But I'd like him aboard as an adviser." "Well that settles that," said FDR. Then looking at Admiral Nimitz he said, "Old gimlet eye is out. But I can't give you Captain Sherman yet. Coded intercepts from the Japanese have a small fleet of theirs headed for the Coral Sea. I'll be sending Admiral Fletcher over there with the Lexington and Yorktown. Captain Sherman will be commanding the Lexington." "Mr. President," said Admiral Wilkes, "I don't think that's a good idea." Wilkes looks at Hawk, and getting a nod, he continued, "According to history, in ten days the Lexington and Yorktown will be in the Coral Sea, with their supporting battle group. There they will find the Japanese fleet, 3 enemy carriers, the Shokaku, Zuikaku and the Shoho, she's a light carrier. Our airmen will sink the Shoho and damage the Zuikaku. But we're going to lose the Lexington, the destroyer Sims and the oiler Neosho. The Yorktown will be heavily damaged." "So," said FDR, "What do you propose I do?" "Keep the Lexington and Yorktown battle groups away." said Hawk, "we know where the enemy will be and when he'll be there and in what strength." "And you know this how," asked Nimitz? "It's in the history books, Admiral," answered Admiral Sherman. Nimitz still wasn't convinced. Turning to Hawk, he asked, "Am I to believe that our navy in the future gives fleet commands to junior officers?" "No sir," said Hawk. "But since I was already in command of Des Ron 3, it seemed appropriate to give me command of the fleet. The President and Naval Chief of Staff felt that an officer of 1942 would have a better chance of successfully completing the mission. But because of my inexperience in combat planning and maneuvers I was given the services of Captain, now Admiral Sherman who is a combat decorated officer, or will be in 59 years." Turning to Sherm, Nimitz says, "So you're claiming to be Captain Sherman's great grandson?" "I am sir," said Sherm. Now turning back to Hawk, Nimitz says, "So not only do you expect us to believe your story, you expect us to sit back and watch while you two Lt.'s and an old man with no history sail us into the Pacific to supposedly fight a battle that nobody else knows about? And then I'm supposed to spot promote you, a Lt., to

Admiral and give you fuel and supplies." "Admiral," said Hawk, "I am an Admiral in the United States Navy already. I have my pennant to prove it. I don't give a rats ass if you promote me or not. Nor do I care if you acknowledge my rank or not. If this wasn't such an important mission, I'd tell you where you can put that fuel and supplies. Furthermore, you're aboard my ship and in my fleet. Here, whether you believe me or not, you will address me by my rank, or I'll put you in irons and have you removed from this ship." "I'll have your stars for that," sneered Nimitz as he spun on his heels and left, heading for the gang plank." "What stars," Hawk yelled back at him, "I'm a Lt., remember?" Then, realizing that FDR was watching him, Hawk apologized. "Mr. President, please forgive me for my outburst. I didn't mean to sound disrespectful." FDR nodded, and then asked, "So then Admiral, what do you suggest we do about this upcoming operation?" "Mr. President," Hawk said, "history has reported that the Lexington is sunk and Yorktown heavily damaged during the battle in the Coral Sea. But that can't happen if they're not there. Give me Captain Sherman and the fuel and supplies I need and I'll take my task force into the Coral Sea. I'll get those jap carriers for you." As FDR thought about it, Hawk continued, "Mr. President, two battleships, two heavy cruisers, three light cruisers and seven destroyers chased three WW 1 era destroyers into a rain squall, one of which was severely damaged, and the other two were heavily damaged. Those fourteen enemy warships waited for us to emerge so they could sink us. Instead three battle cruisers, twelve destroyers, ten heavy and light cruisers and three battleships came out. And all fourteen enemy warships now rest at the bottom of the Java Sea. That happened because we knew they would be there and we planned for it. And we surprised them by being more powerful than they thought we'd be. Imagine what we could do to them in the Coral Sea?" Convinced, FDR asked, "OK son, what do you need?" "Fuel, for our escorts and aircraft," said Hawk, "and 5, 6 and 8 inch ammunition to replenish what we've already used. Also 20mm and 40mm ammunition and 500 and 1000 pound armor piercing bombs to be loaded onto the carrier." "You'll have it. One other thing," continued FDR, "This carrier of yours, you know it was named after my uncle. Does one get named after me as well?" Yes sir," answered Admiral Sherman. "We had a choice of four carriers to send that met the specifications for what we needed. We chose the Teddy R., because we felt sending the Franklin D. Roosevelt might complicate things." "I see," said FDR. "And what were the other two named?" "The Nimitz and the Halsey." said Sherm.

Later, at Naval Headquarters, Admiral Nimitz sat with FDR and Admiral Halsey. "Do you believe any of this?" asked Halsey. "Frankly no," said Nimitz, "and I plan to bring that Lt. up on insubordination charges." "That Lt." said FDR, "is an Admiral, recommended and authorized by two presidents, Chet." "Well, Admiral or not, I'll see him broken," said Nimitz. "They must be from the future," said Halsey. "Did you see the weaponry on that carrier?" "And the electronics," said FDR. "Computer and radar controlled guns that don't require men to man them. Anti aircraft guns that fire three thousand rounds a minute. Effective to four thousand yards! And twenty two hundred of them on the carrier alone, plus many more on the other ships. No enemy plane can survive an attack on that carrier." " You're not actually going to give them the supplies, are you, Mr. President?" asked Nimitz. "Yes I am," said FDR, "But there's one thing I don't understand." "What's that?" asked Halsey. "He asked for 5, 6 and 8 inch ammunition," said FDR. "But he's got 28 inch guns also." "I don't understand," said Halsey. "Where is he getting the 28 inch ammunition to replenish his battleships?" asked Nimitz.

Two days later, Task Force 1 pulled up it's anchors and proceeded to the Coral Sea. One hundred miles from Pearl Harbor, with the radar and sonar scopes clear, Hawk ordered the Wahoo, Tang and Archerfish to the surface and replenish the battleships 28" ammunition. Captain Sherman was kept busy all day on the hanger deck. One hellcat caught his eye. The plane, belonging to Lt. Radcliff, had a meatball painted on his plane. As he spoke to Lt. Radcliff, he explained to Captain Sherman that it was no big deal, he also had 37 kills from the war with Great Britain, (2030- 2033) the same war that his great grandson had won the 2nd Navy Cross. Lt. Radcliff then began telling him how well liked his great grandson was and how much the fleet respected him. Captain Sherman spoke to many of the crew that afternoon; he studied the planes, then took a turn in the aircraft simulator. An experienced flier himself, he was surprised at how familiar the Hellcat was to the

Wildcat, yet how much faster and more powerful the Hellcat was. By the time he came up on the bridge, the re-supplying was finished, the battleships were back in position and the subs were back in deep water.

As the fleet neared the Coral Sea, and the hour of battle drew near, Hawk held a briefing with all of his captains, then all of the pilots. Over confident of victory, the Japanese commander continually broke radio silence, giving his position, which the radio operators picked up and the code breakers translated. What wasn't recorded in the history books was then recorded in the computers in the Combat Information Center (CIC). Once within range, (300 miles) Hawk would launch his Hellcats to bomb the hell out of the Japanese fleet, with two hundred aircraft, one hundred fifty with bombs. Four of his subs, Sea Wolf, Tang, Scorpion and Wahoo were already ahead of the fleet. By the time the aircraft reached the enemy fleet, the subs would also be in position to attack with their wakeless torpedoes. The subs would attack from 1,000 feet down (with torpedoes Radar guided) so the japs sonar couldn't find them. Since the torpedoes were wakeless, the japs would never know the subs were there. After launching the attacking aircraft, the fleet would continue on a collision course with the enemy position so the surface ships could mop up. One hundred aircraft would be kept on the deck in case any enemy aircraft found the Teddy R., and tried to attack. In addition, 40 aircraft would be kept aloft over the fleet at all times as a combat air patrol. (Cap) Should any enemy planes attack, the 100 aircraft held in reserve would attack and annihilate them 100 miles and 75 miles ahead of the carrier. If any aircraft were unfortunate enough to get through to the fleet Hawk was confident the (AA) anti aircraft batteries and the (cap) combat airpatrol would take care of them. Unlike the battle recorded in the history books, this time there would be no invariables. Every move the enemy would make was known. Stupidly, the Japanese commander continued to radio Tokyo with his current position, so as the planes flew to attack, the carrier radioed the planes, giving any needed course corrections. Not that it made any difference. At a distance of 300 miles, the enemy was on the radar scope anyway. Forty minutes after launching, the Hellcats were over the target. As they prepared to begin their dive bombing attack, an enemy cruiser was seen to explode, break in two and begin to sink. The subs were also starting their attack. Lt. Radcliff was in the bombing group. He radioed that the enemy anti aircraft fire was horrendous. He began his dive from 6,000 feet to 1,500, and dropped his bomb, a thousand pounder, square in the center of the flight deck of the Zuikaku, alongside the island. As the carrier's flight deck erupted, his plane, damaged by the blast, caught fire. As he pulled up from his dive, his plane was attacked by a zero. His wing-man Lt. Jim McCain shot down the zero, but Lt. Radcliff's plane was too damaged to continue. Maybe Lt. Radcliff was wounded also. No one would ever know. As others watched, his plane did a wing over and dove into the Zuikaku's stern which was crowded with parked planes. The explosion was cataclysmic. A ball of flame erupted, pieces of the flight deck were blown a hundred feet in the air where they disintegrated, then fell into the water. Seconds later her fuel tank blew up followed by what must have been her bomb stowage. The whole ship seemed to rise out of the water as it was engulfed in smoke and flame. When the smoke cleared the carrier was gone. And 32,000 tons of jap scrap lay on the bottom of the Coral Sea. Meanwhile, unable to see the torpedoes, the enemy fleet began to scatter. This had the effect of dispersing the anti-aircraft fire, which the pilots immediately noticed as they began pressing their attacks. Marksmanship was good. Seven 1,000 pounders struck the Shoho, transforming the ship into a crematorium, and her crew into crispy critters. A Nagato class battleship was struck by tree 1,000 pound and two 500 pound bombs that blew off her stern and toppled her pagoda structure. When the Akatsakazi class destroyer tried to tow her, one of the subs put two torpedoes into the destroyers bow, blowing it off and leaving her to sink as well. Also hit by the subs were the Kumano class heavy cruiser and two Tone class light cruisers and at least three other destroyers. Then the Shokaku got hit. Three 500 pound and one 1,000 pound bombs struck her forward blasting her deck and leaving her down at the head. Before the smoke cleared she took three torpedoes in the bow, which blew off seventy feet of her nose, bursting her aviation fuel tanks. Fuel from the fractured tanks spread out across the water, transforming her crew into charred chunks of flame broiled meat. Shokaku and Zuikaku had both been part of the Pearl Harbor strike force. The pilot who had dropped the bomb on the Arizona (causing it to explode) came from the Shokaku. The 1102 men lost on the Arizona was only a third of the number lost on the jap carrier. The U.S.S. Arizona had been avenged. And the sharks were treated to fried jap that day.

As Hawk watched one blip after another disappear from the radar scope, he also watched two waves of enemy aircraft approach. The first wave contained 22 torpedo bombers, 18 high level bombers, 15 dive bombers and 30 fighters. The second wave consisted of 20 torpedo planes, 24 high level bombers, 9 dive bombers and 34 fighters. Since the enemy C.A.P. had been wiped out right away, Hawk had ordered the fighters from the attack force to return A.S.A.P. To assist in shooting down the enemy approaching the fleet. Until then, Hawk launched the 100 fighters that he had retained for just this purpose. Then, all Hellcats completing their attacks on the enemy fleet were ordered to return to the carrier immediately, which was now only 70 miles from the enemy fleet. As they flew back to the Teddy R., they caught up with the slower enemy planes. But many of the Hellcats were low or out of ammunition. About this time another warship formation appeared on the radar scope, coming from behind Task Force One. T.F. 1 appeared to be trapped! Ahead lay the remnants of the Coral Sea Strike Force, minus it's carriers, 1 battleship, 3-4 cruisers and 4 destroyers. Between it and T.F. 1 was it's attacking aircraft, already being decimated by over 300 Hellcats. And behind T.F. 1 (and coming up fast) were what appeared to be 2 aircraft carriers, 7 or 8 cruisers and about 20 destroyers. Hawk decided to continue his attack. His surface force would mop up the cripples of the enemy Coral Sea Force, then take on the enemy behind him. A bold move, but what other choice did he have. If he changed course now, his planes, unable to find him, would crash into the ocean when they ran out of fuel. In the meantime, Hellcats returning from their attack on the enemy carriers were refueled and rearmed. As soon as they numbered 100, Hawk sent them east to take on the enemy force behind them, now 280 miles away. Submarines Hake and Seahorse had also been dispatched immediately as they came on the radar screen. Command of the eastern strike force fell to Lt. Cmdr. Eugene Minson. Twenty five minutes later the bridge radio crackled, "Green one to Teddy, Green One to Teddy, come in please." "This is Teddy," said Hawk, "come in Green one" "Green one unable to complete mission.

Strike force is friendly. Repeat, strike force is friendly." Hawk turning to Sherm, guessed, "Lexington and Yorktown?" "Couldn't be anyone else" shrugged Sherm. Disgusted with the waste of munitions and fuel, Hawk ordered, "Green one return to carrier. Jettison bombs en-route. Repeat jettison bombs en-route Teddy R. out." Then, "radio man, get me the Lexington." Minutes later, "Sir, Lexington isn't answering." "Perhaps" said Sherm, "she's keeping radio silence, sir." Visibly pissed off, Hawk left the bridge, and went to his cabin. Thirty minutes later Lt. Commander Eugene Minson and his strike force began landing on the Teddy R.

Making an entry in the log book, Hawk called radar plot and asked the radar operator for the Japanese position. "They're 240 miles away, sir. They don't appear to be advancing or leaving the area. Sir, they seem to be just milling about." Next Hawk called the bridge, "Ask Admiral Sherman to report to my wardroom as soon as possible." "Aye aye sir," answered the bridge talker. In the wardroom, Hawk called Magic, his steward. He thought about ordering a bourbon, but instead asked him to bring in some coffee and BLT sandwiches. Minutes later Sherm came in. "You sent for me sir?" "Yes" said Hawk, "have a seat. I'll have some coffee and sandwiches in a moment." "Thank you sir," said Sherm. Five minutes later Majic came in with a thermos of coffee, and a tray of sandwiches. (Hawk called him Majic because of the steward's ability to make something tasty with whatever was available. Majic came from the Stewart with Hawk). After he had left and Hawk had poured Sherm a cup of coffee and given him a sandwich, Hawk asked his exec., "any idea why the Lexington and the Yorktown are shadowing us?" "No sir," said Sherm, "we asked the president not to send them. History records the Lexington sinking today on this mission. Maybe Admiral Nimitz didn't believe us." Hawk nodded, and then continued, "Radar reports the enemy fleet to the west has stopped, but haven't begun a retreat yet." "Yes sir," said Sherm, "they're undoubtedly picking up their survivors. Half of their fleet is sitting on the bottom of the Coral Sea." "Yes" said Hawk, "we did much better this time around. Is there any information as to what they still have afloat, what our surface warships will be facing"? "Sir" Sherm asked, "Are you still planning to send our heavy escorts in to mop up in a surface engagement"? "Hell yes, Admiral," said Hawk, "unless they attempt to run away tonight, I figure we'll reach the target area about 0530 tomorrow morning. You don't think it's a good idea, Sherm?" "No sir, I don't." "Sherm," said Hawk, "we knocked out fourteen enemy ships as we came out of the squall. That's fourteen ships that would still be afloat if we hadn't intervened and changed history. The last time we fought here, the enemy only lost a small carrier and a destroyer. Today they lost that small one again, plus two large ones, at least one battleship, three cruisers and four destroyers. That's eleven ships, nine of which would still be afloat. That's 23 ships sunk. The japs have to use other ships in their coming operations. They can't keep taking loses like that. When they run out of ships the war will soon be over. And that is our mission". "Yes sir," said Sherm, "It's just that, the japs of 2042 know we're here and what our mission is. They know that if we succeed, not only do they lose the war again, but they also lose everything they gained over the last 100 years after the war. Admiral, they have history books too. Whether they come through the squall in a lifeboat, or large warships they've purchased, they could use those books and records to set up a trap for us". "They don't know the coordinates of the squall," countered Hawk. "If they watched you enter the squall on a satellite, they know exactly where the squall is". said Sherm. "Sir, even if the squall appears and disappears randomly," said Sherm, "they need only wait for it to show up. Admiral Yamamoto, like Admiral Nimitz may not believe them, so he sends this carrier force to the Coral Sea. But let's say like Nimitz, he sends another force behind them. They'd know your radar has a four hundred mile range. So if they stayed just out of the range, they could hit us when and where we don't expect them". Hawk thought a minute or so, and then said, "Call the radar room. Tell them to contact the Trout and Harder. I want them to reconnoiter up to 200 miles beyond the enemy, west. Contact the Archerfish and Seawolf, tell them to break off contact. Send the Seawolf 200 miles north and Archerfish 200 miles south. Report any enemy or suspicions warships." Sherm went to the phone and called the radio room. Getting up, Hawk called the radar room, "What's the distance of the Lexington/Yorktown force?" "Three hundred seventy one miles, sir" Said the radar operator. Putting down the phone, Hawk said to Sherm, "Order the Hake and

Seahorse to patrol 200 miles beyond the Lexington and Yorktown. Tell all subs to stay at maximum depth." "Yes sir" said Sherm. "Sir" Sherm continued, "Wahoo and Tang are still in the enemy area. Do you have orders for them?" "Yes" said Hawk, "tell them they can fire at any large warships they can find. Tell them to reload immediately. They may be going after large units if another fleet is detected by our search subs." "Yes sir," said Sherm. When Sherm was finished, he came back to the table, sat down and ate his sandwich with Hawk.

"Sir, radar reports two blips have disappeared from the Lexington/Yorktown strike force." Hawk had gone to his cabin to lie down after the sandwiches and coffee. He had just nodded off, when the radar operator had called him. Jolted awake, Hawk picked up his cabin phone and called the radio room. "Call the Lexington; find out what's going on." A minute later the radio man called back, "Sir, the Lexington doesn't answer, but I got through to the Yorktown. They report the Lexington hit by three torpedoes. They're under attack, sir." Running to the bridge, Hawk got more bad news. "Sir, radar reports the skies over the Lexington and Yorktown are full of enemy planes. At least 200 more are on the way here, range under 180 miles." Turning to Sherm, Hawk asked, "Why didn't we pick them up at 400 miles?" "I don't know sir," Said Sherm, "maybe they're able to jam the radar for short periods of time." "Are all our aircraft aboard?" asked Hawk. "Yes sir" said Sherm, "except for 20 cats over the fleet as C.A.P." "Reinforce them with 100 more, send another 100 to the Lexington and Yorktown." ordered Hawk. "Sir," said Sherm, "I suggest that we keep a couple hundred aboard in case our scout subs turn up something." "That's a good idea admiral, after the 200 cats are launched, I want the flight deck clear. Put all other aircraft on the hangar deck, under the armored flight deck. "Aye aye sir", said Sherm as he left the bridge to personally carry out the orders. (Both of the admirals were reminded of Lt. Cmdr. Radcliff, how he had crashed his plane aboard the Zuikaku earlier that day and had single handedly pulverized her and directly caused the sinking. They could almost envision the same thing happening to the Teddy R.)The 20 cat (CAP.) cover flew towards the 200 strong attacking forces, quickly re-enforced by additional fighters. Lt. Cmdr. Minson was amongst the first to take off. He flew directly for the oncoming enemy closely followed by more Hellcats. All six catapults launched as fast as was humanly and mechanically possible, Upon reaching the enemy, Lt. Cmdr. Minson mixed it up with the enemy for 15 minutes, shooting down 3 enemy bombers, (per orders) then flew onward to the Lexington/Yorktown. The first 100 pilots carried those orders. Upon reaching the carriers, Minson reported, "Green one to Teddy, Green one to Teddy, (Minson knew the Teddy R. wouldn't respond- they didn't know if the enemy could home in on the transmission) Lexington afire & listing to port approximately 6 degrees, Yorktown also smoking". The skies above the American fleet were clear of enemy planes, but the Lt. Cmdr. could see many planes coming in, riding the waves. Torpedo planes! Pushing the stick forward, he dived his plane from 11,000 feet down to the wave tops. From 8,000 down he had zeros on his tail, but his plane-heavier and with a more powerful engine-ran away from them, though his tail did pick up some jap lead. Flying head on into the torpedo planes (attacking alone for a few minutes) he took out one of the frontal assault, circled back behind them and took down another before a zero got on his tail and he had to disengage to shake off the enemy plane. By then there were a couple more Hellcats attacking the low flying planes. Climbing, Lt. Cmdr. Minson was able to quickly out distance himself from the zero, and at that point he realized two things. First, more enemy higher level (dive bombers) were coming in, and second, all of Lexington's and Yorktown's CAP had been shot down. Except for their meager AA protection, the carriers were defenseless. Looking down, he could see the Lexington's list had grown worse, and Yorktown was engulfed in heavy smoke. Neither carrier would be able to launch any supporting aircraft for quite awhile, if ever. Pressing his mic (microphone) button, he called, "green 1 to purple and silver 1, enemy dive-bombers coming in from southeast, 50 strong. Repeat 50 strong. Request assistance." "Silver one acknowledges, coming up." Silver squadron, 25 cats in all, pulled back on their sticks and began climbing. Flying through a pack of zeros, they blew nine out of the sky, but lost one of their own; Lt. Fisher didn't make it through. At the 6,000 level, they met the dive-bombers, the first nine plane formation. Nine dive-bombers never pulled out of there dives. But many more were on their way. Then another Hellcat went down, Ensign Lister, his plane struck by friendly fire from the

Chapter 8

An hour after the air-attack on TF 1, the submarine Scorpian (Cmdr. Grimley) radioed the presence of enemy ships, 160 miles south of the Lexington/Yorktown force. However these ships were not of the WW II era, but of the atomic age (approximately 1990). Escorting destroyers picked the subs up on sonar, even at 22,000 feet deep. However, they had no means to attack the Scorpian at that depth. The fact that the enemy changed course before the sub could fire showed they had some advanced sonar equipment. Also, three enemy subs were picked up at 1,700 feet. At that depth, the pressure would have crushed the hulls of a WW II submarine. When the presence of the subs was radioed to Hawk, he sent out his now famous order, "Kill them". It was an order he had already sent several times, and would send out many more times before this fracas was over. Radio reception from the Seahorse, even more than 500 miles away was amazing. From the bridge of the Teddy R., everyone could hear everything that the crew of the Scorpian could hear, including the bulk heads bursting on the atomic subs as the guided torpedoes stuck their hulls and the screams of the crew as they died. They had tried to escape, but with the fish locked onto them, the only escape open to them was the bottom of the sea with big holes blown into the hulls of their boats. All three atomic subs were destroyed. The Teddy R. took three bomb hits, but armor piercing or not they failed to penetrate the flight deck. And with all aircraft on the hanger deck, there were virtually no fires resulting from the hits. One phalanx gun was put out of action, but was repaired an hour after the attack. One destroyer reported a near miss that started some flooding, but the water was being pumped out. Task Force 1 continued to advance on the enemy surface force. At 0217 a radio call came in from submarine Harder. It reported no enemy presence west of the known enemy force. Then the Wahoo radioed in, "Enemy surface force retreating S.W. No major units survived. Radar reports one heavy cruiser, five light cruisers and twelve destroyers. All cripples sunk. Requesting orders." Hawk thought only a few seconds, and then ordered, "Hawk orders Wahoo and Tang, sink all cruisers. Upon their destruction proceed east to TF 1. Acknowledge receipt of orders." Then, "TF 1 to Trout and Harder, proceed S.E. Find and engage remnants of enemy unit. Link up with Seawolf and Archerfish, and proceed N.E. To TF 1's position. Acknowledge receipt of orders." As soon as Hawk got an affirmative from Seawolf, Archerfish, Wahoo and Tang, he returned to the bridge. TF 1 had done remarkable well. His only casualties were cats over TF 1 and Lexington/Yorktown. Five Hellcats were lost, and three pilots, one over TF 1 (missing) and two over the Yorktown, whose planes had exploded before they could get out. Since the enemy ahead had begun to retire, Hawk ordered TF 1 to turn about and head east towards the Lexington/Yorktown. Hawk had considered going after the retiring enemy, but the enemy ships east of Lexington and Yorktown bothered him. First they shouldn't have been there, and second, he had no answers as to how their planes had got to the Lexington without being spotted at the 400 mile radar range. Sherm had suggested they may have had some stealth capabilities, or were somehow able to jam the radar. That kind of technology was unheard of in 1942. Then there were the three atomic subs. But if the enemy had more modern ships, why were the attacking aircraft planes and not jets? At 0300, Hawk sent out a fleet order for all friendly units to converge on the Lexington/Yorktown position, at full speed.

At 0543, as the sun began rising from the surface, Task Force 1 began seeing smoke on the horizon. Hawk fought off the temptation to ride his helicopter ahead to see where the smoke was coming from. At 0630 TF 1 rendezvoused with Admiral Spruance. No enemy warships were on the radar scope, but since the enemy had shown they had the ability to get close undetected, Hawk kept his ships at battle stations. Coming in, what Hawk saw made his stomach sick. The U.S.S.

Lexington lay abandoned, listing nearly fourteen degrees to port; the port side of the flight deck was only a couple feet above the water. A mile away, Yorktown lay dead in the water. Dead except for the flames and smoke spewing from her flight deck from bow to stern.

"I don't understand," said Admiral Sherman, "the Lexington, OK. But the Yorktown wasn't destined to sink here." Hawk turned to his executive officer and replied, "Neither were Shokaku and Zuikaku. We changed history. If they had remained at Pearl, they wouldn't be sinking here now." After a brief moment of thought Hawk spoke again, "Well if we know history can be changed, then we'll do it again. Sherm get a couple of crews over to the Yorktown, get the fires put out and repair whatever has to be repaired so we can tow her back."

A few minutes later Admiral Spruance radioed the Teddy R. He said he was on the cruiser Chicago, which was going to drop a launch to take him to the Teddy R., which he was going to take command of. (Admiral Spruance was of the same rank as Hawk, but had held his longer, so he outranked both Hawk and Sherm). "Send the Chicago a signal," said Hawk. "The hell you are. Any launches or vessels approaching any ships of Task Force 1 will be fired upon and sunk, by order on Com Task Force One. Any vessel wanting to join screen of TF 1 as escorts may do so. TF 1 departing area in thirty minutes for Pearl Harbor. Suggest you take Lexington in tow, or we will." "Sir" said the starboard lookout, "There's a launch 150 yards to starboard, approaching." Stepping to the starboard railing to confirm the sighting, Hawk ordered, "Main computer, enemy launch approaching starboard side, 150 yards. Phalanx S-120 open fire 100 rounds 50 ft in front of the launch. Authorization code TUC 411." "Disregard that order," ordered Sherm as he ran to the starboard bridge rail. "Sir" he told Hawk, "you cannot open fire on a United States Officer, much less an Admiral." "I can't allow him, I won't allow him to take command. Our special orders prohibit it," said Hawk. "Yes sir, I know," said Sherm. "And we'll explain that to him when he's aboard. But, if you open up on that launch, not even god will be able to help you." Thinking it over, Hawk turned to the bridge and said, "Computer disregard order TUC 411." Then going to the ships phone he called, "Marine detachment, report to starboard gangway #125, combat armed." Then to Sherm, "Follow me please, Admiral," as he left the bridge. At the gangway, Hawk ordered the yeoman to lower the gangplank ladder when the launch tied off. As Admiral Spruance walked up the ladder to the landing off the hanger deck accompanied by his exec and several aides and staff members, he was met by a wall comprising of 60 armed and very serious looking marines. "Admiral," said Admiral Spruance, "Request permission to come aboard." "Permission denied," said Hawk. As the four Admirals stared each other down, Spruance spoke first. "Admiral, I am a superior officer, your commanding officer. I am ordering you and your marines to stand down. I am taking command of this vessel." "Sir" answered Hawk, "You are a superior officer, but not my commanding officer. If you attempt to board this vessel, my marines will cut you to ribbons and we will throw your bloody carcasses overboard. May I suggest you call your launch back and return to the Chicago." Admiral Spruance glared at Hawk, then at the marines. Seeing their unflinching determination he addressed the highest ranking marine and said, "Lt., you're making a bad career move here. If you arrest Admiral Hawkins now, I'll forget...." That's as far as he got. Sixty automatic rifles came to shoulders, all aimed at him, as the Lt. Spoke, "Sir, I believe Admiral Hawkins suggested you leave. It sounds like healthy advice to me." Fuming, Admiral Spruance turned to Hawk and said, "I'll have your flag for this Admiral." "Admiral," said Hawk, "My flag was given to me by President Williams, year 2042. And unless you have orders from him, Admiral William Halsey III and Chester W. Nimitz III of 2042, telling me to hand my ship over to you, I will not relinquish my command. Now if you don't mind, TF 1's leaving the area in twenty minutes. You can either join my screen or not. I don't give a damned. Just get the hell off my ship or I'll throw you overboard myself." If looks could kill, Hawk would've dropped dead. Turning, Admiral Spruance called for the launches return, and when it did, he left with his exec., staff and aides. It was only after he had gone that Hawk noticed crewmen from the Teddy R. and its escort ships watching him. Hawk watched as the crew of the Lexington abandoned ship, and when he was certain all were off the ship, Hawk's next order was to place damage control men aboard the Lexington and his next was to take the heavily damaged carrier in tow.

True to his word, twenty minutes later Hawk signaled TF 1 to prepare to leave, course 010, speed 36 knots. (Too fast for Admiral Spruance's ship to keep up.) By then, all of his subs had radioed their returns and Hawk had then sent them ahead to scout for the fleet. Also by then, the damage control men had put out most of the fires and plugged enough of the holes below the waterline to get the Lexington back on an even keel. Trailing behind the destroyer Phelps, the fires burned for another couple of hours. The damage to the Lexington and Yorktown left the U.S. Navy with only four fleet carriers left. Hornet (too small) Wasp, (too slow) Saratoga, (at Mare Island being repaired from torpedo damage) and the Enterprise. Lost that day were three destroyers from the Lexington / Yorktown screen, torpedo sunk before the Hellcats arrived.

As the fleet began its long trek back to base, Hawk sent his action report to Washington, to FDR, bypassing Nimitz, reporting the loss of the three destroyers and the massive damage to the Lexington and Yorktown, as well as the attempted commandeering of TF 1, (and stated what his actions would be the next time anybody attempted to take command of his task force.) He summed up the losses owing to the complete negligence of its fleet commander, (Admiral Spruance) and pointed out if they (FDR and Admiral Nimitz) had followed his advice, the Lexington and Yorktown would still be of use to them and all their escorts would still be afloat and anchored at Pearl Harbor. Also, if TF 1 had not intervened the Lexington/Yorktown would have sunk with their escorts. He further concluded that" his ships do not fall under the command of the United States Navy-1942. Any further attempt to gain control of Task Force One will result in its return to 2042." Hawk had Admiral Sherman look over each report and advise. Then Hawk said to Sherm, "I appreciate you stepping in and stopping me from carrying out that order to open fire on the launch. It was an order borne out of anger at their losing those ships due to their egos. But Sherm, don't ever countermand my orders again in the crews presence. I'm sure you'll agree there can be only one commanding officer. I don't want the crew looking for your OK every time I give an order." "Yes sir," said Sherm, "I'm sorry, sir. It won't happen again." "Good" said Hawk, embarrassed at having to chew out his executive officer. He had nothing but respect for Sherman. "Let's eat," he said to Sherm, "I'm starved." Later in his cabin, Sherm thought about the order he countermanded. He knew if it happened again he would do the same thing. Next time, if it happened again, he'd be closer to the Hawk, to stop him before he issued the order, and advise him. As exec that was his job. And he fully agreed with Hawk. To maintain discipline, there could only be one commanding officer.

Four days later TF 1 arrived at Pearl. Hawk anchored his fleet outside the anchorage, partly because he didn't know what kind of reception he would get, but mainly to keep his ships from being scrutinized. He was sure Japan had spies within the harbor. Upon dropping the hook, Hawk advised naval headquarters he would remain aboard the Teddy R. until sent for. The following day Admiral Spruance arrived with the remnants of his fleet. The cruiser Chicago was in the rear of the formation. She listed heavily to starboard. Obviously she had taken additional damage as she had steamed for home.

For three days Hawk waited to be summoned. He was sure his wait was due to processing the charges for his court martial. For three days he waited, fully expecting every marine on the base to perform an amphibious assault on the Teddy R. And he wasn't alone. A day after they arrived, two cruisers came out of the channel followed by the battleship Pennsylvania. It was only after they had steamed past that Hawk noticed the main armaments of his three battleships were trained on them. Hawk had sent them a radio message, "Stand down," followed by "Thanks". One of the first things Hawk did upon his return to port was request (to his computer) that Lt. Cmdr. Radcliff be decorated (posthumously) with the Congressional Medal of Honor. He also ordered every sub skipper and Lt. Cmdr. Eugene Minson receive the Navy Cross. One hundred sixty eight other pilots were awarded silver and bronze stars and distinguished flying crosses. Hawk personally spent the first day in port (actually outside the port) handing out medals. Admiral Wilkes and Cmdr. Hunt, as well as all the TF 1 captains also got authorizations to decorate members of their crews who had distinguished themselves in combat. In addition to the decorations, one hundred and two men were promoted. The last man promoted was Cmdr. Hunt, to Rear Admiral, for "Conspicuous gallantry in the face of an overwhelming air attack," for shadowing the Teddy R. (with the battleship Texas) thus adding her AA guns to those of the Teddy R., resulting in minimal damage to the carrier, during an air attack. Hunt also received another navy Cross.* At 0930 of the fourth day following the arrival to Pearl Harbor, Hawk received an order to send his helicopter to Naval Headquarters (NHQ). Fifteen minutes later it returned with 10 armed marines, Admiral Halsey, another Admiral, two Cmdr.'s and FDR. While the marines waited on the deck, (half at the helicopter and half at the armored island) the two cmdr.'s, the two Admirals and the president took the elevator up, then down to the Admirals wardroom where Admirals Hawkins and Sherman awaited them. "Hello sir," greeted Hawk to FDR. "Welcome aboard Mr. President." "Thank you," said FDR "and congratulations for a very successful mission." "Thank you sir," returned Hawk, "but while the Lexington and the Yorktown didn't sink out there, with the damage they took they might as well have, they'll be useless to us for quite some time until repairs can be made." "No. No son," said FDR, Admirals Nimitz and Spruance were responsible for their near destruction. Admiral Nimitz disobeyed my direct order and sent them out of port. I've relieved both of them from their commands pending a Naval Board of Inquiry." *That made three. Over the next week, as the navy's code breakers intercepted radio messages between the Imperial Naval Headquarters and the Admirals Yammamoto and Osaki concerning a move on Australia, Hawks subs returned to the Hawaiian Islands and their captains turned in their patrol reports. Only then did the reason why the enemy carrier force behind the Lexington/Yorktown fiasco breaking off action and retreating make any sense.

While the Teddy R's planes were blowing the hell out of the enemy carriers to the west, the subs were torpedoing them as well. Once the Hellcats were finished with their deadly work and had left the battle area, the japs attempted to regroup their ships. They knew a second carrier force had been dispatched to augment their force, and assumed it would join them from astern, so they waited in the area for it. Instead the submarines Seawolf, Tang, Scorpian and Wahoo continued their attacks. The wakeless torpedoes flashed in disabling and sinking the enemy ships. Their escorts, the destroyers, unable to find wakes, had no idea where to hunt the American subs. Once the decision was made to break off and retreat, the subs still hunted them down. The enemy, unable to find anything to shoot at or depth charge could only run the gauntlet in the hope they could make it. Of the force of 26 ships that left the Japanese waters for the Coral Sea, 3 carriers, 1 battleship, 3 cruisers and 2 destroyers were sunk by Hellcats. 2 battleships, 6 cruisers and 1 destroyer were sunk by subs. Eight destroyers, (2 damaged) returned to their bases. Of the enemy force behind the Lexington/Yorktown, 1 carrier was sunk by torpedoes from submarines Hake & Seahorse. Additionally, 1 battleship was damaged. They were long range (lucky) shots. Lucky, because the range was so extreme they shouldn't have been able to lock on. The Seahorse's skipper, (Cmdr. Arlington) had only fired so the enemy commander, seeing the torpedo, would scatter, and withdraw his forces. And that's precisely what he did.

Upon hearing reports of the primary attack forces losses, the commander of the Secondary attack force lost his nerve and retreated. The loss of one of his carriers and the damaging of one of his battleships hastened his decision. He sent out a small aerial attack force to cover his withdrawal. It was those planes that damaged the Chicago, nearly sinking her. They would learn later that they lost 3 atomic Subs when they didn't return. Hawk, however, learned of their existence when the submarine Seahorse turned in their combat report. *An examination of the wrecks (later) would show the 3 atomic subs to be Russian made Alpha models built in the early 1970's with a maximum dive depth of 2200 feet. Crush depth was unknown, but suspected near 2500 feet. *Compressed Steel Technology (CST) was not adopted until 2020. Now Hawk knew. The Japanese now had technology of the 20th century- the capability to jam radar reception to within 200 miles. (Hawk ruled out stealth capabilities, since they would've been masked all the way in). They also had atomic subs though. And he knew that the enemy had far more warships than they were known to have had at the beginning of the war. So much history had changed, far more than they should have been responsible for.

After reading the patrol and mission reports, Hawk called a conference on the carrier. Present were Admirals Sherman, Wilkes, Hunt, Donaldson, (Nimitz's replacement) Erickson, (FDR's representative) and Generals MacArthur, and Buckner. (U.S.M.C.) After drinks and cocktails were served, (by now there was no surprise at alcohol being served on the Teddy R. Word had spread.) Admiral Hawkins stepped to the front of the wardroom to address everyone. There were as many stars in the room as in the evening sky. "Gentlemen," Hawk began, "The purpose of this conference is tri-fold. Firstly, we have reason to believe that Japan has entered the Atomic age". There were murmurs among the generals and admirals amounting to confusion as to what the Atomic age was. "In the year of 1950, a sub will be built, that utilizing an atomic power plant, will allow it to circle the world without having the need to surface to charge its batteries, Soon after our navy began putting them into warships that would allow them to remain at sea for years at a time, needing only replenishing of ammunition & food stores consumed or used during the time at sea. In other words, a vessel with an atomic power plant need only be re-fueled once every 2-4 years, or as the press wrote, they needed to return to port only to allow its crew to re enlist." Now the murmurs were louder as the generals and admirals voiced their disbelief. "Gentlemen", Hawk continued, "The carrier you're aboard is nuclear powered, needing re-fueling every 4-6 years". Hawk took a deep breath, knowing he had just disobeyed his primary orders. But, he told himself, it was necessary since Japan most likely had atomic and maybe nuclear vessels as well. "Gentlemen, I understand your confusion and disbelief. The battleships, cruisers and destroyers have conventional engines and are oil fueled. But the only fuel you will find aboard this carrier is aviation fuel for the aircraft. The aircraft aboard are F6F Hellcats, and you'll find that they're similar to your F4F Wildcats. That's because they're the next generation, which are not even on the drawing boards yet, and won't be for another two years. They're designed to carry conventional bombs." Hawk didn't tell them about the F-173 because it was absolutely necessary at that time. "What sort of fantasy are you trying to feed us", said General MacArthur. "A ship that can steam across the world without refueling? Planes that are aboard this carrier that don't exist and won't for two years? Perhaps you've been taking too many liberties with the alcohol aboard". Nearly all the officers began laughing and then stood to leave. That's when the hatch (door) opened and FDR entered the room. As the laughter died down, the President spoke. "Gentlemen, what you're hearing is true. We've just began experimenting with the technology. We're years from manufacturing a workable power plant, but apparently the enemy may not be". A dead silence filled the room, until General Buckner broke the silence. "If we're years away from a break through, how is it that you have ships utilizing power from it, Admiral Hawkins?" "Sirs", said Hawk, "You know now of the survival of Des Ron 3 in the Java Sea. What you don't know is ultra top secret. Not one word of what you have & will hear in this room today must ever leave this room." Now Hawk was really digging a hole for himself. "What you don't know about the survival of Des Ron 3, is the how. Des Ron 3 entered a rain squall, coming out 100 years into the future. Upon arriving at the Cavite Naval Base, following the sinking of a Japanese merchant ship, the 3 destroyers of Des Ron 3 were interned outside the anchorage, much like we have been here at Pearl. To make a long story short, the Chief of Naval Operations and the President of the United States devised a plan to rebuild the destroyers Pope, Jackson and Stewart. They were re-designed, re-armed, and re-armored, and given a modern (2042) power plant. The plan was for Des Ron 3 to return and use its new weaponry to win the war quicker." Admiral Donaldson spoke next, "How much quicker could three re-conditioned destroyers win the war? How much difference could they make?" "Precisely our question," said Hawk. "That's when they came up with the idea to send 3 battleships, 10 cruisers and 12 destroyers. The battleships and cruisers were already built, still belonging to the navy; they had been loaned out as memorial ships to the public. Reconstruction on Des Ron 3 took 6 months. Construction of the 12 destroyers and re-building of the battleships & cruisers finished ahead of schedule in 10 months. All of the warships in Task Force I have been modified to carry a heavier armament and are heavily armored. The destroyers of DesRon 3 came out of the ship yards, classified as battle cruisers, carrying a main armament of twelve inch guns and a secondary armament of ten inch and eight inch guns.Then during sea trials, 2 radio controlled jets attempted to crash dive into the Pope. One succeeded. It was assumed to be a terrorist attack. Pope was repaired from damage sustained by the one jet that managed to hit her. A year to the date that we emerged from the squall, we re-entered it. When we again emerged, we faced

8 enemy warships, which we promptly sank, then 6 more that came to their assistance. After mopping up and as we prepared to leave, the Teddy R. emerged from the squall and joined TF1. She carried news that the enemy knew about our mission and was trying to purchase warships to come into this era and stop us." "General MacArthur spoke again". "So if they're here to stop you, why don't you just leave? Then they'll leave too". Sherm answered MacArthur. "No General, they won't leave. You won this war the last time. Even if TF1 left now, they'd stay here and try to win it this time around". "So", said MacArthur, "they're here because you're here, and even if you left, they'd stay here. It sounds to me like this is all your fault. Yours and the navy and idiot government of the future. So why don't you fix it?" "One of those idiots, general," lied Hawk, "was a descendant of yours"! That shut the general up and others in the room quietly chuckled. "Yes, we know the MacArthur's have always been ambitious", said FDR. "So what do we do?" asked Admiral Erickson. "We position subs in a scouting arc along the borders of the jap naval bases, to attack and report." said Admiral Sherman. "They'd be detected and sunk when they surface to recharge their batteries, if they could get there at all", said Admiral Donaldson. "They'll get there", said Sherm. "And they'll be too deep to be detected, and they don't need to surface to recharge batteries." said Hawk. "You said the enemy has atomic powered subs. How do you know this," asked General Buckner. "Because", said Sherm, "we detected them at 1700 feet". "Impossible", said Donaldson. "No sub can go that deep without being crushed like an egg". These can, said Adm. Sherman. "And you sank them," asked Adm. Erickson. Hawk nodded. "How, "asked Adm. Erickson, with depth charges?" "No sir", said Hawk. "with torpedoes". Hawk knew he had divulged so much now that it didn't matter if he gave them little more. "With torpedoes from my subs." answered Hawk. "Your subs," asked FDR. "Yes sir Mr. President. I have 10 nuclear subs that I use as scouts and supply ships. In addition to being filled with 28 inch ammunition for my battleships they also carry 24 inch sonar guided wakeless torpedoes, and unlike your fish, mine actually explode upon striking its target." Ignoring the snub, FDR asked Hawk, "And how deep can your subs go?" "That's top secret," said Hawk. Then realizing how deep he was anyway,

he said, "twenty two thousand feet sir." As Hawk looked around, a hush silence filled the room.

When the briefing finished Majic produced a meal the likes of which nobody had eaten since the war began. Real beef steak, pork and chicken, baked potatoes, corn and ice cream. Hawks liquor cabinet was greatly reduced. Following the meal, Tours were given on the carrier, including sonar, radar and radio. After the Phalanx demonstration they were shown the laser guided system and the computerized gunnery control system. They weren't allowed to see the electronics compartment, but they were shown the nuclear propulsion and control room. Then to complete the tour, they were shown the helicopter, and then flown outside the harbor to view Task Force One. And finally, as an encore, on an order from Hawk, 6 nuclear subs surfaced (the other four were on patrols N, E, S and W, deep covering the island from 200 miles out). When asked for a tour aboard one of the subs, Hawk answered, "maybe another time, they're making preparations to depart."

"Just when were you going to tell me about the submarines?" asked FDR, "I'm sorry sir," said Hawk. "I was ordered not to divulge their existence, for fear I'd be pressured to use them in a capacity beyond what I was authorized to use them for, to re-supply ammunition for my battleships and torpedoes to the rest of the fleet." Then changing the subject, Hawk inquired, "Sir, what's going to become of Admiral's Nimitz and Spruance?" "I don't know," said FDR, "he committed a severe breach of orders, costing us one third of our carrier strength. Why?" "Well sir, I'd like to take him aboard as sort of a military adviser," said Hawk. "Son," said FDR, "he has a very negative attitude where you're concerned. He doesn't like you. When you first arrived here, he wanted to arrest you and take over Task Force One." "Yes sir," said Hawk, "I got that from him." "And still you want him aboard?" "Yes sir, as long as I out rank him. I think he has a lot of knowledge. If I can learn from him, I think he'd still be an incredible asset to the war effort." "OK," said FDR "If I take one of his stars away from him, you'll outrank him. But I don't think he'll be very helpful or forth coming towards you following a demotion." The president thought a moment then said, "So I guess I'll have to give you a fifth star."

* During the war, many officers would receive temporary battle promotions. Following the end of the hostilities, their ranks would be reduced to their original ranks or a lower rank than that which they carried in the war. This was especially common with flag ranks, or Admiral with up to four stars. But Admirals with five stars got to keep them. A four star Admiral was a fleet Admiral, Admiral Nimitz was a four star. Admiral Halsey had three, Admiral Spruance had two. Captain Buckmaster, commander of the Yorktown would soon have one. Five star Admirals were typically the big guy upstairs, the man who controlled the entire Navy. For Hawk to be a five star in command of only Task Force One, it took a presidential order. The day following the briefing, Hawk wore five stars on his collar. He was now the third highest ranking man, the second highest officer in the Navy, and the only five star in naval history to command a fleet unit in wartime, (typically, five stars commanded a desk).

A week later a freshly painted launch approached the side of the Teddy R. At gang plank #125, the launch tied up and Admiral Nimitz ascended the ladder to the hanger deck. Saluting, he stepped aboard and threw a smart salute to Admiral Hawkins. "Request permission to come aboard, sir." "Permission granted, Admiral," said Hawk, as he then put out a hand to Adm. Nimitz. Nimitz was slow to offer his hand to shake Hawks, but after some 10 seconds he stuck it out, still confused why he was ordered to report to Hawk's carrier. Maybe he was afraid Hawk would take his hand and throw him overboard. "Welcome aboard sir, please follow me," said Hawk as he led Admiral Nimitz to the wardroom.

Sitting inside, Hawk asked him, "DO you know why you're here Admiral?" Nimitz was slow to answer, his eyes were locked on Hawk's collar insignia that he had only then noticed. "No sir. I received a presidential order to report to you. What is this all about, Admiral?" "Look, I believe we got off to a bad start. I know you have a problem with me and my rank. You'll just have to accept it and get past it; otherwise your career in the navy is over. Just about every officer and man in the navy blames you for the near destruction of the Lexington. The president and every officer you've pissed off over the years want your flag. And the president wants you cashiered from the navy." "Then why am I here?" asked Nimitz. Hawk calmly answered, "Because I asked for you. I believe you're one of the greatest Admirals the navy has ever had. I think you can still be an asset to the navy. If you feel you can respect my rank and position on this ship, in this fleet and in the navy, I want you to serve aboard the Teddy R. as my military adviser. You'll retain your stars and stand fifth in line to command the fleet. As my military adviser, your first assignment will be to learn everything you can about the systems aboard the carrier and battleships. Only when you know their capabilities can you advise me how best to use them." "Excuse me sir," said Nimitz, "You seem to be doing fine without me. Your fleet actions thus far have been exceptionally thought out, and planned. What makes you think you need me?" Hawk thought a minute and replied, "Chet, Do you mind if I call you Chet? Look, I have Admiral's Wilkes and Sherman to advise me now. Admiral Wilkes knows as much as I do about planning an operation. But his experiences are about the same as mine. Admiral Sherman is from another time, a great tactician and an asset to me. But you are from this era, and also a great tactician. What's more, you know how Admiral Yammamoto thinks. You have the experiences in this era that Admiral Sherman has only read about. Between you, Admiral Sherman and Admiral Wilkes, all the different aspects of planning an operation are covered. Between the four of us, I believe we can outwit Admiral Yammamoto. But in order for us to work together, we have to be able to get along. Think about it Admiral. Report back here in twenty-four hours. Whether you accept this assignment or not, your stars are safe. I'll speak to the president." Standing, Hawk led Nimitz back to the hanger deck and gangway #125. Admiral Nimitz saluted, and then left the ship to his waiting launch. Circling the carrier, he marveled at her lines. She was a beautiful ship. "Fifth in line to command," he said quietly, his mind already made up.

an appearance. Many thought the enemy was gathering muscle for a big push, somewhere.

In the wardroom of the Big Stick, Hawk sat in conference with his officers and staff. "I don't understand it," said Hawk, "Since we returned, we've encountered nearly a dozen battleships, and sunk them. Yet according to our information, Japan only started the war with twelve, two of them half converted to carriers." "So we've beaten them. That's why they didn't send any warships to contest the Guadalcanal landings." said Admiral Nimitz. "I don't think so," said Admiral Sherman. "According to history, when the marines landed at Guadalcanal there were fewer than a thousand troops on the island. The rest were construction crews working on the airstrip. That's why they retreated into the hills. They waited there for reinforcements and didn't attack the marines until they had been sufficiently reinforced. This time when the marines landed, the enemy didn't retreat, but instead fought tooth and nail on the beaches. Intel has reported the presence of more than twenty seven thousand enemy troops killed by the time the island was secured." "That's what I mean," said Hawk. "It is expected that what we do here changes history. The battles we fight in changes the course of the war," said Admiral Wilkes. "Yes," said Hawk, "but we hadn't taken part in any land battles yet, so it doesn't make sense that the enemy would know we were going to invade Guadalcanal." "Could they have been fore warned?" suggested Admiral Nimitz. All attention turned to their senior staff member. "What do you mean," asked Hunt. Admiral Sherman looked at Hawk, and when Hawk nodded in consent, Sherm continued. "Shortly after Des Ron 3 arrived at Cavite, merchant ships began disappearing in the Pacific. Some managed to send calls for assistance before they were sunk. Very short messages. Whatever happened to them, happened very fast. These brief reports, put together, told of a monstrous 19th century warship. It was picked up on satellites and confirmed. A Yamato class battleship, previously reported sunk in 1945 was in the Central Pacific in "2042". "I've never heard of a Yamato Class battleship," said Wilkes. "That's because they were built in secrecy," said Hawk. "I read about them when we were in Cavite. They built three of them. The Yamato, Musashi, and the Shinano. The Shinano was converted into an aircraft carrier when the Japanese lost four carriers at Midway, in 1942. She was sunk by one of our subs in 1945 before it could be put into action."

"As I recall, the Yamato was commissioned on December 16th, 1941. If she followed you through the portal, she must have been on her maiden voyage." Admiral Sherman continued, "Now if she returned through the squall sometime after us and returned to Japan, she may have reported our existence."

"There's another possibility to consider." All eyes turned to Hunt. "Remember those scientists that interviewed us at Cavite? They took a research vessel out to the coordinates we gave them for the location of the squall, and they never returned. What if they passed through the portal, and came out in 1942 or before. What if they were captured by the japs? They're not military men. They would've spilled their guts about everything they knew." "But they didn't know about your mission, or our intentions to modify your ships," said Admiral Sherman. "No," said Hunt. "but if they captured the research vessel intact, they'd have to believe the scientists were from the future. There's no way of guessing what year they came out of the squall. If they came out before the attack on Pearl Harbor...say years before.... and they looked at the implications, they may have built many more ships in secrecy. If they better prepared themselves for the war, they would've put many more troops on islands they knew we were going to invade. That could account for the extra 26,000 troops we encountered at Guadalcanal." "It could also account," said Nimitz, "for the losses of the ABDA fleet, and the number of warships present at your last battle before you went into the squall." Hawk had never considered that. He had assumed that history didn't change until Des Ron 3 had reemerged from the squall. If the scientists did emerge pre 1941, then everything would have changed from then onwards, as apparently it had. Now, it seemed, the historical records were useless. Perhaps the escape of Des Ron 3 had put a sequence of events into motion that could change history all together. Maybe even lose the war. "But if that's true," said Wilkes "Why didn't the jap navy intercede at Guadalcanal." "Maybe," said Nimitz, They're gathering muscle for our next encounter." "We're into new territory there," said Hawk. "According to history, we should still be fighting over Guadalcanal. If history were to repeat itself, the japs would've sent a cruiser task force under Admiral Mikawa down the slot immediately following our landing. Where he should have ...or would have sunk four cruisers had it not been for our intervention. We need more information." Turning to Admiral Sherman, Hawk ordered, "Un-ship the F-173. We need it flown to Pearl, through the squall, to find out what's going on." "Aye, aye sir," answered Sherm, who left the wardroom to carry out Hawks order. Looking at Admiral Nimitz, Hawk saw the confusion. "Admiral," said Hawk, "There are some details about our mission that you haven't been let in on. My orders were to not divulge any more information than I had to." "Need to know," said Nimitz, "I understand." "Well," said Hawk, "now you need to know." Over the next twenty minutes, Hawk explained the presence of the supersonic jet hidden away in the hanger deck of the carrier, its capabilities, and the allowed parameters of its use. He didn't, however mention that he could program it to explode over Japan. While Hawk explained, the confused expression on Nimitz's face quickly turned to disbelief. When Hawk had finished, Nimitz asked, "If it's as fast as you claim, why can't we use it to bomb Japan?" "My orders are specific," explained Hawk, "There are only certain conditions for which I can use that aircraft. Besides, if the japs did score a lucky hit, or a mechanical failure caused it to crash, then the enemy would have the technology to build and use it against us." "If the Yamato returned from the future," said Hunt, "They may already have the technology." Hawk thought for a few seconds then answered, "I don't think so. In 2042 the jet is so new only the United States has it. That's why the SEC NAV was only able to give us one."

Sherm came into the wardroom and announced, "Sir, the F-173 is ready for launching. Lt. Lister has volunteered for the mission." Hawk thought a moment. Yes, Lt. Lister, shot down by the cruiser Chattanooga, recovered by the U.S.S. O'Bannon. A navy jet ace, he shot down six Havoc's during the war with Great Britain. "Yes," said Hawk, "I couldn't have picked a better man. Please inform Lt. Lister before he leaves that he'll be returning to the Big Stick a Captain, with a silver star." "Aye, aye sir," said Sherm, smiling. As he left he thought to himself, "Nobody gives a better incentive to fulfill a mission than Hawk." But incentive or not, Sherm knew Hawk had earned the personal admiration of every officer and man, seaman and marine in Task Force One. Each and everyone would follow him into the gates of hell. And soon Captain Lister may well find himself flying there. For with all of the changes that had so far occurred, nobody could guess how those changes had affected the future. A rumble on the deck below told Sherm that Capt. Lister was on his way. Realizing that the F-173 flies at the speed of light, Hawk expected the plane to return the same day.

In the wardroom of the "Big Stick," Hawk held a conference with his senior officers. "According to the historic records," said Hawk, "Japan started the war with only twelve battleships. We've already sunk more than that. If history had changed prior to our arrival, that would account for the enemy having more warships than history recorded. We know that the japs secretly built three super battleships before the war." "Yes sir, "said Sherm, "But we knew about them shortly before the war started." Thinking a moment, Sherm continued, "We know that they modernized most of their ships in the 30's. What if instead of modernizing them, they were actually building others in their shipyards?" "OK," said Hawk, "Even if they suspected they'd be at war within 10 years, how would they have known it?" "The scientists," said Admiral Wilkes. Everybody's attention turned to Wilkes. "Remember when the scientists came to Cavite to question us on how we traveled through time a hundred years? They said they needed that type of technology for their space program." "Yes," said Admiral Nimitz, "but according to the report you filed, they didn't get any useful information." "We had no idea how we had traveled through time," said Hawk. "They were reported overdue and missing at sea on their next assignment," said Admiral Hunt. "Where was their next assignment," asked Hawk. "I don't know sir," answered Hunt. There was a momentary silence in the room, and then it was broken by Wilkes."What if they got the coordinates of the squall from our log and went out there? Do you think they'd have been foolish enough to enter?" "To further science, hell yes," said Hawk. "Oh lord," said Wilkes, "If they entered the squall, there's no way of telling when they came out." "Yes there is," said Hawk. "They must have come out in the late 20's or early 30's. "The captain of the of the research ship was Japanese," said Sherman. "If they were uncertain of the date, they may have steamed to

Japan for answers." "Or maybe they were captured in Japanese waters," said Wilkes. "Remember, they were secretly doing a lot of building on their islands. That's why President Roosevelt asked Amelia Earhart to divert her around the world flight, so she could photograph some of the islands from the air. It was rumored that they shot her plane down." "That was never proven." said Nimitz. "No it wasn't," said Hawk. "No wreckage was ever found as I remember." "Maybe they forced her down," said Sherm. "Either way," said Wilkes, "if they somehow came into possession of the research vessel, with all of its future technology They'd have to believe it was from the future. And if they interrogated the crew".... "Or if the Japanese captain volunteered the information," interrupted Sherm. "If they found out they were going to be in a war with the United States in the early 40's," said Hawk, " and were told they were going to lose it, what would they do?" asked Hawk. Looks went around the room. Hawk continued, "They'd start a building program to radically enlarge their fleet. That would explain why we're facing far more warships than the enemy was supposed to have." "I wonder how much technology the scientists gave up," said Nimitz. All attention turned to him and as he finished, "What if they told the enemy how to build the atomic bomb?" Everybody in the room felt a shiver go down their spine, as a shroud of silence filled the room.

Several hours later Hawk was in his cabin, lying on his bunk, contemplating the earlier meeting with his officers. "What if," he thought to himself, "they do know about the A-bomb? If they were told they'd be losing a war, surly they'd be told how. The scientists wouldn't have to know how to build one. The information would be available on any one of the ships main computers. They could be building one right now. Obviously, if they already had one, they would've dropped it on Pearl Harbor." A knock at his cabin door interrupted his thoughts. "Sir." said Sherm, "we're picking up an I.F.F.(identification, friend or foe) from the F-173. Lt. Lister is requesting landing instructions." "Order all flight operations ceased and the flight deck cleared. He's never landed an F-173 on a moving flight deck before. Have crash crews and medical staff standing by." "Aye, aye sir," said Sherm. As Sherm turned to leave, Hawk said, "Just a minute, I'll go up to the bridge with you." As they made their way to the bridge they heard a loud whine, and then felt a thud. By the time they reached the bridge, (less than three minutes after leaving Hawks cabin) the F-173 was safely aboard. No longer a shiny silver color, it looked a cloudy white, and a vapor appeared to be coming off the skin of the jet plane. Once on the deck, Capt. Lister collapsed. Corpsmen, standing by, caught him and placed him on a stretcher. After giving him a quick physical check they looked up at the Hawk with a confused expression. Giving thumbs up, they proceeded with the pilot to the sick bay.

An hour later Lt. Lister reported to the admiral's wardroom to give his report. Admiral's Hawkins, Nimitz, Sherman, Hunt and Wilkes were present. As the door opened and Captain Lister entered, Hawk and all of the staff officers were aghast. The captain looked as though he had aged fifty years! "Captain Lister reporting as ordered, sir." "Captain Lister, welcome back." said Hawk. "Thank you sir," said Captain Lister. Hawk motioned him to sit down, and Sherm stepped over to help him. But, despite looking very old, Captain Lister moved with the agility of his actual twenty-four years. "Begin your report, Capt.," said Hawk. "Yes sir," said Capt. Lister. "My flight to the squall was quick and uneventful, as was my transient flight through the squall. However, once I emerged through the other side, my plane was frequently buffeted as though by strong winds. But it was calm. It was as though I was flying through A.A., but there wasn't any of that either. When I darkened the cockpit, I was able to see red streams of light coming from above, as though the light was trying to track me. Each time I saw the light my plane was bounced around. Once I fed the information into the on-board computer, the Nav Com took over, and diverted the plane on an assortment of diversionary courses, so when ever the beam searched for me, the plane would bank away. From then onwards it was a pretty smooth flight. As ordered, I stayed away from other ships and planes, and maintained an altitude of eighty thousand feet. But sir, I didn't see a single jet aircraft. All the planes radar picked up were planes of this era, mostly bombers and transport planes. As I overflew Wake Island, the computer scanned the surface and photographed the base there. The planes radio picked up military stations from Wake, all in Japanese, but everything east of Wake appeared to be jammed. I flew onward west towards Pearl Harbor. As I approached, my radio picked up warnings, first in Japanese, then in English, warning me that I was approaching a military base off limits to non military ships and planes. I had the computer scan the base, photo's showed several hundred aircraft and about a hundred ships. I flew on toward the west coast of the United States. Computer images show Japanese control of the United States as far as Billings, Montana. The computer picked up high levels of radiation. I flew further east where the computer picked up high levels near the coasts. My radar picked up several planes in aerial combat, propeller driven planes. On the way back I had the computer scan all civilian radio stations from the east coast to the west coast. From the east coast to the center of the country, I picked up several that warned of a laser beam, and certain times of the day that it fired more often. I asked the computer to query it and the information is stored on the flight computers data base. I removed the disc for you as soon as I landed." Captain Lister handed the disc to Hawk and continued." From the center of the country, west to the coast, there were no other civilian transmissions. Sir, Wake Island, Pearl Harbor, and the west coast of the United States as far east as Billings, Montana seem to be under Japanese control. From Billings, east to Louisville Kentucky the computer picked up very high levels of radiation, levels much too high to allow any life to exist. From Louisville to the east coast there seem to be pockets of American resistance. These areas picked up very little radiation. The computers estimate that by the high levels of radiation picked up in the center of the country, the bombs were probably dropped close to 1944. One last thing, sir. According to Doc Webb, the side effect of flying the F-173 is advanced, irreversible aging. In the event that we have to use the plane again, I request that I be assigned the flight so nobody else has to endure the effects." "Thank you, Captain. That was a very concise report. I'm sorry for the ill effect of the flight. The plane was still in the experimental stage when we got it. Those effects were not known to us at the time when we were given the plane. As a result of that effect, I'll have to remove you from flight status pending a complete physical evaluation. I'm sure you understand." "Yes sir, "answered Captain Lister. Hawk continued, "Until I get the results of that exam, your duties will be limited to that of a consultant on the F-173. I'm upgrading your silver star to a Congressional Medal of Honor. Congratulations Captain.

When Captain Lister had left, Admiral Nimitz spoke first. "You know admiral, that only the President of the United States can authorize the CMH, don't you?" Hawk thought a moment and answered, "If his report is accurate, there is no President of the United States." After a moment of reflection, Hawk went over to the command console and inserted the disc that Captain Lister had given him. Then he sat down with his flag officers and listened to the end of their world.

According to historic data, in 1944, atomic bombs were dropped on Wake Island and Pearl Harbor, destroying the bases and the ships stationed there. Survivors were left to die from the effects of the radiation. Six months later seven more atomic bombs were dropped on the United States, from north east of Yellowstone, from Billings to Louisville. A month later eleven more were dropped on the Central United States, destroying the farm belt in an obvious attempt to starve out the country. Two more were dropped on Northern Minnesota and Montana as well as Southern Canada where the iron ore is mined to make the steel for the production of weapons and ships. The U.S. military retreated to the east coast and their remaining naval bases, while the Japanese advanced to within three hundred miles of Billings, Montana. In 1946, a very technologically advanced Japan launched a series of weapons platforms into the stratosphere. Computer controlled, it was designed to fire a laser beam at any target the Japanese programmed it to fire at, thus condemning the east coast of the U.S. without putting their own pilots at risk. Americans began to die by the thousands without the cost of a single Japanese life. Then in 1947 a meteor shower occurred. Though they missed all of the actual weapons platforms, (28 total), several struck the command platform, damaging the command module and destroying all of its backup systems. When Japan attempted to repair the platform, the laser platforms blew the repair ship up as soon as the jet engines fired. Since then, no jet aircraft had taken to the skies. Suddenly every country on the planet found themselves searching their lands for propeller powered aircraft. The laser was indiscriminate, shooting down aircraft and firing on targets all over the world. By 2042 the weapons platform was even more formidable than when first launched, because the computer learned and adapted as time went by. All these years later war is still being waged, with aircraft a hundred years old. America is still fighting the Japanese, despite Japans belief that the U.S. would surrender as soon as they invaded the west coast. Now they knew, the Americans would never surrender. The computers aboard the F-173 could "read" when and where the lasers would strike. Perhaps it could be reprogrammed to order the laser to fire on the Japanese and only the Japanese. It was a long shot. When the disc report was finished as well as its theories, Hawk and his officers sat in silence for several minutes, contemplating the information. No words could describe the feelings they felt. The silence said it all.

Admiral Hawkins rose early the next morning, though he hadn't slept much at all. He was pretty sure he was going to have a busy day, certain that news of Captain Lister's flight had already gotten out. He knew he would have to address the crew. And not just the crew of the "Big Stick", but the whole fleet. What would he tell them? That they were fighting for a country that in seventeen months would nearly cease to exist? That the country that half of them left a few months ago had been blown apart and was hanging on by the skin of their teeth? Or that the history they had come to change had changed for the worst? Of one thing Hawk was sure of, the news Captain Lister had brought back would fill them with a hatred that would never die. Maybe he could tell them about an idea he had had during the night. A plan that just might set things straight again. Hawk knew that this was all his fault. His, the CNO's, and those damned politicians. If only they had left well enough alone. But no, they had to mess with the future. If only they could've foreseen what their meddling would do. And those damned scientists, had they lived long enough to see what they had done, by handing over their research ship with all its data to the enemy? As Hawk had breakfast, ham, scrambled eggs and milk, all of it powdered, tasteless and slimy, another thought occurred to him. All of those battleships and cruisers that seemed to be waiting at Surabaya, as though they knew admiral Doorman would be there, and when. Waiting to spring the trap on the ABDA fleet. Did they know Admiral Doorman would be there from the data files on the research ship? If they gained that information, how far back had the future been changed? So was it the scientists and the research ship or DesRon3 that changed history? With breakfast done, Hawk suddenly felt sick. Unsure whether it was the eggs and milk or his thoughts, he decided to stop at the sick bay before heading for the bridge.

Every officer and man had heard scuttlebutt that somehow the japs had managed to change history to their favor. Every man knew that the japs would drop atomic bombs on our country in less than two years, all but destroying it. And every man knew that up to ninety percent of all Americans would die in the war as it continued well beyond a hundred years. And every man knew one other thing, Hawk would never let that happen. He knew they knew that. Now he had to figure out a way to set things right again. A week later T.F.1 returned to Pearl, and planned the next mission with Admiral's Halsey, Nimitz and Sherman. Hawk sent out an order to all C.O.'s and X.O.'s to report to the carrier at 1800. (Having gone from Ensign to Admiral in a very short time). Hawk was a great believer in telling his subordinate officers what to expect from upcoming missions. It wasn't too long ago that he was a shave-tail Lt. And clearly remembered how much he disliked being kept in the dark before a mission, not knowing what to expect until it was upon him. *As soon as the fleet was refueled and replenished, (food stores and ammunition)* Hawk ordered one end of the massive Hangar deck cleared. Next he had every chair, table and bench taken from the mess hall and brought to the hangar deck. Coffee, sandwiches and cokes were brought in. At 1730 officers began to arrive. Hawk had first planned to have a nice steak supper served, but after discussing it with Sherm, it was decided to go with the snack sandwiches. Hawk realized that once the mission was explained after a heavy meal, there would probably be some very upset stomachs. No, a heavy meal first was definitely not a good idea.

As the officers began to filter in, Hawk stood at the entrance to welcome them aboard, as his aides prepared maps and slides. Slides taken from aerial photographs, which had been taken by the F-173. Both over the Japanese islands and the previous flight by Captain Lister to Pearl Harbor, then the west coast of the U.S. To the east coast. The computer had taken several hundred feet of video footage that showed the atomic bomb surface (ground level) and effects. Within hours after Captain Lister's return, word of what he had seen and learned had already begun to circulate within the fleet. But until now, nothing had been confirmed by command. Part of the purpose of this mission was to inform the officers of the mission's findings, so they could explain it to their crews. The crews would then understand the reasons behind the mission. That mission would be explained in the second half of the conference. Hawk knew nobody would turn down a good meal before the briefing, but would certainly regret having the meal once they were briefed. So the steak was out and sandwiches and coffee were in. Hawk spent a few hours moving from table to table, conversing with the crewmen he knew. He knew most of the crew. This idea stemmed from a book he had read while he was a youth. Books he had read about a famous admiral named Horatio Nelson, one of England's most famous admirals. Lord Nelson would dine with his officers within his command, giving him a chance to get to know them, and his officers could get to know him. Only Hawk included his crew as well. Every day Hawk would take a casual walk along the flight and hangar decks, and down through the engineering spaces of the ship. He liked to stop and talk to the men (regardless of rank) asking them how things were going, both aboard ship and at home. (From the beginning, whenever an SSBN emptied its cargo of twenty eight inch ammunition, the sub would load up with mail sacks to bring to Pearl Harbor which would be mailed to families and loved ones. Upon its return it would be carrying mail for the task force. However, the last sub returned empty of both mail and cargo. Its captain had reported that things didn't appear quite right at Pearl. That was one of the reasons for the mission that Captain Lister had flown.) It wasn't uncommon for Hawk to invite members of his crew to dine with him while he was on these walks. To say that Hawk was loved and admired by his crew was such a gross understatement that it was uncommon to hear otherwise. Any and all would gladly follow him to and through the gates of hell, confident that he would get them back out again. Unbeknownst to them, they soon would be doing just that.

Amongst the officers in his task force, there were some that he had taken a shine to. In much the same way his first captain had taken Hawk under his wing, Hawk now did the same. Hawk found that talking to his men on subjects besides duty related issues; he could learn more about their characters than by looking at their service records. An officer that "ran a taut ship" but didn't fraternize with his men wasn't a reliable officer in combat. The men had to like and respect their officers, or they wouldn't risk their lives to the extent that was often necessary. Most crewmen won't go above and beyond for an officer they don't like. Hawk's method was proven by the results he had gained since taking command. But it's not that he was over lenient or babied them, for crewmen don't respect an easy captain either. And in combat, the hero's are usually a member of the crew and not the captain that decides whether a battle is won or lost. The order that a captain gives the ordinary seaman is more often than not a life or death decision.

Chapter 10

Lt. John Smyth was the captain of the destroyer U.S.S. Ladd, and one of Hawk's favorite escort captains. The Ladd's patrol position was a thousand yards to starboard of the Big Stick. The A.A. guns of the Ladd had thus far shot down more enemy aircraft than any other escort ship in the fleet. Painted on the ships bridge were twenty six jap flags representing planes shot down, one sub sunk and two half flags representing shared kills. As Hawk and Sherm approached Lt. Smyth's table, he stood and saluted the admirals. Hawk seemed to ignore him and instead turned to Sherm and took a small box from his exec. Turning back to face Lt. Smyth, Hawk returned his salute then said, "Lt. John Michael Smyth, commander of the destroyer U.S.S. Ladd, for conspicuous gallantry in the line of duty on 28, June, 1942. In a surface and air action against Task Force 1, by enemy aircraft, The destroyer under your command provided deadly anti aircraft support to the aircraft carrier U.S.S. Theodore Roosevelt as well as formidable screening tactics that discouraged enemy attacks and damage to said aircraft carrier. Lt. Smyth and his crew exemplified their courage and devotion to duty by shooting down seven enemy aircraft that attempted to crash into the flagship and above mentioned carrier. For your heroic service and that of your crew, this command recognizes you, your crew and the Destroyer Ladd with the Commanders Unit Citation and awards the advancement of rank to Lt. Smyth to the rank of Lt. Cmdr." Hawk then snapped a crisp salute to the captain of the Ladd and said, "Congratulations Lt. Cmdr.," He then shook hands with both Hawk and Sherm as more than four thousand men applauded. The applause was thunderous in the enclosed hangar. Lt.Cmdr Smyth was as surprised as dumbfounded and could only mutter "Thank you sir." Hawk and Sherm then continued down the front of each table. Hawk promoted one hundred and seventeen other officers and gave out over two hundred medals. He covered every table on the hangar deck. During this time the sandwiches and cokes and coffee were served. It seemed like a festive occasion and everyone seemed to be enjoying themselves, but Hawk knew he had to put an end to it. There were far more serious matters that had to be discussed. As the crew members continued to eat and joke around, Hawk began calling the names of his officers and MP's began escorting them to the after third of the hangar deck, where the briefing would take place. Once everyone was seated, Hawk stood at his table and looked around, making sure there wasn't anybody there that wasn't supposed to be there. Still at his table, he addressed them, "Gentlemen, we'll now start the briefing." The lights went out leaving them in utter darkness for a few seconds before the film projector came on. Hawk narrated, "Our F-173, flown by Captain Lister flew through the portal three days ago. His mission was to fly to Cavite to hand deliver top secret documents to the SecNav. Upon his arrival, he found the base deserted. On his own initiative, he flew over Wake Island, where the planes sensors picked up the same things. He then continued on to Pearl Harbor." While Hawk is speaking, all eyes are glued to the bulkhead where a film taken by the stealth plane is showing what Captain Lister saw and what was picked up on the ultra sensitive monitors and camera's of the plane. "All buildings have been reduced to rubble. Weeds and small trees grow within the rubble giving the impression that whatever happened, happened quite a while ago. Of the warships there, all are sunk; half sunk or have been reduced to rusted hulks. The sensors on the plane estimate that based on the levels of radiation, the base was destroyed nearly a hundred years ago, or within the next couple of years. The levels of radiation far exceed the level of human endurance." Hawk stopped speaking to allow his audience to concentrate on the vast desolation pictured on the screen. "No longer a green vegetative paradise, the hills around the base were a dirty brown and black, with trees toppled and burnt where they fell to the ground. Like the buildings at Cavite, these too have been reduced to rubble. The base runways show wreckage long ago bombed. Weeds growing through cracks in the pavement give the impression that the base hasn't been used for a very long time. There's not a sign of life, human or animal. Flying east, to the continental United States, Captain Lister found that the west coast was occupied by forces of the Imperial Japanese army." Hawk again stopped talking to let this information sink in, watching the expressions on the faces of his men. With all eyes on the film, the officers saw building after building flying the flags of Japan. The men looked intently, as though they were attempting to recognize a particular business or residence. There were some buildings that looked like they had been burnt up or blown up, but most appeared to be newly rebuilt in the style of the Japanese people. That meant that the invasion and occupation had happened so long ago that there had been time to clear away the rubble and rebuild. As the film continued, Hawk began narrating again. "The northern parts of the country, north central, central, south central and southern parts of the country have all been destroyed. Since the northern part is where we mined the materials to build our warships and produce the steel to make our weapons, we are no longer able to access the ore due to the high levels of radiation. The central part of the country is where a vast majority of our farm goods came from, they destroyed that part of the country, in an obvious attempt to starve us out. In the south, they destroyed our ports and oil fields, reducing our ability to put our ships to sea to combat them. They didn't appear to have fought for it, just flew in and dropped their atomic bombs. According to the sensors aboard the F-173, from Billings, Montana to Louisville, Kentucky and from the Gulf of Mexico to five hundred miles into Canada everything has been neutralized. Wiped from the face of the earth! As Captain Lister approached the east coast, the planes radars picked up aircraft involved in dog fighting. Here we apparently are still fighting the enemy. We seem to still possess some of our naval bases and a few of our warships. What struck us as strange is that the warships being used in battle are of this period, that is to say the era of this war. The planes long range sensors picked up a battle in progress six hundred miles south of Florida. The japs seemed to be getting the worst of it. Either way, since the F-173 is unarmed, there was nothing that Captain Lister could've done to help. Since the captains return, it took a couple of days to extract the data from the planes on board computers and record the computer sensors, as well as down load the data taken when the captain reprogrammed the planes computer to mate with the enemy and friendly computers on the east and west coasts. I know the question on everybody's mind is, how could this have happened? Well, this is what we believe happened. After DesRon 3 emerged from the squall and returned to Cavite, a group of scientists arrived with questions as to how we were able to travel through time and escape destruction at the hands of the Japanese armada. We had no idea and left them with their questions unanswered. Apparently they boarded a research ship and cruised to the then top secret location of the squall. According to the documentation taken from the Japanese computers, the scientists entered the squall and emerged in the year of 1933. Steaming about and trying to ascertain the date, they sent out a call to any nearby vessel. They were soon met by a Japanese destroyer that boarded and captured the ship and towed the ship to Japan under the auspice that it was a spy ship, the crew and scientists being spies. Since the United States of 1933 had no idea of the research ships existence and subsequent capture, there was no rescue attempt or scandal, and the Japanese were able to keep the ship and crew, whom they no doubt interrogated. Obviously they told their captors they were from the future, and obviously they wouldn't have been believed except that the equipment aboard the research ship was much more advanced to what technology they had at the time. We're not sure of the nationalities of the scientists and crew, but we do know that the captain was a native of Japan, highly educated, and more than capable of extracting data from the computers. The crew was probably disposed of right away, the scientists kept alive as long as they were useful. We know from the historical records that Japan started the war with twelve battleships. But since we returned to 1942, we've sank sixteen. As of now, we have no idea of what ships the enemy has, much less, how many. Information taken from the Japanese computers tell us that Japan began a naval build up in 1933. Japan also began experimenting, then building atomic bombs. In 1943 they dropped two bombs on Cavite, and two on Pearl Harbor. In 1944, they dropped one on Canada and three on Mexico, despite Mexico's neutrality. We believe this was to show the United States their capability in the hopes that we would sue for peace. We didn't. In July 1944, they invaded the west coast of the U.S., forcing the armed forces back with the threat of dropping an atomic bomb. The result was that the enemy only had to fight civilians. According to the enemy computers, they're still finding pockets of resistance in 2042. In December of 1944 they began dropping the A-bombs on the Central United States, all told, fifteen. Over kill, but radiating that part of the country, so humans couldn't live there for one hundred years. And the computers show the level is still too high for human endurance. The computers also picked up some information from the enemy computers about some sort of laser weapons platform in orbit over the planet. Our computers on the Big Stick are still working on the translation.

Apparently the U.S. Navy and Air force are still in combat with the enemy on our east coast. The fact that the last three SSBN's sent to Pearl to re-supply us with 28 inch ammunition, returned empty, explains the loss of Cavite and Pearl Harbor. What we find perplexing is this." The lights went out again, and a slide was shown of the two planes (shown in aerial combat) over the east coast. "This photograph, blown up showed the Japanese plane as a Nakajima Kate, and the American plane as a P-40 Tomahawk. There were several other planes that were picked up by the camera that weren't noticed by the plot, but were picked up later." The slide projector changed photo's to reveal a Kawanishi flying boat (Recon) and several Japanese float planes that appeared to be spotting (for the naval engagement) for the Japanese battleships 600 miles from Florida. "The Kawanishi is a land based plane, with a range of six hundred miles. The computers didn't pick up any sign of an enemy base within three thousand miles. We haven't figured out where it came from yet, possibly an underground airbase. It's no doubt something we'll have to deal with once we defeat the enemy and return to the future. So gentlemen, you know as much as I do about what has happened to our country since we emerged from the squall to change history. Unfortunately we now know that history changed in 1933 and we now must set things right or forget about the world as we knew it. Since there's no chance of re-supply, we must go with what we have. And the sooner the better before we run low on our 28 inch ammunition. We have six subs full and one a little more than half full of our main battery ammunition. Here is my plan." Hawk motioned to an aide and as the lights came on, he continued.

"According to the data from the computers, Japan began dropping A-Bombs on our bases in1944. We're going to attack Japan now, in 1943. We're going to take every carrier, battleship, cruiser, and destroyer the U.S. Navy will give us. We'll surround them with TF1, and steam directly for Japan, destroying every enemy aircraft, ship and sub we come across. Our subs will patrol ahead of us and help clear the way. We don't know where the enemy is developing the bombs, but we feel it will be the area they fight the hardest to protect. Once known, we'll pull back as far as possible, then send in the F-173, which is nuclear powered. We can program its computer to fly the plane and explode it over the bomb building location. Once that is done, all surviving TF1 vessels (and any vessels from this area that want to) will return to 2042 to combat any enemy there. Make no mistake, gentlemen, there will be casualties. I expect the enemy will send out everything they have to keep us away from their coast." "Sir," an officer stood. "Yes Lt. Erickson," "Sir, if the F-173 has that capability, why not just send it over and explode it. Don't get me wrong, admiral. I have no problem cruising to Japan and having my can blow the hell out of the bastards. But if we can send one plane to destroy the japs, why risk losing our warships when we can return to 2042 with more ships?" "Good question Lt." said Hawk. "The problem is that though the explosion created by the F-173 will decimate Japan, it won't necessarily destroy the bomb factory. We have to know exactly where the bombs are being built, then explode the F-173 over it. If we don't destroy the bomb factory completely, and we return to 2042, we can expect to have several A-Bombs dropped on us as we emerge from the squall in 2042." "Yes sir", said Lt. Erickson as he sat down. "Any more questions?" asked Hawk. "Yes sir," said Lt. Cmdr. Baskill. (Heavy Cruiser Duluth) "Yes Cmdr. Baskill," said Hawk. "Sir, how do we know that as we close on Japan, we won't have to engage warships like ours? If the enemy knew we were coming, they may have built more powerful ships during their re-building program in 1933." "A good question," answered Hawk. "At the time the scientists ended up in Japan, no plans had yet been discussed regarding our disposition. We don't believe the japs knew about us, or we would've faced them already. The japs would've sent their most powerful ships to engage and defeat us as we came out of the squall. But instead of sending more powerful ships, they just sent out enough to do the trick." "Sir," asked Lt. Henry. (Light cruiser U.S.S. Esko) "How will we re-fuel the fleet from Pearl to Japan?" "Our carrier will carry a half million gallons of fuel for the ships. We'll refuel from the Teddy R. and any carrier we can get from the Navy. Then we plan to have at least four tankers that will stay with us up to a thousand miles from Japan. Any other questions?" "Yes sir," said Cmdr. Obrien. (Heavy Cruiser Adak) "When will our attack begin?" "We have to report to the Admiral, and show him our evidence, then ask for whatever ships they can give us. Either way, we leave for Japan within ten days. Any other questions?" "Yes sir," (Cmdr. Talbot, Heavy Cruiser Minneapolis) "Sir, how much of this can we tell our crews?" "That," answered Hawk, "I'll leave to your discretion. Personally, I'd tell them all of it. "But sir," continued Cmdr. Talbot, "what about panic?" "Cmdr. Talbot", explained Hawk, "I don't believe the truth will panic our men. I think it will fill them with a resolve to want to kill every yellow bastard they can. Now then gentlemen, if there's no more questions, you can return to your ships and await further orders. As soon as we know what, if any, ships we'll be taking with us, I'll write up a more detailed plan of attack. Then each of you will get your orders and the time/date of sortie." Hawk stood as Sherm announced, "Gentlemen, you're excused."

With Task Force One anchored outside the harbor, Hawk ordered the whaleboat lowered over the side, then he and Admirals Nimitz and Sherman got in. A motion of his hand and the Bosun's mate started the engine and pulled the swift craft away from the carrier's side and proceeded to the entrance of the harbor. "You know sir," said Sherm,"the chopper would've been quicker." "Yes it would've, "said Hawk,"but I'm in no hurry." Nothing else was said as the small boat entered the channel and made a right turn and slowly glided past the sunken Arizona, as per Hawk's instructions. Turning to the admirals, he said, "The sight of the gallant battleship and the thoughts of her lost crew always gives me the strength I need to do what I need to do. Once past the wreck, Hawk had the bosun make a hairpin turn and circle back and headed for the administration building. Speaking to no one in particular, Hawk softly said, "Within an hour I have to stand before Admiral Kincaid and ask him to give me all the ships and men that he has so I can put them in an action that I have to convince him is crucial to the survival of our country, an action that could cost us every ship and man that he can give us, including every ship and man in Task Force One. Don't let these fool you," Hawk said, pointing to the stars on his shoulder, "I may be an admiral, but to most of the navy, I'm still a shavetail Lt." "Do you think it'll be as bad as that, admiral," asked Admiral Nimitz. Hawk thought a moment and answered," "We don't have any idea what the japs built when they re armed. As we come at them, they'll be warned by their picket boats. If they come out, we'll split our forces and try to take them from several directions, dispersing their fire. We'll hit them with air and surface fire simultaneously. But casualties will be high if they come out to contest us." Hawk looked at his admiral's and saw their expressions. "I don't like it any more than you do. If there was any other way, I'd do it. I love these men. But sometimes a commander has to give an order that costs men their lives. That responsibility goes with command. If an officer can't do it, he has no right to command." Sherm nodded. That was a lesson he had learned a long time ago. And he knew how difficult a lesson it had been for Hawk to learn. Mostly, he knew how close Hawk was to his men. Above all, he knew Hawk wouldn't waste their lives. The japs would pay dearly for every man Hawk lost. His men knew this, that's why they would follow him, unquestioningly.

Admiral Nimitz sat in the back of the boat behind admiral's Hawkins and Sherman. His thoughts drifted back to when he had first met Hawk. He had wanted to arrest Hawk, steal his command and throw him into the brig for insubordination and impersonating a flag officer. He hadn't liked Hawk at all, thought he was an opportunist. But President Roosevelt had sided with him. Then there was the order he had countermanded. Roosevelt had made it clearer, disobeyed. Then the near losses of the Yorktown and Lexington that resulted from those disobeyed orders. His arrest and the proceedings of the court martial. Then, surprisingly, Admiral Hawkins who came to his rescue. Result? No court martial and duty aboard the super carrier Theodore Roosevelt and 5th in line of succession for command. In the months that followed, he had seen the man he didn't know existed. Inexperienced? Yes. But willing to learn and a rapid learner. Since coming aboard he had seen Hawk's task force take on units of the Japanese Navy, (sometimes outnumbered), and always by surprise, leaving the enemy bloody, and always with minimal damage to his own fleet. Thus far, despite heavy and continuous action, Hawk hadn't lost a single ship, and had lost only 13 aircraft. Did he respect him? Hell yes! What's more, he was one of thousands who would die for him.

"Sir," said Sherm, "We've got to assume that the enemy at least suspects our existence. They've lost too many ships to not wonder." Hawk nodded, as Sherm continued. "And if they know about us, but don't have enough navy to stop us, what's to stop them from developing and dropping the bombs on us sooner than 1944?" "That's why we need to attack them with every ship and plane we can lay our hands on," said Nimitz (before Hawk could answer) who had until then, remained silent with his thoughts. Sherm and Hawk looked at him for a minute or so, but nothing else was said. The three admirals concentrated on the ships in the harbor, making mental notes of what was available, as the whale boat pulled up to the dock in front of the Naval Headquarters and Administration Building. The whale boat bumped the dock a couple times before the bosun's mate stopped the boat and tied it off. As the admirals left the boat, neither noticed the nervousness of the sailor manning the boat.

Seated outside the door marked ComSoWesPac, the cmdr. spoke into the intercom, "Sir, Admirals Sherman, Nimitz and Hawkins to see you." "Very well," said a voice, "show them in." The cmdr. rose and let them into a door. Beyond it was a long hallway with forty marine guards along the wall, twenty per side. The marines, wearing camouflage utilities and combat helmets also camouflaged, stood at attention, but as the officers passed, the brought their M- 1 carbines up in salute. The marine at the end of the hallway, the only one without a rifle, saluted, then after checking their ID's, saluted again then opened the door and let them inside. "An awful lot of security." said Sherm quietly. To Hawk, it was strangely reminiscent of his first meeting with Admirals Nimitz and Halsey when TF1 first arrived at Pearl Harbor after emerging from the squall. They entered the open door and it was pulled shut behind them. Inside Hawk saw a long table to his right and a desk directly in front of him. Admiral Simms (Nimitz's replacement) sat at the desk. Standing next to him was Admiral William (Bull) Halsey, Commander of Task Force 53. "It's damned good to see you again, Admiral Hawkins," Bull said, extending a hand to Hawk. "and congratulations on your last patrol." "It's good to see you too, admiral," said Hawk, taking Halsey's hand and firmly shaking it. "did you receive our action report?" "Yes we did, I've been looking forward to meeting you. "said Admiral Simms, without addressing Hawk by his rank or even offering to shake his hand. Hawk ignored him. He noticed there was no friendliness in his voice. "These action reports of yours seem a little farfetched." "Farfetched?" asked Hawk. "Sir," responded Admiral Nimitz," every one of those ships we reported sunk can be collaborated by the gun cameras of our aircraft. I assure you, if we reported them sunk, they're sunk." "Yes," said Admiral Simms, "but how many times?" (making it clear that he no longer considered Admiral Nimitz an equal since the Coral Sea debacle.)When neither Hawk, Sherm nor Nimitz spoke, Simms continued. "Gentlemen, you claim to have sunk thirteen enemy battleships, but we know that the enemy started the war with only twelve. So even if they built one more, are you claiming to have sunk his entire battleship force?" "No sir," answered Hawk, "not even a third." Admiral Simms stood abruptly, pushing his chair back so it hit the wall behind him. "Are you going to stand there and tell me that the japs started the war with forty battleships, Lt. Do you think I'm an idiot?" asked Simms angrily. Suddenly very angry, Hawk ignored the Lt. quip for the second time and turning to Sherm he said, " We're wasting our time here with this moron, I'm going to fly to Washington and speak to the President himself." "Moron? I'll have you busted for insubordination you little fuck." Then yelled, "Lt. send in a dozen of those marines outside." The door flew open and ten or twelve marines came rushing into the room. "Arrest that officer." screamed Admiral Simms. "Enough!" bellowed a voice from the table to the right. It was only then, in the dim light that Hawk saw his Commander in Chief seated at the long table. "Sir." sounded Admirals Hawkins, Nimitz, Sherman, Halsey and Simms. The marines stopped in their tracks, and stood at attention. Silence permeated the room.

"At ease, Gentlemen," said F.D.R. "as you can see, admiral, there's no need for you to fly to Washington." Then speaking to the marines, "Gentlemen, you're excused." Hawk walked to the table and spoke to the president. "Sir, I can assure you that our combat reports are very accurate. What's more, we've uncovered evidence that Japan began an enormous naval build up in 1933 that resulted in a navy of unprecedented proportions. In addition to this, we have further evidence that not only does Japan know about the Manhattan Project, they're actually in the process of building several that they will drop on us within eighteen months. Maybe sooner." "Admiral," said F.D.R., "I wasn't aware you knew about the Manhattan Project?" "What's the Manhattan Project," sneered Admiral Simms. "I've never heard about it." "I'm sorry, Admiral," said FDR, "I can't tell you. Your security clearance isn't high enough." Simms, still visibly pissed off, suddenly got even angrier as he heard Hawk snicker. "It doesn't matter, Mr. President," said Admiral Nimitz. "In eighteen months or less, we'll all be dead and the United States will no longer exist." Hawk saw that they had everybody's attention. Taking the canister from Admiral Nimitz, Hawk asked if there was a projector available that he could use. Simms went to the door and spoke to a marine. Minutes later a Lt. Cmdr. came into the room pushing a cart with a projector on it. In minutes he had it set up with the film that Hawk handed him. One of FDR's aides turned off the lights and the film started. This time there was no narration from Hawk. The film said it all without words. The President, five admirals, the Lt. Cmdr. and the three aides sat in silence for seventy five minutes as the horror unfolded on the screen before them. When the film was finished, the Lt. Cmdr. stopped it with the last frame frozen on the wall. It showed the devastation of the White House, blasted apart and the rubble fire blackened and obviously deserted for a very long time. And in the background, the spire of the Washington Memorial, now lying on the ground, also blown apart and fire blackened. Washington D.C. had the appearance of the Roman Coliseum, with parts of the buildings gone and pieces scattered about on the ground.

When the lights finally came on, Simms was the first to speak. "That's impossible. It has to be some sort of fabrication. You can't expect us to believe...." "Admirals," said FDR, cutting off Admiral

Simms. "I know all of you to be honorable and trustworthy officers. If you're telling me this is real, I've got to believe it." Admiral Nimitz stood and walked to Admiral Simms and stood face to face with him, close enough to kiss him, and looking him straight in the eyes, close enough to spit in his face, (and later he claimed that he did.) he said, " It's all true, Mr. President. If we don't hit Japan now, with everything we have, we're all dead. The United States of America will become another Atlantis to be studied by people of future generations." Still looking at the grotesque picture on the wall showing the destruction of Washington D.C., FDR asked, "What do you need?" Hawks answer was equally brief, "Everything you've got, sir."

Over the next seven days, many warships began arriving, warships of all types, from aircraft carriers to destroyers and subs. Tankers, merchant ships, anything with a bottom. Two days after the conference with Admiral Simms, Hawk had a surprise visitor aboard the carrier. As FDR was piped aboard, every available crewman, dressed in whites, stood the rails and saluted their Commander in Chief. FDR had been aboard before but still got a grand tour. Admiral Simms had come along with the President, but hadn't been allowed to board. FDR had tried to talk to Hawk, but he was adamant. "If that son of a bitch comes aboard," Hawk told his marines "Shoot him." Admiral Simms returned to the launch. After the second tour, lunch was served on the hangar deck, with the "Big Stick's" officers and men eating in shifts. FDR, surrounded by armed marines, graciously allowed the carrier men to step to his table and speak to him, to the chagrin of his armed protectors. As the mess attendants served the crew, the ships chefs served the President and Hawk, Sherm and Nimitz. First came the porterhouse steaks (grilled to order) and baked potatoes, (with butter or sour cream) mixed veggies, (corn, peas and carrots) followed by coffee, coke and/or orange juice. Dessert was apple, cherry or blueberry pie with real whip cream. As surprised as FDR was over the meal, he was astonished that every crew man aboard was having the same meal for lunch as they were. "Where the devil did you find enough for the crew," asked FDR. "Sir" answered Hawk sheepishly, "You wouldn't believe the size of the reefers on this ship. I figured it would be a good surprise for you, sir." "Well admiral, I have a better one for you. In the time you've been gone, we've had our munitions specialists working around the clock to produce the 28 inch ammunition for you. We've been somewhat successful. We haven't been able to build any 28 inch barrels nor any armor piercing or high explosive rounds for you." Hawk was about to ask him what was left that they could've been successful at, but FDR held up his hand to stop him. "From what I understand, your 28 inch guns are useless in an air attack." Hawk nodded. "Well our munitions experts have developed an anti-aircraft shell for your 28 inch guns. Same principal as buckshot, I'm told. Supposed to be deadly. No aircraft can fly through it without being shredded. The bad part is that it can't differentiate between friendly and enemy air craft. I have five merchantmen en-route, filled with these 28 inch AA shells. I'll let you have them if you let Admiral Simms aboard. He's got to be hungry, sitting alone in the launch. My guards tell me your men invited the boat pilot to lunch, but the marines still wouldn't let the Admiral aboard." Those were my orders, sir, "said Hawk, "But I'll tell you what. I'll send a mess attendant over with a plate for Admiral Simms." Hawk then motioned for the attention of an attendant and ordered him to send a plate to the launch. Before the attendant left, he heard FDR say, "Please don't poison him, Admiral Hawkins." The attendant laughed as he walked away but then realized, the President was serious.

And the ships kept coming in. Admiral Simms began placing them in anchorages all over the Hawaiian Islands. There were still enemy spies about, and the many ships arriving were a security nightmare. 14 battleships, (New York-14 inch guns, Nevada-14 inch, New Mexico-14 inch, Idaho-14 inch, Tennessee-14 inch, California-14inch, West Virginia-16 inch, HMS's Renown-14 inch, Vanguard-14 inch, King George V-15 inch, Queen Elizabeth-15 inch, Valient-15 inch, Rodney-15 inch, and Ranier-16 inch guns. Seven aircraft carriers, Saratoga, Enterprise, Lexington, Wasp, (HMS) Leviathan (HMS), Ark Royal (HMS), and Glory (HMS), 36 heavy and light cruisers (20 British) and 77 destroyers (11 British). Apparently Roosevelt and Churchill had canibalized the Pacific and Atlantic fleets as well as Britains Home fleet. In 7 days the largest armada ever assembled was ringed around Pearl Harbor. Seven carriers plus the Big Stick, over a thousand five hundred aircraft. However, FDR and Admiral Simms were only able to scrape together 38 subs, which though seeming a lot, was really a thin forward guard considering the size of the fleet behind them. With 14 battleships in addition to his three (Texas, Colorado and Mississippi), Hawk built 3-5 ship divisions, placing each of his battleships as a command ship over the other 4 that made up the 5 ship division. Over all command of the BatDivs went to Admiral Halsey. Hawk kept Texas to support his carriers starboard side. Additionally, Hawk elected to keep all of his destroyers and cruisers with him and the Big Stick.

Since the enemy had demonstrated the ability to jam his radars, Hawk ordered twenty of the subs a hundred miles out on each quarter, to protect his sides in case the enemy attacked. The other eighteen scouted a hundred and two hundred miles ahead. His boomers (SSBN's) scouted beyond that at deep submergence. All were emptied of 28 inch ammunition before setting out 3 days ahead of the fleet.

Chapter 11

Hawk sent for Cmdr. Smyth, of the destroyer, U.S.S. Ladd. "John," he said, "I want you to take command of your destroyer, the Smith, Jolie, and Shaver, drop back 60 miles astern of the fleet and cover the rear. "But sir," said Cmdr. Smyth, "we won't see any action. Sir, I've got the best gunners in the fleet. We should be alongside the carrier, where we always are." "Look John," said Hawk, "I would like nothing more than to have you along side me. Your gunners have been invaluable protecting the carrier. But I need someone behind me that I can trust. If the enemy makes an end around and attacks from behind, I need to know I have someone covering my ass that I can depend on. When the fighting starts, I can't be worried about my rear." "Very well sir," said the young cmdr., "I'll be proud to cover your ass." Three days before the fleet was due to sortie, Hawk received a radio message from the fleet H.Q. "FDR requests assignment of these 4 officers. Adm's Norman Scott (great grandfather of the future SecNav.) Daniel Callaghan and Frank Simms, and Cmdr. Bill Hunt. Hawk sent back, "Will take Admiral D. Callaghan and Cmdr. Bill Hunt. Simms will be shot if he attempts to board. N. Scott can't come either. If he dies, we loose our future Sec Nav." At the Admiralty Head Quarters, FDR turned to Admiral Simms and said, "Sorry Admiral. He just doesn't like you. I can't say as I blame him, I'm not too fond of you either."

Next, Hawk sent for his old friend, Admiral Hunt. As he entered Hawks wardroom, Hawk handed him a bourbon. "How are things shaping up, Bob?" "Well sir," said Admiral Hunt, I've had the crews of the additional heavy and light cruisers drilling but, they're still not up to par with our cruisers. I'm thinking it'd be safer for us if we put them outside of our screen, let them play by themselves. And then, when they depart the screen to go out with the surface action force (the Bat Div's) they won't reduce the efficiency of our screens." "Alright Bob, whatever you decide, put it in writing, and on my desk within 24 hours." "Aye aye sir," said Hunt. As he turned to leave, Hawk stopped him, "Say Bob, don't you have a brother out here somewhere?" "Yes sir, he's on the Tennessee, she's slated for Europe. I'm sure glad he won't be in this mess." "I'm sorry to hear you say that, Bob," said Hawk, motioning Hunt to the port side port hole. "That's the Tennessee 500 yards to the port. I just approved a transfer to the Big Stick. I believe the name on the request was Cmdr. William Hunt!"

For Bill and Bob Hunt it was like old home week, all rolled up into two hours. "Billy," said Admiral Hunt, " I want you to rescind your transfer. Request a hardship discharge. Go home, take care of the folks. I'll see that you get your discharge, by presidential order." "What? What are you talking about. I'm not going home. The word is, this task force is going into battle," said Cmdr. Hunt. "I'm where I want to be, sir." "Yeah Bill, were going into battle. A battle the world has never seen. And if we don't win, America loses. Every man, woman and child loses. If we lose, somebody has to be home to help the folks. Go home!" "Look Bob, if this battle is so crucial, so important, then this is where I want to be." "I can't talk you into going home?," asked Admiral Hunt. "Hell no Bob, I'm staying right here." "Then you leave me no choice Bob?" The quizzical expression on Cmdr. Hunts face was replaced with anger, when Admiral Hunt called in the sentry at the door and ordered, "Sgt., place this officer under arrest for insubordination. I want him escorted off this ship and placed in the brig until he can be sent stateside for trial." "Aye aye sir," said the sgt., then led Cmdr. Hunt (who was speechless) out of the hanger area and off the ship.

Admiral Hunt and Hawkins sat in the wardroom minutes later. "You know Bob; he's going to hate you for that." "Yes sir," said Hunt. "But it was the only way I could think of to keep him alive. Do you think the President will discharge him if I ask?" "I don't think there's anything FDR wouldn't do for us at this point," said Hawk. "Good," said

Hunt, "but I'll bet you he goes off and re-enlists in the Army. And they'll take him. They'd take Al Capone if he enlisted." "You know Bob," said Hawk, "If we fail, he'd be better off here dying in combat than burning alive in the radiation from the A-bombs. And there's not much he'd be able to do in the way of helping your folks, if it comes to that." "I know," said Hunt, "but he's my kid brother, I don't know what else I can do for him." "Look Bob," said Hawk, "We've been friends a long time. I don't claim to have all the answers. I'm responsible for the lives of more than a hundred thousand men. But I can't worry about them now. Neither can you. We have to concentrate on the mission and trust that the men will do their jobs and come through it ok. Their lives are in good hands. Drop the charges, reverse the orders and I'll put him on my staff. He'll do his duty from the inside of the armored bridge. It's the safest place in the whole task force. I give you my word he'll survive." Hunt thought a moment, then nodded his ascent. "You're right, Admiral," said Hunt. "If he has to die, better here where he has some control over his destiny, than at home just waiting for the bombs to drop." "I'll notify the brig that all charges have been dropped," said Hawk, "And leave orders for him to report to me aboard the Big Stick for duty. Any ideas as to what duty I should give him?" "Yeah," answered Admiral Hunt, "Make him Captain of the heads!"

Two days before sortie, Hawk took his three battleships NW of Pearl and off loaded the 28 inch AA ammunition from the cargo ships. Hawk didn't want to do it within sight of possible spies, and Admiral Simms wouldn't allow the cargo ships in the harbor because of their explosive nature. In that regard, Hawk agreed with Simms. If any cargo ships exploded in the harbor, the death toll would be unimaginable. Once the cargo ships were emptied, they began their long trek back to the west coast of the United States. As they passed the entrance of Pearl Harbor, they picked up their escort of two destroyers. It was a light escort, but all available destroyers were committed to the big mission at hand. Besides, as Cmdr. Hunt had pointed out to Hawk, there was little doubt that the spies had already informed Japan of the massive build up of warships in the Pacific. Japan was surely recalling all of her warships to the Japanese Islands and the Truk Naval Base until they knew where the American warships were heading. There probably wasn't an enemy warship anywhere between California and Pearl Harbor. And with 94 destroyers (including Hawks Des Flot 1,2 and 3) deployed around the massive fleet, there was little chance an enemy could sneak in undetected to torpedo anything but a corvette (British). In fact Cmdr. Hunt felt that Japans days of sneaking into anything were long over. Hawk almost gave him a reality check.

The day before sortie, was a day of feast for the men of the "Salvation Fleet" as they were now calling themselves. There wasn't a man present who didn't know where they were going and why. The feast was a miracle in itself, put on courtesy of FDR. Every steer, pig, chicken, duck and turkey within 100,000 miles must have been butchered and brought in for the feast. Every fruit and vegetable gathered and shipped to Pearl. "Better than ground beef and powdered eggs," thought Hawk. All that was missing was FDR, who had returned to Washington to await the end.

The feast was better than any Thanksgiving any man could remember. Fresh pumpkin, apple and blueberry pies. Fresh whip cream and milk. It was impossible to imagine where it all came from, or to what lengths FDR had gone through to get it all here. But Hawk also knew it would be the last such meal for many men within the fleet. Even though the men in the battleships Texas, Colorado and Mississippi, his DesRon 3, and his own cruisers and destroyers (the ships he took with him through the squall) would be safer due to heavier armor, the men in the ships that FDR supplied would face the most danger. Those ships had only the armor protection they were built with. And they would be the ships closest to the enemy coast. Also they didn't have the STARS, the heavier fish or the more potent depth charge. Also, though Hawk placed one of his battleships with each division, the other two battleships in each division were only armed with 14" and 15" guns, so they couldn't use the 28 inch AA ammunition. As it is, Hawks battle plan called for the Colorado, Mississippi and Texas to be placed within the carrier groups to add their 28" AA fire to protect the carriers. The "Big Stick," carried 8 inch to 28 inch guns, so they also had aboard the new ammunition. The ships in the most danger would be the destroyers. They would be the furthest away from the heavy ships (patrol and escort duty) and so the furthest away from the AA protection supplied by the big ships. Hawk had considered putting his more heavily armored ships in the patrol positions-especially if the Japanese came out with the Kamikaze attack (suicide) corps again. But Hawk knew he'd need his own forces when/if the Japanese fleet came out to do battle. No, he'd have to keep his heavy ships for that eventuality. War is full of danger, and they'd have to face it. He couldn't protect them all. Besides, at the moment, he had other problems on his mind. His idea was not just to attack the Japanese Islands, but the main island of Japan. He needed to know exactly where the enemy was developing the atomic bombs. There was nothing in the computer data banks that gave even a clue. He knew the enemy would send everything they have against his fleet, both as it approached and as it came to their coast. Even with 7 CV's, (aircraft carriers) the Teddy R. would be needed. Five of the seven carriers carried only dive-bombers (300), the sixth and seventh (Saratoga/Lexington), carried only fighters (135). The Teddy R. carried (600) fighters, which meant she would be closer to the action-about 400 miles from the coast of Japan, along with the other seven carriers. That put all eight carriers within range of the enemy aircraft. It also put their F-173 in range of their attacking aircraft. This didn't worry Hawk. He knew the Teddy R. could take care of herself. Especially with the new 28 inch AA (anti-aircraft) rounds she and her battleships carried. No, what concerned Hawk was that he had only one ace up his sleeve, and no idea where to put it.

When the fleet left Pearl, the anchorage seemed almost deserted. There were several submarines left that had already been assigned to other missions, possibly keeping an eye on the sea lanes between Pearl Harbor and the west coast. A couple of tankers were in the harbor that hadn't left yet for the states, as there wasn't an available escort for them. Two cruisers were left in the harbor for protection of the dozen or so auxiliaries that remained anchored. As the fleet steamed away, it picked up other units that had been staged around the Hawaiian Islands and the fleet began to slowly grow in size. From the Teddy R's bridge, warships could be seen in any direction for as far as the eye could see. It would take several hours for the escorts to take up their proper stations around the formation. It was the largest and most powerful fleet that the United States had ever amassed up to that time. In warship count, it dwarfed even the Japanese Pearl Harbor attack strike force. For three days the fleet steamed nearly due west, then turned north west on a more direct course towards the target, the course meant to by pass the normal patrols of enemy submarines. No enemy subs were detected, more likely because the enemy seemed to have recalled them until the fleets intention was revealed. Aboard the ships, pilots studied the photographs provided of the large cities, including Kure, Tokyo, Hiroshima, Nagasaki, Yokohama and many others to attempt to locate anything that could be ventilators for feeding oxygen underground. The vents would have to be large. Anti aircraft crews drilled constantly, though with the standard ammunition. The new 28 inch AA ammunition was too precious to waste on practice. Plane crews worked on their planes, then looked them over and searched for potential problems. Between AA practice, machinists worked on the guns, replacing barrels. Everyone was kept busy with the duties that would keep the ships and guns in working order during the fight to come. Even Hawk was keeping busy. When he tired of studying blueprints and schematics of the ship, he walked along the decks, speaking to the thousands of his crew men about everything from their duties to the upcoming battle, from the lowliest sailor to his own admirals. Hawk was continually on the TBS, speaking with Admirals Hunt, Nimitz, Sherman, and Wilkes with suggestions and ideas. They seemed to be relaxed and unconcerned in the knowledge and belief that Hawk knew what he was doing and would lead them to victory. It was this belief of theirs that had Hawk concerned. The Teddy R. had been built to be unsinkable. She had been designed and built to even withstand a nuclear attack. The only other ship Hawk could remember as being unsinkable was a liner built in1912. "God himself couldn't sink this ship" they said. But that ship, the R.M.S. Titanic sank on its maiden voyage after striking an iceberg. Obviously, the Titanic wasn't designed to withstand the damage of a near head on collision with an iceberg. As he walked the decks of the Teddy R., he wondered what kind of damage his carrier wasn't built to withstand. At 0816, as he walked along the hanger deck, he was called to the bridge. "This is Admiral Hawkins," "Sir," said his newest aid, Cmdr. Hunt, "We've just received a radio from the DD (destroyer) Willis, she's been hit by two torpedoes and needs assistance. She says she's sinking." "Did our sonar pickup anything?," asked Hawk. "No sir, they must have sonar jamming capabilities," said Hunt. "Very well," said Hawk, "Detach the three nearest destroyers to hunt down the enemy sub and assist the Willis and her crew. And Bill, send the nearest SSBN to the scene to help find and sink the enemy sub." "Yes sir," said Hunt. Hawk hung up the phone, although he hesitated for although a moment or two, then continued his stroll. By 1015, his inspection completed, Hawk went to the bridge.

"Admiral on the bridge," sounded as Hawk pushed open the heavy door and entered the bridge. Normally the door was left open, but given the serious nature of this mission, the ship was set to be sealed and water tight at a moments notice. "At ease men, continue your duties," Hawk ordered. Going to the radar station, Hawk asked Hunt, "What's the word on the Willis?" "She's gone sir. By the time the O'Bannon, Ridley and Moore got out there, the Willis had already sunk. The O'Bannon and Moore began an under water sweep to locate the sub, soon joined by the SSBN Skipjack, but thus far they haven't found it yet." "And the survivors of the Willis?" asked Hawk. "Picked up by the destroyer Ridley sir, they picked up 173 officers and men sir." "Very well Cmdr., order the Ridley to transfer the crew of the Willis to the Teddy R.." As Hawk turned to leave the bridge, he was stopped by Cmdr. Hunt, "Sir, I've been going over the designs and the capabilities of the TF 1 ships under your command, and it occurred to me that if Japan had any subs like your SSBN's, it would account for why we haven't been able to locate it in the vicinity of the sinking ship. I think they may have better luck searching five to seven miles from the Willis sinking. If the enemy sub is an SSBN, her torpedoes would have a five mile range." Speaking aloud, but to himself rather than Cmdr. Hunt, Hawk said, "The japs aren't supposed to have any war ships of their own in 2042, but with history changed, God knows what they may have." "Excuse me sir?" asked Hunt. "Never mind," answered Hawk, "I'm just thinking out loud. You're right Cmdr., order the O'Bannon, Moore and Skipjack to widen their search. And tell them they may be up against an SSBN with ultra modern weaponry. No, belay that. Order the O'Bannon and the Moore to rejoin the fleet. Get me two more SSBN's and send them out to assist the Skipjack. Tell them to search from deep submergence. And tell them I want it sunk before it attacks again." "Aye aye, sir," said Hunt. Moving to the command computer, Hawk punched in his personal command code, then typed in a change of orders, recalling four of his boomers (Tang, Wahoo, Archerfish and Flasher) to take up positions fifty miles out to port and starboard of the fleet and to be alert for possible enemy SSBN's. Then going to the bridge telephone, he called, "Admiral Sherman, please report to the bridge." When Sherm arrived, Hawk told him about the Willis sinking, Cmdr. Hunts suspicions and the recalling of the four SSBN's and their new orders. (Admiral Sherman commanded the subs and was third in the line of command of the fleet). "Sherm," Hawk said, "I want you to take Cmdr. Hunt to my cabin and bring him up to speed on everything." "Everything?," asked Sherm. "Yes," said Hawk, "Every thing." "Yes sir, follow me Cmdr.," said Sherm. Fifteen minutes later an explosion was heard within the fleet. It seemed to originate somewhere off the port side, astern. Sailors on the deck reported seeing a small white mushroom shaped cloud. However, since the expected wave failed to materialize, Hawk decided the explosion must have come from the depths of the ocean. This was substantiated a half hour later when the U.S.S. (SSBN) Skip Jack radio'ed the carrier confirming thee sinking of the enemy sub responsible for sinking the destroyer U.S.S. Willis. The enemy sub was sunk at the depth of four thousand feet, and because of the depth, none of her crew survived. Hawk sent his congratulations, to the captain and crew of the Skip Jack, and forewarned them that the Tang, Wahoo, Archerfish and Flasher would soon be patrolling 50 miles from the fleet, port and starboard. "Stay deep and keep an eye and ear on your scopes. They may be able to jam our radars and sonars, but they can't jam yours." "Aye aye sir," said Cmdr. Warren.

For the next four days, as the fleet moved closer to Japan, life was quiet aboard the carrier. Two other enemy subs had been spotted and sunk. One was a nuke, sunk deep, and the second was an I-boat, sunk on the surface, recharging its batteries before dawn. The C.A.P. was vectored to the area by the U.S.S. Enterprise. A five hundred pound bomb, dropped on their conning tower, blew the sub to the bottom before any of her crew could get out. The Enterprise, destined to be the most famous aircraft carrier in the U.S. Naval History was just adding to her score. Even at this time, she had already seen more combat, and been in more campaigns than any U.S. carrier except the Big Stick.

The one thing that worried Hawk about most of his carriers, (the Big E), Enterprise, Wasp, Saratoga, YorkTown and Lexington, was their flight decks were comprised of wood (cedar). The British carriers flight deck was armored (steel), like the Teddy R., but not nearly as heavily armored. The U.S. Navy used wood so the flight decks could be repaired at sea, between attacks. Hawk remembered reading at Cavite (after emerging from the squall and while his Des Ron 3 was being rebuilt) that the Yorktown had been hit hard during an attack at the battle of Midway. By the time the next enemy raid appeared, the flight deck had been repaired and the enemy thought they were attacking another carrier, having sunk Yorktown in the last attack. Great Britain put armored flight decks on their carriers. As a result, all of their carrier losses were due to torpedoes instead of bombs.

According to the original history, before it was changed, seven of the British carriers would be lost in the war. Of the American carriers, Wasp would have been lost during the Guadalcanal campaign, torpedoed by a Japanese I-boat. Saratoga, though torpedoed several times, survived the war, but was sunk as a target ship at Bikini, during the atomic bomb tests after the war. Not a very respectful end to America's 2nd aircraft carrier (the U.S.S. Langley was converted from a freighter. The Lexington and Saratoga were supposed to be battle cruisers, but following the terms of the 1927 Washington Arms Agreement, work was suspended on the battle cruisers and begun as carriers CV 1 and CV 2). Tragically, the most famous aircraft carrier in the U.S. Naval history ended her days in a scrap yard. Surely not a fitting end for the U.S.S. Enterprise.

Seven hundred miles from Japan, the fleet began coming upon Japanese fishing boats, obviously picket boats. They were quickly dispatched while the Teddy R. jammed radios. Several attempted to send a sighting report, but according to the RadCom, (translations) no complete contact reports were sent. And no survivors were picked up. Just the same, Hawk ordered condition two watches, (eight on, four off.) and crews went to battle stations from 0500 to 2300. Hawk knew it would be hard on the crew, but getting caught off guard would be much worse. The next afternoon, as the fleet neared to within 520 miles, Hawk ordered the fleet to prepare for battle. Pilots began getting their final briefings on which targets were the biggest priority. Some were merchant and others were naval. The airfields were a big priority because command of the skies were all important. The mission called for massive bombing attacks on the harbors, targeting any warships that could conceivably present a danger to the surface forces of the task force. Tankers (fuel) were also a priority as well as ammunition (merchant) ships. As soon as the large enemy warships were disabled or sunk, and air supremacy was achieved, Hawks battleships would steam along the coast and into the harbors to pulverize the shoreline with 14, 15, 16 and 28 inch gunfire to destroy any enemy warships that had thus far survived. These attacks would coincide with the bombing strikes against their airfields to ensure that the enemy wouldn't be in a position to counter attack. Finally the naval air armada would concentrate their bombing on the large cities to reduce them to ashes, hopefully destroying the location of the atomic bomb factories. The chances of success were very slim. But the chances of the United States surviving the atomic bomb assaults were non existent.

At 0400, the following morning, Admirals Hawkins, Sherman and Wilkes began an inspection tour of the Teddy Roosevelt's hanger and flight decks. Of her six hundred fighters, one hundred would be carrying bombs, five hundred pounder's for use on the battleships and carriers that were known to be in the enemies harbors. Scout planes that had returned from the early morning reconnaissance missions had reported the IJN Shinano, (80,000 ton aircraft carrier) and the IJN Musashi and Yamato, (78,000 ton battleships). The carrier was virtually defenseless, as she was so new that she didn't have her full complement of aircraft aboard. Actually she hadn't even been commissioned yet. The super battleships carried 18 inch guns and with the exception of Hawk's battleships, were the most powerful battleships in the world. In addition to these monster warships, the scouts reported four Nagato class, and seven Fuso class battleships,(28,000 and 39,000 tons respectively) thirteen heavy and eleven light cruisers, and at least twenty destroyers in Hiroshima bay. The harbors of Kure, Tokyo and Ominato were reported to have as many warships as well. There was also a report that a large enemy fleet was anchored on the other side of the Japanese islands in the Sea of Japan. More than twenty battleships, proof that the enemy had started the war with more than the reported twelve battleships. In addition to the Shinano, seventeen other enemy aircraft carriers were spotted. However, the scouts reported that the carriers had few planes aboard. Hawk guessed the planes had been staged at airfields throughout the islands. (Actually, the enemy carriers aircrews had suffered heavy casualties in recent battles with Hawk's squadrons and were badly depleted.) Hawk would've liked to send more of his fighters with bombs, but he knew he would need to send in as many fighters to protect his "bombers" as well as the dive bombers from the other carriers. According to the plan, Lexington would stay with the Teddy R., the other six carriers wouldn't close on the Japanese islands any closer than four hundred miles, in case the enemy had any atomic bombs ready to drop. Once it was ascertained that they didn't, Hawk would decide whether to risk bringing them any closer. The Teddy R. would close as near as necessary. If the enemy attacked with swarms of bombers, Hawk felt confident that the carriers combat air patrol (CAP) along with the carriers phalanx and 28 inch anti aircraft guns and the stars could handle anything the enemy could throw at the fleet. His only real concern was an attack by stealth submarine attack.

Speaking to the pilots on the flight and hangar decks, Hawk found them in high spirits, a little nervous, but not afraid. At 0500 the order to attack was given and the attack computer began sending the command to the other carriers in the fleet. Pilots on all of the fleets carriers began climbing into their cockpits and preparing to take off. The carriers then began sending orders to each of the accompanying warships within their divisions. The computers negated the use of the TBS (talk between ships) that had caused so much confusion in battles early in the war, according to the historic documents. No confusion this time, within minutes every captain on every allied warship knew exactly what his part of the mission entailed, from the battleships, cruisers, destroyers and subs.

On the radar scopes, Hunt watched as each division separated from the main task force and began converging on their assigned positions to carry out their respective missions. Task Force One forged ahead, minus her battleships, which were assigned to the other carrier groups for anti aircraft protection. Later, when air superiority was attained, they would be dispatched with their escorts to proceed with their off shore bombardment assignments. Hawk had planned to keep the Texas with him, but after the sighting of the twenty enemy battleships, he decided it would be more prudent to send her with the Lexington carrier group. For now, all of the carrier groups were within sight, but that would soon change as each took divergent courses to the Japanese home islands. At 0530 Hawk returned to the bridge. "Sir," said Cmdr. Hunt, "request permission to airlift to one of the battleship divisions." Taking the younger Hunt aside, he said," "Permission denied, the only reason you're not still in the brig is I promised your brother that I'd keep you out of harms way." "Sir," said Hunt, "I appreciate that, but I didn't join the navy to be coddled. I expect to face the same dangers as every other man in this task force. I think...." Hawk interrupted him. " Cmdr., didn't you request duty with this task force so you could serve with your brother?" "No sir," said the cmdr., "I requested duty here so I could fight with my brother." "Look son," said Hawk. "I sympathize with you, and I respect your desire to fight. But your brother is one of my best officers and one of my closest and dearest friends. I gave him my word that I would keep you aboard ship. He has a very difficult job ahead of him, and he can't be worried about whether or not you're safe. But you are right about one thing. You deserve to share the same risk as any other man in this force. If responsibility is what you want, I can make you my second on the bridge. You'll remain in the safety of the armored citadel bridge where you'll be as safe as I am, but still in the fighting. That's the best I can do without breaking my word to your brother." "I'll take it,"said cmdr. Hunt. "Thank you sir." "Sir," said the bridge talker,"RadCom (radio communications) reports receiving a message that the cruiser Nashville has picked up two enemy destroyers three thousand yards off his port quarter. He's requesting permission to open fire." "Damn," said Hawk. "What's his position?" "Sir the Nashville is two hundred and twenty miles south east of the Japanese islands." "Shit," said Hawk. "Tell the Nashville to blow them out of the water before they can radio in a sighting report." "Aye aye sir." said the bridge talker. A couple minutes later the bridge talker reported that the two destroyers had been sunk. Hawk turned to the bridge talker and asked," Ask RadCom if the destroyers were able to send in a sighting report." "Sir," said the talker,"RadCom reports that all radio communications were jammed by the Colorado." Turning to cmdr. Hunt, Hawk said, "Your brother is commanding the Colorado/Saratoga battle group. Cmdr., send to all divisions, permission to fire upon and dispatch is given to all vessels as come upon. No further permission required. Hawk sends, send them to hell." "Aye aye sir," answered cmdr. Hunt. Going to the bridge phone, Hawk picked it up and called, "ComCom, this is Admiral Hawkins. From now onwards and until further notice Cmdr. Hunt has command control, level one. Command verification 178BPV." Turning to Cmdr. Hunt, Hawk said, "Well cmdr., for all practical purposes you now carry the responsibilities of the fleet admiral and the authorization to command the fleet. If I am incapable of command, you will take over command until relieved by either Admiral Wilkes or Admiral Hunt. You're now temporarily promoted to the rank of Captain. Congratulations Captain." Returning to the command computer, Hawk keyed in his verification number, then the cmdr's promotion and responsibilities, then re-verified his command verification. Finished, Hawk called the radio room. "Sparks, send to all divisions, enemy air attacks possible. Be alert. Lets not get caught with our pants down. All carriers begin launching at 180 miles. Hawk sends, kill em all." "Aye aye sir," said Sparks. "Sir," asked capt. Hunt, "when will our troops land?" "They won't." said Hawk. " We have twenty one troop transports at sea. But at this point we feel they'll be facing every man, woman and child as well as the enemy soldiers if we put them ashore. Perhaps later, when we've destroyed everything they have that flies and floats and we have their bomb factory's location narrowed down, maybe we'll land some forces with close air and sea support. But for now, I think they're safer at sea." "Sir,"asked capt. Hunt, "What happens if the japs have any atomic bombs already to drop?" "We've considered that," said Hawk, "but we don't think they do. Just the same, that's why the other carrier groups are staying out to sea four hundred miles. We're the only carrier going in close for now. We'll be within fifty miles if we can get that close. With the number of fighters we'll have in the air, we should be able to shoot down any enemy aircraft while still over the islands. But that's another reason I don't want to land troops. The Japanese are suicidal fanatics. I wouldn't put it past them to drop one of those monsters on their homeland to kill our troops. According to the historic documents, it was thought that we would incur a million casualties if we had invaded Japan. Instead we dropped the two atomic bombs. We didn't actually occupy the islands until after the surrender." "So all that changed when your destroyers entered the squall," asked Hunt? "So it would appear,"said Hawk, thinking about the many millions of innocent Americans who would die if the enemy was allowed to drop those bombs on the United States. And then there were the bombs they would drop on Mexico and Canada and the millions they would kill there. Ultimately the continent of North America would become a Japanese bastion. The future of more than America depended on this battle.

Chapter 12

The skies over Japan were soon marked with the dirty blackish brown smudges of smoke and debris as anti aircraft guns fired at the allied planes as they dove down to drop their ordinances. Then there were the grayish black trails that led from the sky and trailed to the ground as aircraft were shot down. So many planes were falling out of the sky that it was difficult to tell whether they were friendly or enemy. There would be a flash in the sky, then pieces of a plane would flutter down, closely followed by a shattered, burning wreck. The plane would strike the ground and explode in ball of fire, leaving only a plume of smoke and a deep hole in the ground to mark the grave where our pilots planted the enemy. Because of the volume of anti aircraft fire coming from the cities and towns, our bombers concentrated on them as well as the harbors. (The plan was to bomb the naval targets first.) Their cities and towns were soon ablaze, and the little yellow men burned with the targets. Planes that attacked the naval targets fared no better. Anti aircraft fire from the warships was very heavy and deadly. Several American planes were hit. (Knowing what the enemy would do to any captured pilots, the pilots were instructed to attempt to head to sea, where our subs would pick them up.) But as the bombs struck their targets, the AA began to slacken. As the planes descended upon the harbors, ships of every size began to attempt to escape the holocaust that the harbors became. In addition to falling bombs, torpedoes from the subs provided by Roosevelt began to strike the hulls of the enemy ships as well. And unlike the torpedoes Hawk's squadron had started with (following the

Pearl Harbor attack), these fish exploded. (Video footage taken from the gun camera's of the fighters and viewed later would reveal one enemy warship exploding every four minutes.) Main targets were the Yamato and Musashi as they put up the greatest volume of AA than any other warships. Their 18 inch guns, useless in an air attack, fired at the attacking planes, their shells dropping on the city of Hiroshima. Soon they ceased firing when they were struck by the heavy bombs. A Fuso class battleship took at least two bombs to its pagoda mast. The resulting explosions toppled it, causing many casualties. Seconds later a bomb landed about fifty feet off its port side, close enough to rip open its side and the ship took on an immediate list. A destroyer took a bomb between the funnels and when the smoke cleared, the only visible part of the ship was its bottom. Seconds later another bomb struck its bottom, blowing a huge hole into it. This time when the smoke cleared, the ship was gone. A cruiser, steaming for the entrance of the harbor, took a torpedo amidships. In a flash of hot flame, it was gone, leaving a hole in the water and very few survivors. The Shinano, not yet commissioned, lived but a few minutes after the attack began, Six low level planes from a British carrier fanned out and dropped their fish at fifteen hundred yards. There was no way they could miss. They didn't. Spaced nearly perfect, the fish drilled the huge ship from bow to stern. With virtually her entire port side opened up to the sea, she rolled over in less than a minute. Then three Kaga class carriers,(38,200 tons) pulled out in an attempt to escape to the open sea. Obviously thinking of safety in numbers, they soon see the futility in it. Two flights of fighters,armed with bombs, converge on the flattops. There are a few splashes from near misses, but enough bombs land on the flight decks blowing enormous holes into them. The bow of one is blown clean off. It veers to starboard and collides with another carrier. Then suddenly there are explosions all over the carriers. The carriers are taken under fire by the battleship Colorado, twenty six miles off the harbor entrance. Shells, twenty eight inch, are guided by computer control, shells that don't miss begin landing on the 812 foot long flight decks with maniacal precision and accuracy. The three carriers become crematoriums for their crews. There are few survivors. Within ten minutes the carriers are sinking, effectively bottling up the harbor. When the Colorado ceased fire, it was only because there wasn't anything left for the shells to home on to. With the harbor mouth blocked, there wasn't going to be any other targets trying to escape, so she and her escorts changed course and steamed down the coast looking for other targets.

The Japanese navy fought valiantly, but they were so completely overwhelmed that they didn't stand a chance. High explosive armor piercing shells struck Japanese armor and the armor lost. The few defending planes that rose to protect the ships were quickly dispatched. If ever a fleet were sitting ducks, this was it. Hawk sent four waves of aircraft to attack the enemy fleet that day. As the sun began to set, all American planes returned to their carriers. Returning pilots were debriefed and results were recorded to be delivered to command to ascertain which targets needed further attention. Hawk was curious whether there was any location that seemed as though the enemy was trying to protect it more than an other. (It would make sense that the enemy would try to protect the bomb factory.) But as the results were tallied, it became apparent that finding the location where the bombs were being manufactured wasn't going to be that easy. The enemy fought fiercely over every target. At 2300, (11:00 pm) Admiral Davidson sent a few planes over the jap targets, equipped with night vision to determine how much damage was done to the enemy. The enemy anti aircraft guns remained silent, perhaps not wanting to reveal their location to night bombing. Not that that mattered, Admiral Davidson's planes were also equipped with infra red bombing capabilities. But on this mission, only photo's were taken. By 0100, (1:00 am) the photo's were spread out on the table in the wardroom aboard the Teddy R. Admiral's Hawkins and Sherman were looking at them attentively. The days bombing results were impressive. Both the Shinano and the Musashi were sunk. In addition to the three Kaga class carriers sunk, four Zuikaku class carriers were sunk in the other harbors and bays. Three Fuso class battleships were sunk, eleven heavy and light cruisers and six destroyers were also sunk. Also, air supremacy had been achieved. Impressive as the results were, Hawk was no closer to knowing the location of the bomb factory as he was a week ago. From the flagships position, seventy miles off the enemy coast, the sky over the island of Japan was still lit up as fires continued to devour the wood structures that made up the cities. Crewmen, off duty, stood on the flight deck and watched Japan burn. Occasionally, explosions would go off as fires reached ammunition stock piles or flames breached bulkheads and set off the magazines of the ships that were hit by bombs and/or torpedoes. Judging by the pilots reports and the photo's taken, close to half of the enemy warships present had been sunk or heavily damaged in the days attack. As impressive as the results were, Hawk couldn't be sure if the attacks had destroyed or even damaged the enemy's bomb making capabilities. Hawk called a conference aboard the Teddy R. for 0200 to decide whether another day would be needed to bomb or if an amphibious landing would be necessary.

By 0145 the admirals began arriving aboard the carrier. Hawk apologized for the late hour, but made it clear that the reason was very important. As soon as the admirals came in, they began looking at the photos, attempting to determine which targets had been plastered and which needed to be hit again. As soon as all were present, (Admirals Nimitz, Capt. and Admiral Hunt, Admirals Sherman, Wilkes, Davidson, Smyth, Halsey and Callaghan.) Hawk posed the question to them. "Where would you put a bomb factory if you didn't want to risk the enemy finding it?" The room fell silent as the officers looked at one another. They had seen the photos. There wasn't any part of the island that hadn't been hit. What had they missed? Admiral Nimitz spoke. "Sir, if I remember the historic documents correctly, The Imperial palace was never bombed. The enemy would've known this if they had access to the research vessels computers. It would make sense then if they were to put a manufacturing plant in a place where it wouldn't be bombed, why not put it there?" Hawk thought a moment. It certainly made sense. Turning to Captain Hunt, he asked, "Capt., do we have any information on the building plans on the structure of the palace?" "I'll check the computer, sir," said Hunt. He left to check. Admiral Wilkes spoke next. "Sir, we have a battalion of Filipino troops aboard our troopships. Why don't we land them and have them recon the palace? They're pretty blood thirsty. They volunteered for this as soon as word got out that an amphibious landing on Japan might take place." "No," said Hawk. "I discussed that possibility with General Mac Arthur before we left. The consensus was that a landing would only take place as a last resort. The enemy has proven to have a taste for torturing our Filipino allies. Besides, we would want some enemy prisoners, and General MacArthur thinks it's unlikely we would see any live prisoners." "Sir," said Admiral Halsey, "if they may be building the bombs below the Imperial palace, why don't we drop a few five hundred pound bombs on it and see what pops?" "The problem is that the reason why we didn't drop any bombs on the palace originally was that headquarters believed that if we bombed the palace and killed the emperor, the Japanese people would never surrender. That possibility still exists." "Sir," said Nimitz, "weighing the possibilities, I believe the risk is warranted." "Well I don't. Before I commit to that recourse, I'm going to make damned sure we've checked out every other possibility." "And then?" asked Nimitz. "We'll drop so many bombs on that palace that all that'll be left is a very deep hole, and we'll fry every yellow bastard in the process. Emperor be damned."

When the conference was over, Hawk sent several messages to the fleet. Acting on a hunch that the enemy might counter attack in the morning, Hawk ordered all ships to move a hundred miles out to sea, except for the Teddy R. and her escorts as well as the Colorado, Texas and the Mississippi. These ships had been built to withstand a nuclear blast. There was still a possibility that the enemy had a ready atomic bomb that they might try to use against the fleet. Hawk thought it would be a good idea to disperse the fleet. Later in his cabin, Hawk read up a little more on the F-173 and its capabilities. He was still working on a plan in his head, a plan that he might have to put into effect if he couldn't locate the target. It was a plan he didn't want to put into action. It was a plan he wasn't sure he could live with. As he read, he noticed the ship was rolling, the seas were getting rougher. Ready to call it a night, Hawk pulled up the historic documents and checked out the developments. So much had changed that there wasn't much there that could help him anymore at this point. But there was something that caught his eye. Scrolling through the data, Hawk took some notes, then exited the program. Pulling up his command program, and entering his personal code, he issued an order for a conference for all commanders the following morning at 1100, providing the fleet wasn't in action.

Admiral Isoruko Yammamoto stood on the bridge of his flagship, the emperors newest battleship, the Yamato. The ship was a monster, weighing in at seventy eight thousand tons and packing a walloping eighteen inch main battery of nine rifles in three triple turrets. Only one other warship in the entire world was equipped with that kind of fire power, and that ship was the sister ship of the Yamato, the Musashi, which at this moment was moored alongside. Nine years earlier, when rumors spread that an American vessel had been captured that held unheard of information aboard, information that told of a war the Japanese empire had started and ultimately lost due to a bomb that the devilish Americans had devised and dropped on the Japanese islands that had destroyed two of Japan's largest cities, most officers, including Yammamoto, figured it was ruse, planted by the Americans. After all, a bomb that could destroy an entire city was a dream.

Isoruko Yammamoto had risen through the ranks believing strongly in airpower, this in a time when most high ranking officers still believed in the battleship as the queen of the sea's. Anybody believing otherwise, was very unpopular, and seldom made rank in the peace time navy. Decorated in the battle of Tsushima, then duty as a naval attaché in Washington DC, Isoruko emerged as a commander, and placed in command of Japan's newer aircraft carrier, the Akagi. (Red Castle) Originally planned as an Amagi class battle cruiser, following the Washington Naval Treaty, the ship was converted into an aircraft carrier. (Like the American carriers Saratoga and Lexington, that were converted also from battle cruisers after that same treaty.) Originally built with three flight decks forward, between 1936 and 1938 she was completely modernized including hull blisters and a flight deck that sat at the same level and a large stack that canted downwards to vent fumes away from the flight deck. Her aircraft capacity was nearly doubled. Other carriers with multiple level flight decks were soon converted as well.

As far as Isoruko was concerned, if it was a ruse, it backfired. The data on the research ship caused the Japanese to start a naval building program unprecedented in history. That program was responsible for the designing and building of the super battleships Yamato, Musashi and Shinano, (Shinano was converted from a battleship to an aircraft carrier), which this day was in Tokyo Bay, awaiting her aircraft and final preparations to the sealing of her water tight doors. Additional data aboard the captured ship revealed methods to build ships that were heavier as well as techniques to build ships at a faster rate. Information, also aboard the captured ship revealed how to build these fantastic bombs that could destroy cities. These bombs were also being developed. Then word had spread that a large American fleet was bound for the Japanese islands to attack. His advise had been rejected, that he put together a large fleet and meet the enemy fleet and destroy it. Instead, the fleet lay at anchor in several harbors and bays, like the sitting ducks his task force had destroyed at Pearl Harbor. The lessons that the Americans had learned the hard way apparently had not been learned by his superiors. Still, the admiral wasn't unduly concerned. An attack on Japan would be foolhardy. Even with the number of warships that the Americans were rumored to have, which the admiral didn't believe, the volume of anti aircraft fire that his warships could send up against any attacking force would make any attack suicidal. Then this morning, as the sun rose off of the sea, the enemy planes came in from all directions, attacking every major harbor and bay. High level bombers, some dive bombers, and fighters, some carrying bombs as well. Mitsubishi (A6M) zeros went up to meet them but were quickly shot down, leaving the skies in the control of the enemy. Anti aircraft fire was thick enough to walk on and several enemy planes were shot down, but the American planes continued to attack the ships. The enemy airmen attacked with ferocity, attacking like samurai warriors. Like an unstoppable force, their planes flew through the wall of AA, and planted their bombs on the emperor's warships. Watching from the bridge of his mighty flagship, he was astounded to see the planes break through the AA patterns and strike the BB Musashi. One bomb after another struck her. Then he saw several torpedo strikes, even though he had not seen any enemy sub activity. As suddenly as the attack began, the air just as suddenly seemed to clear. A torpedo struck the Musashi on her port side, just aft of "B" turret. It penetrated the shattered torpedo bulges and exploded, setting off the forward magazine. The resulting blast seemed to suck the oxygen from around the ship. Seamen around the ship found an inability to breath, and the breath they did take in was super heated and roasted their lungs. It was an excruciating death. Most simply vanished in the explosion. Parts of the ship blew out in every direction, followed by men and pieces of men. The water around the hull glistened a crimson red, tainted and stained by oil and blood. When the smoke and flame cleared, the mighty Musashi was gone. The skies had long ago been cleared of zero's and with the Musashi gone, as well as all the other ships that had thus far been sunk or disabled, the AA fire had eased considerably. The American planes could now attack without a certainty of being shot down. The attacks continued. From the bridge, the admiral saw three of the fleets carriers make for the harbor entrance. Planes pulled out of dives and converged on the carriers. Isoruku looked on as the three ships were enveloped in flames and eruptions from the bombs that landed on their decks. Again the oxygen seemed to disappear around the ships. Once again, when the smoke cleared, the carriers had been reduced to wrecks. Now the harbor mouth was blocked and nobody would escape the smoking harbor. Not that it mattered, from what the admiral could see, there wasn't many ships left that were able to escape the crucible anyhow. Tokyo Bay had effectively become another Pearl Harbor.

The following morning the pilots were up and having chow by 0430. Briefing was at 0600, planes were being armed during the briefing. At 0700 the carriers began launching, fighters first,(because they would be circling the carrier until all of the planes carrying bombs were airborne) then the rest of the air armada. At 1100 Hawk held a conference in his wardroom to go over the missions. As the admirals began to arrive, they checked out the historic photos that Hawk had printed out of the documented damage that the coming storm would inflict. Ofcourse at this point they didn't know what they were looking at. The Sherman's arrived first, then Wilkes, the brothers Hunt, Nimitz, Halsey, Smith, Davidson and Callaghan. "Gentlemen," Hawk started, "a development has come up that I feel calls for the personal touch. As you know, the historic documents haven't been of much use to us since we started changing it. Too much has changed as a result of our victories. However, last night I was checking. I found something that no matter what we do, we can't change." Looking around the room, Hawk could see he had everyones attention. " Beginning tonight about 2300, the winds will start to pick up. By 0100 we will have winds sufficient to seriously disrupt operations. Within three hours we'll find ourselves in a class five huricane with reported winds in excess of one hundred and eighty two mile per hour." Hawk let that sink in a moment before continueing. "As you can imagine, that will endanger our destroyers as they try to keep escort positions. Therefore, the fleet will begin moving out away from that enemy coasts at 1500. Any aircraft still on missions will have our carriers courses programmed into their computers so they can safely return to their flight decks. I want all aircraft back on their carriers and stowed below decks by 1400, The carriers with their cruiser escorts will steam four hundred miles from the Japanese Islands and wait for the storm to pass. The battleships, which as you know were modified to withstand heavy damage, will haul off to a hundred miles, so they can serve as picket ships, in case any enemy ships attempt to come out after us or try to escape. Our destroyers will be at the biggest risk. They will follow the carriers at a safe distance, not trying to keep escort stations. I want all destroyers refueled from the carriers by 1300 this afternoon. The lower they sit in the water, the less punishment they'll take. DesRon 3 will stay with the battleships. All warships following the carriers and battleships will stay within protective range of the capital ships, but will not, I repeat will not attempt to keep escort stations with the heavy ships. Are there any questions?" "Sir," said Nimitz," by moving out, you realise that we'll be providing a respite for the enemy to attempt a retaliatory attack on our fleet." "Yes, I realise that Admiral," said Hawk. "But it can't be helped. Our fleet would not survive this storm if we stayed closer to the enemy coast. And any bluejackets that survived a shipwreck would not live very long if he went ashore. According to the historic documents, the damage that the brittish suffered to their battle fleet was mostly due to their trying to keep stations escorting their merchant and naval forces at sea. Even their warships in port suffered damage. Unless they're knowledgable about the coming storm, they'll suffer damage again. As far as leaving ourselves open to an enemy attack when the storm passes, they'll be digging themselves out from the storm and probably won't be in a position to attack us anyway. However, if they do attempt to attack us, it'll be by air, as their harbor entrances have been blocked. Any aircraft they send out against us will have to find us first. We should spot their search planes with radar. Our battleships and DesRon 3 should also be able to warn us." "And if they go after them," asked Davidson. "Our battleships, with their 28 inch AA ammunition, and DesRon 3's stars (surface to air rockets) will have no trouble shooting down any attacking aircraft." said Hawk. "Any other questions?" Hawk looked around the room, but there were no other questions. "Very well," said Hawk. "Today we'll step up our attacks, concentrating on the known ammunition and aircraft factories. I want them levelled. They could be where the enemy is producing the A- bombs. We'll also continue to work over their heavy ships. I don't want to leave them any battleships or carriers to use in a counter attack. We know they have hangars underground, so we'll hit their air fields again also. I'll send the courses to the command ships at 1200. Make certain that any aircraft still on mission at 1300 have those coordinates programmed into their computers. Now then, I'm told my stewards have prepared a special lunch for us, so we'll all have a good meal before you return to your ships. It may be the last good meal any of us get until this storm passes."

By the time the admirals had returned to their commands, Hawk had received an update on the damages they had inflicted on the enemy the previous day. During the night, the enemy had attempted to clear the harbor of Tokyo Bay by setting explosives underwater. Their attempts were partially successful, as they were able to clear a narrow path, wide enough for destroyers and possibly cruisers could safely navigate to the open sea. Several ships that had been left in a sinking condition had been beached. Of the sixteen battleships that were present, six had been sunk and the others were all damaged to some extent. Of the twenty four heavy and light cruisers present, only eight escaped damage. Seven had been blown to pieces. And of the twenty nine destroyers in the various harbors, there were still seventeen left. Since Tokyo Bay had been cleared sufficiently for destroyers and cruisers to escape, and since they held a possible threat, Hawk ordered the attacking planes to concentrate on them. Throughout the day Hawk received further updates on the damages inflicted on the enemy. When the last planes had returned to their carriers, Hawk was informed that Tokyo Bay had again been plugged, when two destroyers had been sunk while trying to flee the flaming harbor. This time it was unlikely they could clear it over night.

By 2300 the fleet was close to three hundred miles from the enemy coast and the seas were already getting very rough, with waves as high as ten feet. By 0100, waves were up to twenty four feet, the roughest seas Hawk had ever seen. Only Admirals Nimitz and Halsey had ever seen anything like it, and still nothing as bad as this. The ships as large as the carriers rolled horribly, making passage through the ships dangerous. Hawk ordered all unnessecary movement halted. Seeing the carnage aboard the Teddy R. caused by the rolling, Hawk dreaded what the crews aboard the destroyers were going through. Even as large as the Teddy R. was and Hawk's standing order to limit movement, the sickbays began filling with sailors with crushed and broken bones. Sea sickness ran rampant throughout the ship. It was going to be a long night.

At 0300 that morning, two hundred and seventy three blue jackets disappeared when their destroyer, the U.S.S. Blue was struck broadside by an unseen wave. The DD was heaved over on her beam ends, hung there for several seconds, then was struck by another that rolled over her, burying her. Twenty seconds after the first wave struck her, the Blue was gone, taking her entire complement with her. A solitary inflatable raft remained to mark her grave. The DD U.S.S. Jarvis fared nearly as bad. She ran headlong into several thirty foot waves that struck her A- turret so hard that it disappeared, causing her forward handling room and magazine to flood. Pumps were started and a distress call went out. The DD U.S.S. O'Bannon heard it and attempted to radio back, but the storm caused too much interference. She was able to steam to the Jarvis's position, but in these seas, there was nothing she could do to assist the sinking destroyer. Still, just being close gave the destroyermen some comfort. Perhaps it wouldn't have had they known the O'Bannon had lost most of her life rafts. Not that rafts could be launched in these seas anyway. Any man in these waters, even with a preserver, would be dead long before he could be rescued. Minutes after her forward turret was washed away, her B- turret was struck, knocking it thirty six degrees to port, destroying her train machinery. At 1430, thirty nine minutes after she lost her A- turret her bow went under and her crew hastily abandoned ship. No further distress call was sent as her radio mast had gone overboard. Flares were fired off but they were extinguished immediately. The crew of the U.S.S. O'Bannon didn't see the ship go down and didn't know her crew was in the water.

Meanwhile, aboard the Teddy R., despite having the aircraft, ordinance carts and maintenance machinery tied down, seamen continued to get injured. The ships sick bay was beginning to fill, even after Hawk ordered that all unnessecary movements cease. He finally ordered that all off duty personnel sack out. By this time the seas had risen to more than fifty feet. From the bridge, ninty three feet above the raging surface, the escorting cruisers didappeared from sight with every wave. Hawk was worried for his destroyers. They were shorter vessels, and despite having their tanks topped with fuel, they were still in grave danger in weather such as this. It was no picnic for the cruisers either. In some ways they had it worse than the destroyers. They were bigger and higher off of the water, but that meant there was more surface to be struck by the waves. (The battleships built to withstand the damage of heavy gunfire and their main deck was thirty eight feet above the flat surface of the sea.) The cruisers were low on ammunition from constant shore bombardments and fighting off the occasional enemy aircraft. Though riding somewhat higher in the water, they were also somewhat unwieldy and more difficult to keep on course in heavy seas. Torpedo mounts; twenty and forty millimeter gun tubs all took damage from the powerful waves. All day long the warships were bounced and buffeted by the monstrous seas. There was no safe haven for the crews or the ships. On the bridge, Hawk could see a cruiser; the U.S.S. Adak was in trouble. Her forward funnel had been washed overboard and she was taking water. TBS (talk between ships) messages were picked up stating that the pumps were being put into action, but the water was gaining and if the storm didn't end soon, the ship would sink. With a twelve degree list to starboard, she had to reduce speed to keep from capsizing. In no time she had dropped out of sight astern. There was nothing Hawk or anybody else could do to assist in this weather, but hope and pray for their safety. At 0800 (8:00 am) the storm still raged and showed no sign of weakening. The escorts (cruisers) began suffering damage that threatened their abilities to keep station and Hawk ordered them to disperse for their own safety. After all, even if there was an enemy sub in the vicinity, it wasn't likely that they would be able to track them in these waters, much less attack. Finally, as the clocks crept up to 1300, (1:00 pm) the seas began to abate and the waves dropped to about forty

Chapter 13

As the fleet closed tentatively on the Japanese Islands, the warships did what repairs they could. The Adak had been at last found, very low in the water and nearly ready to turn turtle. Pumps were hauled over and as water began pouring out of the ship, her list decreased. Soon she was on an even keel and the welders went to work making the ship watertight again. It had been a close call. As the destroyers began to check in, Hawk learned about the fates of the Blue and Jarvis. The light cruiser Cloquet reported picking up survivors from the Jarvis. There were pitifully few. Thirteen blue jackets were the sole survivors. The captain didn't survive, nor any of the officers. Two hundred and seventy nine officers and men perished with the ship. Worse yet, there were no survivors from the Blue. Her entire complement of two hundred and ninety three went down with their ship. For Hawk, the losses were reminiscent of the losses sustained by DesRon 3. Though the enemy wasn't directly responsible, Hawk vowed to avenge the destroyers and their crews.

Meantime, Hawk had other things to worry about. Not that the loss of two destroyers and five hundred and seventy three men wasn't important. It was the blast that the Texas had seen that had him concerned. If it was an atomic bomb that had exploded prematurely, then Hawk could be steaming the task force to their own destruction. The course he was on could result in the loss of not only every man in the fleet, but also every man, woman and child in the United States if Japan was allowed to drop those bombs. As the fleet neared four hundred miles from the enemy coast, Hawk sent out a general order, that all vessels would meet at a point three hundred miles from Japan. By this time, the winds had died down considerably so several scout planes were sent out to fly over Tokyo and take photos. Until the planes returned, the fleet units converged on one another.

At 2100, the Admirals began filing into the wardroom and seated themselves. The stewards brought in coffee and donuts and despite the friendly atmosphere, there was little talk. The officers looked as haggard as though they were getting off of an alcoholic bender. Admiral Wilkes was seated next to Hawk and they were quietly discussing the blast and his suspicions as to its cause. "Gentlemen," said Hawk, "I'm sorry to have to ask you here, I know all of you have gone with little or no sleep for twenty four hours or more, but there have been some developments that need to be addressed. At 0530 this morning an explosion was witnessed from the Texas at ground level along the shores of Japan. At the time the Texas was a hundred and ten miles from Japan. Being seen from that distance means that the explosion was massive. It could only have been caused by an atomic bomb." Hawk stopped to let the weary minds take in this newest threat. Admiral Nimitz spoke first. "So they do have some bombs." Admiral Sherman spoke next, "If they have them, why haven't they dropped them on us before?" "Maybe they didn't have them finished yet," said Admiral Hunt. "Maybe they rushed to complete one and messed up, and it went off on them." "Maybe," said Cmdr. Hunt, "they thought they could come at us hidden by the storm, they couldn't and the high winds forced them down resulting in the bomb going off." All eyes turned to Cmdr. Hunt as he spoke. "Whatever the cause," said Hawk, "we now have to consider the possibility that any enemy plane that attacks us may be carrying an atomic bomb. Even if we shoot it down fifty miles from the fleet, it would still be catastrophic for the fleet. Even if some of our ships survived, the radiation would kill the crews. The only ships equipped to withstand an atomic attack is the Teddy R., and through their modifications, maybe the battleships. Maybe!" "So do we step up our attacks on the enemy from long range?"asked Admiral Smyth. "I sent scouts over Tokyo as soon as it was safe to launch them." said Hawk. "They were checking on something that will give us the answer to that." "Care to let us in on that?" asked Admiral Wilkes. "Our scout planes computers are scanning for residue of the a- bombs." "But," said Cmdr. Hunt, "if they accidently dropped one on themselves the planes would pick up radiation anyway. How does that help us?" Hawk smiled at the younger Hunt, and then looked at his brother. "Plutonium." said Admiral Hunt. Hawk nodded and said, "Exactly. The scout's sensors picked up trace elements of plutonium, the key element in producing an atomic bomb." "So we know where they are producing the bombs!" said Admiral Nimitz. "Yes," said Hawk. "Exactly where Admiral Wilkes thought it was. Right under the Japanese Imperial Palace. The sensors place the bomb making factory at three hundred feet below the surface." There was a few seconds of silence, and then Admiral Nimitz spoke. "Do we have a bomb that can penetrate that deep?" "A bomb, no." said Hawk. All attention turned to Hawk as he spoke. "Gentlemen, I have an idea, but I'm not sure it'll work. As you all know, the F- 173 is nuclear powered." "Yes," interrupted Nimitz. "So we draw straws to see who crash dives the jet into the palace?" "No sir," said Cmdr. Hunt. "The plane can be flown by a pilot in another plane by remote control." Looking icily at Hawk, Nimitz replied," I wasn't told the plane had that capability." "I'm sorry Admiral," said Hawk. "My orders prevented me from disclosing certain aspects and possibilities about my mission." "That's alright, son," said Nimitz. " I understand the importance of following orders. So what's the range of this remote control device?" "It's a very short range, Admiral," said Hawk. "about four to five miles." "And the pilot wouldn't be affected by the radiation?" asked Nimitz. "Yes it will," said Hawk. "It'll kill him." "So it's a suicide mission then." answered Nimitz. "Admiral," said Wilkes, "I thought I had read somewhere that the F- 173 could be remotely controlled from the bridge of the carrier via the command computer." "Yes," said Hawk. "But this would call for pin point accuracy on the palace. Piloting the F- 173 from the bridge computer wouldn't guarantee an accurate strike within six hundred feet." "Maybe that would be close enough." said cmdr.Hunt. Hawk thought a moment, and then answered, "But if it isn't, we've blown our only chance to destroy the bomb factory." Admiral Sherman, quiet for most of the conference now spoke, "We have the 1st Marine Division waiting aboard transports off Wake Island. They could be here in a couple of days. I don't think there's anything those jarheads would like more than landing on the shores of Japan and mixing it up with a couple million nips." Laughter filled the room at the aspect of setting the famed division on the japs. "The trouble with that is we would want some prisoners and the marines don't take prisoners." said Cmdr. Hunt. "Seriously," said Hunt, "we could land troops to set explosives. If they're underground, they would need ventilation ducts to bring in oxygen. If we blew those up, wouldn't they suffocate underground?" "Possibly." said Hawk. "But the radiation already on the ground would kill them." "You know," said Admiral Callaghan, "we already have a most powerful means to destroy the bomb factory. We only have to find a way to set it off. And accuracy isn't necessarily important." All eyes went from Hawk to Callaghan. "I'm listening," said Hawk. "Well sir," continued Admiral Callaghan, "correct me if I'm wrong, but isn't Mount Fuji classified an inactive volcano? What if we crashed the F- 173 into the volcano from the carrier? We wouldn't have to be very accurate, we could hit the volcano just about anywhere. Mount Fuji would be hard to miss, and from the carrier we would be accurate within six hundred feet." Hawk thought a few seconds, surprised he hadn't thought of it himself. "Admiral," said Hawk, "I think you just earned yourself another star." The atmosphere changed instantly in the room. Everyone stood and congratulated Admiral Callaghan on his brilliant idea, and began shaking hands and slapping each other on the back. They all understood the significance of the plan. Maybe, after this attack, the war would end and they could go home. "Gentlemen," said Hawk, "I think we have a plan. Thank you for coming. Now all of you can return to your commands and get some well deserved sleep. I'll get things prepped here and notify you by Com Com as to the time of the flight. Keep in mind that prior to the flight, all surface ships will have to be at least four hundred miles from the target. We'll leave some SSBN's in the area to monitor the results of the attack from a distance. Good evening.

Going to the ComCom after everybody had left, Hawk began feeding data into the computer, pulling up information about the remote controlling of the F- 173. A red light came on in the corner of the screen, but Hawk wasn't familiar enough with the nuclear powered plane to know what the light indicated. With all data fed into the computer, Hawk logged off, and went to bed, confident that the war with Japan would soon be over and without the cost of a single human life. Ok, without the cost of a single American life. And soon the United States would be safe from the threat of atomic annihilation.

Waking the next morning, Hawk quickly dressed and had his breakfast. It was his favorite meal of the day. His mind was fresh and he planned his day as he enjoyed the meal his Filipino steward whipped up. Hawk was always amazed that his cook could do so much with so little. After breakfast, Hawk radioed his commanders, "Admiral Halsey, You'll take command of TF53,(the ships given Hawk by FDR) and steam course 000, six hundred and fifty miles from Japan and await us. Continue A.S. and C.A.P. protections. Admiral Hunt, You'll assume command of the battleship Texas and DesRons 1,2 and 4 and take up screening positions around TF1. Admiral Wilkes, you'll assume command of the Colorado and CruDivs 1 and 2 and take up screening positions around the Teddy R. Admiral Sherman, you'll take command of DesRon 3 and the SSBN's. I want the Pope on my port side, the Jackson on my starboard and the Stewart ahead of me. Send five subs to Japan to monitor the results of the attack. Position the other five between us and the Japanese Islands to watch for any counter attacks from enemy naval forces that may try an end run on us. Admiral Callaghan, you'll take command of the Mississippi and stand off of my port side to provide any AA protection we may need in case the enemy attempts to attack us by air. Admiral Halsey, I want you to detach the carriers Lexington and Saratoga and place them under my command. From now onwards they will be permanent units of TF 1. Does anybody have any questions?" There were none. "Very well gentlemen. Lets refuel our small boys while we have the chance. Good luck. Hawk out."

With the refueling complete, the fleet began to break up. Ships under Admiral Halsey began drawing off, and the escorting ships began pulling in. It was a very impressive sight. With all these ships taking different paths to join their respective forces, it seemed a miracle there were no collisions. But the commanders were too experienced for that. The carriers Lexington and Saratoga nudged into position to port and starboard of the Teddy R. The Mississippi pulled up on the Lexington's starboard side,(Hawk's port side) and the rest took up their screening positions around the capital ships. Admiral Sherman, aboard the Stewart, had the best view of the warships that came together to form the fleet. He felt a shiver of pride go down his back. He was one of the few men in the entire fleet who knew why Hawk had transferred the "Lady Lex" and the "Sara" to his task force. But he wished Hawk had also transferred the "Big E" as well.

As TF1 moved at a speed of twenty eight knots towards the launch position of four hundred and fifty miles from Japan, Hawk sat on the bridge in the chair that his engineers had designed for him and his machinists had built. The previous chair had been uncomfortable and hurt his back. But this chair was so comfortable he could easily sleep in it. He felt as though he could really relax in it. Maybe it was his mood. He wondered if it had been this way for Col. Paul Tibbets as he had flown away from Japan after he had dropped his bomb on Hiroshima. The bomb he had historically dropped, the bomb he would never drop. The ironic part was that Japan was already lit up. They had inadvertently A-Bombed themselves! And soon, the first country to be nuclear bombed as well. Suddenly he felt a shallow wave of depression. The American people had not wanted war. Perhaps the Japanese people had not wanted war as well. Maybe they had been pushed into it by their military. Suddenly he visualized seeing their bodies burnt to a crisp or blown apart, either by the two days bombing, the atomic bomb blast by their own hands or the nuclear blasting to come from the crashing of the F- 173. The thought sickened his stomach and he pushed the thoughts from his mind. "Hell," he thought to himself, "these same people would've massacred his troops had he landed them. Reaching for his bridge phone, he called the hangar deck and ordered the F- 173 prepared for flight. An hour later the bridge phone rang, "Sir, this is Lt. Neilson, were having difficulty getting the aircraft remote on line." "Is the problem on my end," asked Hawk. "maybe I have to log in my command code." "No sir," answered the lt., "We haven't progressed that far yet. The computer says we have to power up the remote device and let it warm up for twenty minutes, feed in the target coordinates, then add your command codes. We can't get the remote to come on line." "Did you ask the computer to run a systems check," asked Hawk. "No sir," said the lt., I'm not familiar with that procedure. I don't think I have a high enough security clearance." "Very well," said Hawk. "Call Capt.

Lister to the hangar deck and I'll be there in a few minutes." "Aye, aye sir." said the lt. Minutes later Hawk was on the hangar deck, walking towards the big jet. He found the captain speaking to the aircraft chief. Hawk was a bit pissed that the captain hadn't versed his chief on the power up procedures and might have said something to him if he hadn't been so surprised at the condition of the captain. Apparently the aging progress hadn't stopped when he had returned from his previous mission, flying the F- 173 at the speed of light, through the squall. The captain had suffered massive aging. As a result the young man found himself in an old mans body. He was a twenty six year old man with the ailments of an eighty year old man. Of one thing Hawk was certain, Captain Lister was the oldest line serving officer in the U.S. Navy. To think that a few months ago he was in the prime of his life. Turning, he faced Hawk and said,"Sir, I'm sorry for this screw up. I should have trained the chief on the procedures." "No captain," said Hawk. "I'm the one who owes you an apology. There was nothing in the computer about health hazards caused by flying this plane. If I had known, you never would have been in that cockpit." "Sir," said the captain, "if we hadn't made that flight, we never would have known about Japan's posession of the bombs or that they would use them on our country. Sir, I consider it an honor to have made that flight." Reaching out, Hawk took his hand and shook it, surprised that he had such a strong grip. "Well captain, do you know why we can't get the planes remote on line? Is it possible it was damaged during that flight?" "Well sir," answered the captain, "anything is possible. I took quite a few near hits until I figured out what was going on and I reprogrammed the planes computer." "So the lasers may have struck the plane in a near miss.?" "Well, there was one that was as near to a strike as you could get without actually getting hit. It came down in front of the nose, so close that it lit up the cockpit. But the plane continued to fly without any extra difficulty, so I figured it had missed me. That's when I began flying evasive and started to reprogram the computer to see the strikes. And that's when I realized the strikes were coming from above and not from the ground." "Well," it appears that that one strike may have disabled the remote device. We can't get it online." "I'll take a look at it sir." said the captain. As Hawk turned to walk away, he heard the captain say, "Sir, one more thing, Please." "Yes Captain," answered Hawk. "Sir, I would have been here sooner, but the marine sentry wouldn't let me pass. My ID doesn't match this old face that I'm carrying around. I need your permission to have it retaken." "You have it, captain. Just tell security to call me. And captain, the next marine that stops you and doesn't let you pass, you call me and give me his name. He'll find himself swimming home." "Aye, aye sir." said the captain, smiling. Back on the bridge, Hawk called the commanding officer in charge of marine security and asked him to report to the bridge. Within minutes Maj. Calvin arrived. " Major Calvin reporting as ordered, sir." "Major," asked Hawk. Are you familiar with one of my pilots named Captain Lister." "Yes sir, isn't he the pilot that flew the super jet through the portal?" "That's right," said Hawk. "As a result of that heroic flight, the captain has sustained some health issues. And as a result of those issues, he has been denied entry to areas of the ship where he has every right to be. That stops now. Do you understand Major?" "Yes sir." answered the officer. "Good," said Hawk angrily. "Because the next man to deny the captain entry is going to be keelhauled by me personally. Are you sure you understand, major?" "Yes sir, I understand." "Then you're excused." Major Calvin saluted and left as quickly as he could. Hawk knew his next stop would be to chew out every marine on the security team.

Hawk returned to the bridge to await word from Captain Lister that the problem had been cleared. He got the call almost an hour later, but it wasn't the news he had hoped for. The remote device had been fried, the needed parts weren't aboard, and could only be replaced in 2043. But as Hawk knew, that 2043 no longer existed, even if he could get there to get the part. "I guess we write off the attack." said Hawk. As he turned to the ComCom, he heard captain Lister say, "Excuse me sir, there is another way." "I'm listening," said Hawk. "Sir, may I speak to you in the wardroom?" "Yes, I'll meet you there in fifteen minutes." It would only take Hawk a couple minutes to get there, but he knew it would take the captain longer due to his ailments.

In the wardroom Hawk had coffee and some carrot cake waitting when the captain arrived. "Sir, there is another way we can carry out this mission." The captain could see that he had the admirals attention, so he continued. "Sir, let me fly the mission." "Absolutely not, captain.

It would be suicide." "Sir, this mission is very important. It could end the war." "Captain,: said Hawk, " this mission, if you flew it would kill you." "Sir," the captain responded, "I'm already as good as dead. The aging didn't stop when I returned. I've continued to get older. At this rate I'll die of advanced age within a week. Two at the most. I surely won't live long enough to see my home again. And if we don't fly this mission, we may not get the opportunity to destroy the bomb factory. If given the time, the enemy may even get the chance to use them against this task force. The mission has to be undertaken. If another pilot flies it, he also will suffer this aging. The mission must be flown and I'm the logical pilot to fly it." Seeing that Hawk was considering it, Captain Lister continued, "Sir, this mission is too important to scrub." Thinking it over, Hawk told the captain, "Captain, wait here for me, I'll be back in a few minutes." As the captain sat down, he winced and groaned in pain. Seeing this Hawk asked, "Are you sure you're up for this, captain?" "Yes sir, these old bones don't move around as good as they used to." "Can I get something from the ships pharmacy for you?" asked Hawk. "No sir, I'm fine. Thank you, sir." Leaving the wardroom, Hawk went to his cabin and called the ships sick bay. "Captain Webb, can you report to my cabin immediately please." In minutes Hawk was speaking to the doctor. "What can you tell me about captain Lister's condition?" "Well sir, I've been monitoring him since he returned from his flight through the portal. I can't explain why his aging hasn't stopped. But according to my calculations, within the next ten to fourteen days he'll pass away from old age. He seems to be in considerable pain, but he's refused pain medications whenever I offer them." Thinking back to the wardroom, Hawk nodded and replied, "Pilots don't like to be medicated in case they have to fly." "Yes sir, but he's not flying anymore." said the doc. "Yes, that's what I had ordered." "Sir?" asked the doctor. "In his present condition, can he fly?" asked Hawk. "Sir, hasn't he done enough? You can't expect…" "Doctor, can he fly?" interrupted Hawk. "Well, I guess he can. But I can't say for how long. He'll start to age more rapidly as soon as he's airborne." "Look doctor, this is very important. If you were going to take a guess, how long could he survive in the cockpit?" Doc Webb thought a moment and answered, "Maybe an hour. Any longer and he would lose consciousness and the plane will crash." "Thank

Chapter 14

One hour later Hawk was back on the hangar deck, standing in front of the supersonic jet. Captain Lister was already in the cockpit, making the final preparations for his flight. Climbing the ladder, Hawk went over the details of the mission. Captain, remember, using the scanners on the plane, you must locate the weakest area on the cone where the crust is the thinnest. If the nuclear explosion doesn't penetrate and set off the volcano, you'll have died for nothing. All we will have succeeded in is losing the only possible means of ending this once and for all." "I understand, admiral. Look, I'm not looking forward to dying like this, although I do prefer this to the alternative. But I won't die for nothing." Reaching up, Hawk extended his hand and shook with Captain Lister. "If anyone ever asks me what a hero looks like, I'll tell them about you, captain. I'll see that you get the Congressional Medal of Honor for this, Captain. It's been an honor knowing you." "Thank you, admiral. It's been an honor serving under you."

Stepping back down the ladder to the deck, Hawk joined a dozen other officers and men behind a thick bulkhead as the pilot started the engines and began easing the throttles to the speed needed for the takeoff. With a final burst of power, the jet screamed down the hangar deck and disappeared off the stern and immediately climbed to sixty thousand feet. According to the operational orders, the captain would fly at low speed (so his aging wouldn't speed up) at nine hundred miles per hour to the Japanese island and circle while the computer scanned the cone of the volcano to find the thinnest surface. Captain Lister would then program that location into the targeting computer, (in case he lost consciousness) then climb another twenty thousand feet (90,000 feet total) and crash dive the jet into the target area located by the computer. It would take seven seconds once the jet was put into the dive.

At the time of takeoff, TF1 was four hundred and eighty miles from the enemy mainland, far enough to be safe from any nuclear blast. However it was unknown whether the strike to the volcano would create a tidal wave that could endanger the task force. Leaving the hangar deck, Hawk raced up to the bridge as fast as he could. Like everyone else, he wanted to see the strike. Of course, at this distance, they were too far away. But it was thought that the blast caused by the volcano's eruption might possibly be evident. Four minutes after Hawk reached the bridge; the radioman came on the bridge and said, "Sir, I have a message from Peacemaker. It reads, God bless America, Task Force One and the United States Navy." Then there was a flash in the direction of Mount Fuji. Then, despite the distance, a dull roar was heard. Seconds later a cloud of black smoke could be seen low on the horizon. The cloud grew and seemed to spread out on the water. Three hours after the strike, radar showed a large wave approaching the fleet. A tidal wave, that as it reached the fleet, seemed to raise each ship about thirty feet, as though going over a hill. For the next eight hours the smoke continued to rise. Then it was dark and the smoke couldn't be seen, replaced by a bright glow, low on the water. At 0630 the following morning Hawk ordered the fleet to reduce speed to wait for the SSBN's to catch up. He also ordered all flags raised at half mast in honor of the sacrifice given by Captain Lister.

At 1000, the first subs rejoined the fleet and reported to the Teddy R., and Admiral Sherman. First to arrive was the U.S.S. Tang, (Cmdr. Morris). He reported that the U.S.S. Silversides had radioed contact with three enemy boomers, atomic subs. apparently their jamming capability was damaged by the Peacemaker strike. The Silversides destroyed two of them with torpedo fire before they themselves were destroyed. The loss was witnessed by the Tang, which was next in line, twenty miles away. The U.S.S. Wahoo, (Cmdr. Marston), came in next. He also reported the Silversides loss and stated that he had fired a homing torpedo from six miles that struck the hull of the third enemy boomer. He reported having heard the war head go off and even heard the sub sink. He said he was impressed with the listening gear, that he could plainly hear the compartments collapsing as the sub sank into deep water. His report finished stating that a huge explosion was heard a couple minutes after the sub sank. He guessed that the crew had set off the subs arsenal when it was certain that they were too deep to escape. Very typical of the enemy. When the U.S.S. Flasher (Cmdr. Riley) came in, she reported that from her position, at 2100 hours many explosions erupted on the main Japanese island. As few as seven and as many as eleven coming from Tokyo and SW as far as forty miles away. Laying submerged, about fifty miles out, he reported an enemy boomer on the surface that was attempting to escape from one of the shallower entrances of the harbor. He reported that it seemed as though the submersible was pulled straight down as though caught in a whirlpool. He further reported that an hour later the bottom of the harbor seemed to come up, and lava began flowing across the harbor and into the city, quickly moving towards the Imperial Palace. He reported that the entire time, Mount Fuji was in a continual state of eruption. When the U.S.S. Seawolf (Cmdr. Rupert) reported in, He said he saw and heard nine separate atomic explosions, and witnessed nine mushroom clouds, resulting in the total devastation of the main island. The Seawolf was positioned on the NW side of the island, in the Yellow Sea, with China astern. Before departing the area, Cmdr. Rupert reported that the whole center and the NW side of the island seemed to drop into itself and disappeared leaving a huge atoll, and creating a seventy foot tidal wave that nearly capsized his boat despite the depth of sixty feet the boat sat in. U.S.S. Harder, (Cmdr. Jared) reported the same thing, except his report included the presence of a magnificent harbor after the tidal wave had passed. U.S.S. Scorpian, (Cmdr. Randolph) reported hundreds of soldiers and civilians running to the water's edge in a vain attempt to extinguish the flames consuming their bodies. According to the subs gauges, the water temperature had risen to five hundred degrees, and they simply boiled to death at the water's edge. In addition to the U.S.S. Silversides, the U.S.S. Growler also failed to return. She went down without a whisper, her final resting place unknown.

Despite his losses, Hawk was very pleased with the success of the Peacemaker mission. From all appearances, the island nation of Japan with all of its military might and fanatical leaders seemed to have disappeared from the face of the earth. And to some extent, destroyed by their own hand. Destroyed by the very bombs that they hoped to drop on the United States and her allies. Hawk hoped that at least some of her citizens had survived. He also worried about China, so close to the atomic and nuclear blasts. "Had the radiation harmed her people? What had the tidal wave done to her shores?" Since the Japanese had invaded from the SW, he fervently hoped he had taken out a large number of enemy soldiers. These questions would be answered later, after their triumphant return. Now his only thoughts were for the safety of his men and the fleet. At 0200 he ordered the task force to form up in combat formation (He had no way of knowing if any enemy subs were around that weren't at Japan and escaped destruction.) and the SSBN's to deep water around the fleet. He ordered a course of 080 degrees to rendezvous with Admiral Halsey. With all enemy jamming ceased, radar showed the rest of the task force a hundred and twenty miles south east of the Teddy R. Sonar was non functional, probably due to the commotion caused on the bottom of the ocean resulting from the atomic and nuclear blasts the day before. Long range radar was also non functional obviously due to the amount of soot in the air. From his wardroom, Hawk sent a message to the commanders of all of the carriers, "Due to the ash and soot in the air, all CAP (combat air patrols) and other flight operations are suspended until further notice." Then to the escorting vessels," Due to the ash and soot conditions at low and high altitudes, all flight operations, including the CAP are suspended. Escorts are our only line of protection against air, surface and sub surface attack. Remain Vigilant. Hawk sends." Two hours later Task Force One joined up with the rest of the fleet.

As exhausted as Hawk was, getting to sleep wasn't easy. The faces of the dead came to him. One hundred and sixty five men from the two subs, who would never go home. He saw Captain Lister's face and heard his final words again. "I'm no hero sir. Just a pilot who knows what's in store for him if he doesn't make this flight." The countless, faceless civilians, screaming in terror as they watched their children die, knew they couldn't stop it, and then died themselves. "What would history say of him? What would history say of a mass murderer that wiped out an entire country? American history may praise him, but what of the rest of the world? No man in history had ever killed that many. Not even Col. Paul Tibbets, who originally dropped the first bomb. He had only killed an estimated hundred thousand. But he, (Hawk) had inadvertently caused one atomic bomb to be dropped accidentally (by the enemy), had ordered a nuclear device set off, then subsequently caused the explosions of nine to eleven other atomic bombs. Would history label him as a mass murderer, as many felt Col. Tibbets had been labeled for the rest of his life." Then the faces of the lost submariners were back, forever entombed in the cold dark water that filled the hulks of their sunken submarines. Men not even of this era, technically not even born yet. Men from a time that wasn't even at war. Men, who at this very moment should be at home, in bed with their sweet hearts a hundred years in the future. Now dead and sealed for all time at the bottom of a cold, cold sea. Was he at fault? You god damned right he was! He led his DesRon 3 into the squall and he led them out. How many Japanese sailors died on the merchantman he had sunk outside of Cavite? How many guardsmen died when he ordered his gunners to open fire on the coast guard cutter, also outside of Cavite?" Now, with the war seemingly won, the dead cried out from their graves. Murderer, Murderer, Murderer!

Dawn came at 0532; a dawn without the sun, for the soot in the air didn't permit its rays to penetrate to the surface. Breakfast, a meal Hawk always looked forward to, seemed tasteless to him this morning. The powdered scrambled eggs felt like a cement concoction that he had to wash down with vile tasting powdered milk. Seeing his commander's displeasure at the meal, the Filipino cook apologized behemothly, explaining that the ships stores had run out of a lot of the fresh supplies and were forced to use the powered variety. Hawk did his best to console him that it wasn't the food, but his mood. On the bridge, Hawk saw the darkened skies and felt it fit his mood perfectly. "This," thought Hawk, "must be what Armageddon will be like. Considering all the destruction he had meted out the day before, maybe this was Armageddon. Maybe they would never see the sun again." He could think of several million people who wouldn't. He had seen their faces in his sleep. Hawk's mood was very somber, nearly suicidal. The majestic sight of the massive fleet did nothing to change his outlook. He felt himself becoming more and more depressed. His only hope was that after all of the death and destruction he had caused the day before, he would find a flourishing United States somewhere on the other side of the squall, that by causing so much death, he had saved so many more of his countrymen's lives.

As the Salvation Fleet closed the distance to the squall, Hawk issued orders that would halt the task force twenty miles short. Once there, speed was slowed to five knots, barely moving so the ships wouldn't drift. First an order was sent to Admiral Halsey, releasing the U.S.S. Enterprise to Task Force 1. Then orders were sent throughout the task force, separating the crews of 1942 from 2042, placing the volunteers on the ships that would return to the future. Many men had expressed wishes to return to the future that were from the past and vice versa. Hawk allowed men of the future to stay in 1942. But men from the past could not return to the future, for obvious reasons. If they were somehow killed in the future, their descendants wouldn't be born. Very few exceptions would be made. Aboard the Teddy R., Hawk held a final conference. What should have been a joyous occasion, turned out to be a depressing affair, due to Hawk's state of mind and mood.

Drawing Hawk aside, Admirals Nimitz and Halsey asked why Hawk wanted the Enterprise and if he would be returning the Lexington and Saratoga. "Admirals," said Hawk, "If left in your time, the Saratoga will be sunk as a target ship, the Lexington was destined to be sunk in the Coral Sea and the Enterprise will be scrapped. These ships deserve a much better end. Ask President Roosevelt to sign a presidential order that places them permanently at Pearl Harbor as memorial ships. History will take care of the rest." Sensing Hawks depression, the admirals asked what the trouble was. "I guess I wasn't thinking how I would feel when it was over." said Hawk. "Admiral," explained Admiral Halsey. "There's a reason why it takes thirty years to reach the rank that you reached so quickly. It takes that long to be able to psychologically deal with the death that our profession forces us to cause." "How do you block out the nightmares?" asked Hawk. "You don't." said Halsey.

"Then how do you sleep?" asked Hawk. "Admiral," said Nimitz," The faces of your vanquished enemies will always stay with you, to remind you of the faithful service you've performed for your country as will the faces of your countrymen you've sent to their deaths. Welcome them; they remind you of your losses and victories.

Attempting to help change Hawk's mood, Admiral Davidson said, "You've won a great victory, Admiral." "Think of the lives you've saved," said Admiral Hunt. "Think of the lives we've taken, "said Hawk. "But they were enemy lives," said Cmdr. Hunt. "But still lives," said Hawk. "How do you justify that sort of killing?" "Sir," said Cmdr. Hunt. "Do you think the enemy would've been concerned about dropping them on the United States? Remember, the bombs that destroyed them were destined for the U.S.A." Raising their glasses, Admirals Davidson, Smyth, Halsey, Nimitz, Callaghan, Wilkes and Hunt and Cmdr. Hunt toasted, "To the greatest Admiral of our time and the savior of the United States of America and all Americans."

Within the next three hours, the fleet had separated, Admirals Halsey and Nimitz were on their way back to Pearl, and Hawk was on his way to the coordinates of the squall. His scanners, radars, sonars and radios were dead due to the ash that still filled the skies, even at this distance. They would remain dead until Hawk reached the other side od the squall. Peering at the horizon, Hawk could see it as they neared the coordinates. As they closed the distance, Hawk recalled the first time DesRon 3 raced into it. His thoughts went back to the desperate situation they were in. "That time it had appeared out of nowhere, a godsend, offering a possible escape from the deluge of enemy shells falling on them. Chasing splashes that were as numerous as the raindrops within the squall. He still believed it had been a miracle that they had actually reached it. Maybe it had been destiny. Maybe it was fate that they reach the safety of the squall and escape the death and destruction of the Japanese guns. Did a higher authority exist that allowed things to change?" Hawk's mood began to change as well. Now entering the squall, Hawk wondered what they would find on the other side." Obviously the war still would rage with Germany. They had done nothing to change that. Would they find the government that had existed before they returned from the future? Would there be some sort of record that they had changed history? If not, would anybody believe their story?" Questions filled Hawk's consciousness. Then as he looked ahead, he realized that his mood and outlook were as bright as the skies were turning ahead of him. A quick glance at the clock on the bulkhead showed that he was emerging from the squall at precisely the same time he had entered it. The clouds disappeared, the sea calmed and then he saw it……..

The End?

Printed in the United States
By Bookmasters